D1197190

Mailbox
by the Sea

Mark Grady

Webster Falls Media™
Great Stories in Books & Films

www.websterfalls.com

This book is a work of fiction. Any use of real locations or people are used only in a fictional sense. The remainder of the characters are the creation of the author.

Published by Webster Falls Media LLC
Wallace, NC · Burbank, CA

www.websterfalls.com

Library of Congress Control Number:
2021906858

ISBN: (Hardcover) 978-0-9816872-5-4
(Paperback) 978-0-98167-3-0

Printed in the USA

To Kristina, wherever you are.

For of all sad words of tongue and pen,
the saddest are these: "It might have been."

- John Greenleaf Whittier
  Editor, Poet, Politician
  (1807 – 1892)

Chapter One

The wind and sea spray being stirred up by a strengthening nor'easter just off the North Carolina coast was worse than the forecast had predicted. It definitely wasn't beach weather. In fact, it was only a few weeks before Christmas.

Mason James could feel the wind against his car as he crossed the bridge onto Sunset Beach. Just how strong the wind was blowing hit him when he opened his car door at a parking area. The wind almost pulled the car door out of his hand. Since the worst winds and rain were still 60 miles away, he wondered how powerful the full force of the storm would be when it arrived onshore.

Mason wished he had brought a heavier coat with him, but that wasn't the most important thing on his mind when he left Wilmington to make the drive down. He pulled the delivery he wanted to make out of his back seat, closed the door and made his way over the access ramp that crossed dunes over to the beach front. He was trying to concentrate on his bearings while dealing with the rapidly deteriorating weather conditions. From the directions he brought with him he knew he had to turn southwest after he crossed the ramp to continue his walking trek to Bird Island. That's where the mailbox is. You can only get there on foot. There were no closer areas to park in order to make the journey.

Everybody's right. I AM crazy! They just don't get it. Maybe they've never loved like I have.

Mason James was heading to Bird Island with a special delivery under his arm. He had written all of what he had been feeling down over the past week in a now-tattered, wire-bound notebook he had picked up for a buck at one of those stores where everything is a dollar. He was likely the only one who had ever walked into one of those stores and left with only one item. He even told the girl at the checkout to keep the bag and throw away the receipt.

Mason was fighting to see as the wind spray came at him head-on while he made the mile-and-a-half journey towards the mailbox, He kept going, slowly. When the wind eased up just a little, he was able to see how much the surf was being affected by the incoming storm. Some waves almost appeared to be breaking sideways.

Who cares if they think I'm crazy. I really will be if I don't do this! The letter said I should be here today so I have to be here. What if she is here? What if she still feels the same I have for all these years? I have to know why the letter said I should be here. What if the letter has nothing to do with her?

Mason's emotions were all over the map on his walk to the Kindred Spirit Mailbox. The winds, now gusting occasionally to 30 knots, were making his journey seem more like ten miles than the actual mile-and-a-half distance.

Finally, during one of the times he forced himself to glance up, he saw it. It was an American flag on a pole atop a dune. He had been looking for the flag. The article he read in *USA Today* said the mailbox could be found on the beach side of that flag.

The force of the wind seemed to be getting worse by the minute. And now, it wasn't just sea spray Mason was battling, the rain was starting to fall more steadily. He was glad he had decided to put the tattered notebook into a large zip-lock bag.

Trying to focus on heading towards the flag, Mason hit a barrier. It caught him just below his kneecap. It hurt. He looked down the best he could and realized he had run into a bench. He had forgotten that benches were also mentioned in the article about the mailbox.

The pain he felt in his leg eased the moment he saw it. There it was. THE mailbox. Just like the article he read had described, letters were on the side of the roadside-style mailbox. They spelled "Kindred Spirit."

When he grabbed the door of the box, he was glad to see it had a snug fit. That way, if no one showed up, he at least could leave his notebook inside the mailbox without worrying if the wind would blow the door open and cast his notebook miles down the beach. He opened the door and saw other papers and envelopes in the mailbox. Fortunately, there was still room enough for the notebook.

Mason placed the notebook inside the box, still inside the zip-lock plastic bag. He closed the door and checked to ensure it was snug. He checked his watch and noticed it was now 15 minutes past the time the letter had told him to be there.

Maybe nobody's supposed to be here. Maybe there is something for me in the mailbox.

Mason opened the Kindred Spirit Mailbox again and pulled out everything that was underneath the notebook he had placed on top. He quickly scanned everything. There was nothing on the envelopes, notes or in the notebooks that were addressed to him or mentioned his name. Disappointed, he put everything back in the box and decided it was time to drive back to Wilmington.

As he turned around to begin the long walk back to his car parked in Sunset Beach. he hoped the wind he encountered on the walk to Bird Island would now be coming from behind him. No such luck.

Good grief! This stuff is coming from everywhere. I just hope that mailbox survives this.

Right after those thoughts crossed his mind, Mason heard something. Everything was about to change forever.

Chapter Two

22 Years Earlier

Mason James was what people called a beach kid or an island boy. He grew up at Carolina Beach, part of what had become known as Pleasure Island. The island reference comes from the fact Carolina Beach is part of an island that also includes Kure Beach and Fort Fisher. It's located in southeastern North Carolina at the point where the Atlantic Ocean meets the Cape Fear River.

Pleasure Island is not an island formed naturally. In 1929, the U.S. Army Corps of Engineers created a man-made passage between the Intracoastal Waterway that ended at the Carolina Beach yacht basin and the Cape Fear River. This cut-through for boats turned Carolina Beach, Kure Beach and Fort Fisher into a barrier island. The cut-through became known as Snow's Cut, named after Maj. William Snow of the Corps of Engineers who supervised some of the dredging process to create the pass.

Mason's dad, Woody, discovered Carolina Beach when he was stationed at Marine Corps Base Camp Lejeune located about 50 miles north in Jacksonville. When he left the Corps, he moved to Carolina Beach. While he liked the beach, he mainly moved there because of a girl. Her name was Joy. Whenever Woody's friends from his military days came to visit, he never admitted Joy was the reason to his military friends, but they all knew better.

Mason was about 12 when his dad's military buddies came for a visit during the summer. Mason remembers that day well.

"How come you picked Carolina Beach over Wrightsville Beach?" Woody's old sergeant, Bill, asked.

"Don't you remember the time we went to Wrightsville on liberty?" Woody responded.

"I doubt he remembers that," another old Marine buddy, Matt Jacobs, chimed in. "Don't you remember how much he kept trying to get us to go to Carolina Beach instead?"

Everybody laughed except Mason. He just sat and listened, completely enthralled with their banter, old stories, and, no doubt, a few lies thrown in for good measure.

"I remember," Bill said. "What did you have against Wrightsville Beach?

"The place is full of a bunch of rich, snooty people," Woody said. "The girls have always been spoiled, conceited got-rocks."

"Got-rocks?" Sgt. Bill blurted out. "What the hell is that?" Bill then glanced Mason's way and modified his question. "I mean, what the heck is that?"

"My mother used to say it all the time about snooty rich people," Woody said. "I think it's in reference to all the high-dollar jewelry they wear to flaunt their wealth, like diamonds. You know, rocks."

"Ohhhh," everybody said in unison.

"You mean that lady you ended up lucky enough to talk into marrying you didn't have a thing to do with you wanting to come here instead? You mean she had nothing to do with you deciding to move here when you got your discharge papers?" Bill said, grinning.

"My discharge papers are a lot more honorable than yours, Mister Sarge. I guess you forgot how I saved your butt in Desert Storm."

"What are you talking about? You never saved me from anything?"

"I guess you forgot about me bailing you out of trouble when you ended up owing that lieutenant all kinds of money after that card game on the flight out to England," Woody said.

Bill laughed and said, "You make it sound like you saved my life on the battlefield. But, you're avoiding the question."

Joy had entered the room as if right on cue carrying a tray full of glasses of iced tea for everybody.

"Bill, I'll answer your question for you since that husband of mine is more worried about his macho Marine image than answering your question."

As she passed out the tea, everybody took turns saying, "Thanks, Joy." Mason followed up with, "Thanks, Mom."

"You all are welcome," Joy said. "When Woody came back for a visit just after his discharge, he begged me to marry him. He said he would find us a house anywhere in the world I wanted to live."

Matt Jacobs interrupted. "Where was he going to get the money for that. He was a Marine. Did he win the lottery or something?"

When the laughter died down, Woody jumped in with, "No, but unlike you, I've always been willing to work."

"All right, boys," Joy said. "Let me finish my story. I told him I didn't want to live anyplace else but here. I was born a beach girl and would always be a beach girl."

Mason was smiling. He loved to hear people tell stories. His dad's old sergeant noticed the look on Mason's face.

"How about you, Mason? You gonna want to stay a beach kid?"

"Yes, sir, I think so."

"You might just meet some beach girl like your dad did and she'll want to stay, too," Bill added.

Mason just smiled.

"You don't say much do you?" Bill asked Mason.

Joy was headed back to the kitchen with her empty tray just as Bill was asking about Mason's quiet demeanor. She stopped and rustled Mason's thick hair.

"No, my son doesn't say much, probably because he can't get a word in edgewise around a bunch of old Marines."

Everybody laughed, including Mason.

"Yeah, he's a quiet guy," Woody said. "But, he's one smart cookie. A lot smarter than you clowns. He reads all the time and I can tell he's a big thinker."

At that moment, Mason was doing exactly what his dad said he was always doing – thinking. He was thinking about what his dad's old sergeant said about meeting a girl on the beach. He was 12 years old and definitely starting to notice the opposite sex.

But how am I supposed to meet a girl down here? None of them in school hardly talk to me.

Mason's observation was accurate, but it wasn't because the girls were not noticing Mason, too. He just seemed too quiet and shy, so they were as scared to talk to him as he was to talk to them.

Mason had no way of knowing Sgt. Bill's prediction would come true. He would meet a girl at Carolina Beach, just like his dad did. The only difference would be she did not live at the beach; but, he would fall in love with her just like his dad had fallen for his mom. Mason also had no idea he would forever love the girl he would meet at the beach, no matter what happened.

Chapter Three

Mason's life at the beach was as one of the lucky kids. While his mom and dad disagreed from time-to-time, he never heard them raise their voices to each other. At his age, he wasn't grasping the significance the atmosphere of his parents' mutual respect for each other was having on him. He also didn't know how a habit his dad had created with him was going to lead to what he would want to do to make a living.

Mason's father, Woody, did not attend college. He decided to enlist in the Marine Corps not long after he graduated high school. While Woody may have not had much of a formal education after high school, he was incredibly self-educated. Woody's father, also a military veteran who served in Vietnam, believed reading was extremely important. He believed knowing what was going on in the country and the world was something every good citizen should do. He became an avid newspaper reader and that rubbed off on Woody.

"I'll watch the evening news on TV, but there's no way they can tell you the whole situation behind a story in two minutes," Woody's father would say. "That doesn't answer all the who, what, where, when, why, and how questions for me."

Since staying informed had been passed down as important to Woody, he wanted to inspire Mason to want to know the who, what, why, where, when, and how of what was happening in the world around him. He knew that you could inspire kids when they're young, but he didn't want to overwhelm Mason too early. So, he started with the comics, especially on Sunday.

Before Mason could talk, his dad would call him to the couch where he would crawl up to listen to Woody read the comics to him. His favorite was always Peanuts. He especially loved Snoopy and always laughed when the comic strip would show Snoopy on top of his doghouse with a typewriter.

Mason thought the typewriter looked like the old, heavy Underwood his dad had on his desk on the enclosed porch at back of their house. Instead of getting frustrated when Mason tried to pound on some of the typewriter keys, Woody came and showed him how to hit them properly. Mason couldn't read yet, but he would spend long periods of time mimicking his dad typing.

By the time Mason was in the first grade, he once asked his dad, "What are you writing?"

"Oh, just some memories I have from Desert Storm and family stuff," Woody said.

"Is it going to be like a book?"

"I don't know. Maybe it's just something I'll do for you guys."

When Mason was in the third grade, he was sitting at dinner with his mom and dad and heard them talking about some changes coming to the boardwalk at the beach.

"I think it's sad," his mom said.

"What's sad?" Mason asked.

"They're talking about tearing down the Ocean Plaza Ballroom. You know, that big white building right at the curve at the boardwalk."

"Why are they tearing it down?"

"Because people don't understand the value of historic places," Woody chimed in.

Mason stopped to think a minute before asking another question.

"How do you know they want to tear it down?"

"Because it was in the paper," Woody said.

"The one with the comics?"

"Yep, the same one. There is a lot more in there than the funnies."

When they finished eating, Woody led Mason into his office on the porch and showed him the story in the newspaper about the Ocean Plaza Ballroom. There was a photo of the building with the story. Woody read some of the story to him.

"How did the paper know people wanted to tear down the building?"

"That's a great question, Son. There are people who work for the paper called reporters. They are always asking questions and listening for people talking about rumors around town. Then, if they hear something interesting, they start asking more questions to see if the rumor is true. The reporters also ask the police about any crimes that happen and report on that, too."

Woody held the paper closer to Mason to show him the byline of the reporter.

"See, this is the reporter's name that wrote the story."

"So, he writes the news story and it ends up in the paper?"

"That's right."

"That sounds like a really cool job. Your name is in the paper every day you write a story."

"Yep, maybe you'll want to be a newspaper reporter when you grow up."

"That's what I want to do, Dad. I want to be a newspaper dude."

Woody laughed at Mason's choice of words.

"Dude, huh?"

Neither of them realized that moment contained a very accurate prediction.

By the time Mason hit the 8th grade, he would be writing for the small school paper that was printed once a month. In high school, he would become the best reporter on the school newspaper staff and would write some great stories in the yearbook. He was the school newspaper's most prolific writer. He turned down the editor position because he was afraid it would keep him from writing stories.

Chapter Four

Not long after Mason turned 16 years old, he landed his first official job. He had worked some odd jobs for people since he was twelve, including yard work and walking dogs. He also had a small paper route for a few years delivering the *Star-News* newspaper from Wilmington, the closest city located 15 miles north of the beach.

Mason liked delivering along his route because, in addition to making some spending money, he got to have his very own copy of the daily paper. After throwing his last paper from his bike, he rode home and read his copy before heading off to school. Just as he had first done when he was in the third grade, he dreamed of seeing his byline at the top of some of the stories that caught his interest.

His friends were relentless when they would catch him pouring over the *Star-News* at school.

"Why do you like reading that thing? It's boring," one of them would inevitably say.

In his usually quiet nature, Mason would just shrug and say, "I don't really know."

The reality was Mason knew it was his dad who had inspired him to want to write for a newspaper. Woody's father had inspired him to take an interest in politics and world affairs, if for no other reason than to know how it would affect him as a man in the military. Then Woody's overseas deployment during Operation Desert Storm only ramped up the interest his dad had passed on to him. Now, Mason was inspired to take that interest to another level, too. Instead of just reading the news, Mason wanted to be one who reported it.

Mason began working at Britt's Donuts during summer break following the 10th grade. Britt's Donuts was a Carolina Beach institution located in the heart of the boardwalk. The small shop had been around since the 1930s and had gained a reputation almost across the country for the only kind of donut they served. It was right out of the cooker, light and dipped in glaze. Britt's Donuts is open only during the summer months and judging by the lines waiting to buy the donuts by the dozen, you'd think they'd added some kind of highly-addictive substance to their closely-guarded recipe. The reality is they are simply the best donuts on the planet.

Mason had grown up having frequent trips to the boardwalk during the summers. After he and his parents enjoyed the ocean a while, they would venture up to Britt's for a few donuts and then they would cross to the other side of the boardwalk so Mason could play some games in a large arcade.

The owner of Britt's, a man named Bobby, was more than glad to hire Mason the minute he asked if they had any openings for the summer. Bobby had known Mason's parents since long before Mason was born and had seen him grow up on the beach. Bobby always said Mason "sure is a good boy."

After getting through the 11th grade, he was back to working at the donut shop the following summer.

Britt's Donuts stayed busy on weekdays during the summer, but not anywhere near as swamped as the small shop was on weekends when there were all-day lines from the time they opened until they closed for the evening. It was a Tuesday and business had slowed down a little. Most people were enjoying being in the water or laying out on the beach.

"Hey, Mason," his boss, Bobby, said. "Why don't you go ahead and take a 15-minute break. You've been working mighty hard over there."

Mason's job that day involved flipping the donuts in the cooker using wooden sticks, just like the shop had been doing it since its creation. Then, when they were done, he would line the donuts up on another stick and dip them generously in the glaze before hanging the donuts on a rack. They didn't last long there before one of the girls working the counter would come and place them in white paper bags to deliver them to the next in line.

After turning over his duties to another guy working in the kitchen area, he went to the back where he kept his personal items and grabbed a copy of today's newspaper he had brought from the house.

The long counter with stools on one side where customers who ate in the shop sat to enjoy their donuts was not very full for the afternoon. Mason ventured down to the last stool in the back of the shop and sat down to start reading.

In less than a minute, Mason became engrossed in a story about the dredging operation going on just offshore. He had seen the huge ships off the Carolina Beach coast for several days. The story had his undivided attention which kept him from noticing someone had sat down on the stool right beside him.

"Wow, that must be some story you're reading," the voice said, breaking Mason's concentration. He looked up from the paper he had in front of him on the counter to find a girl sitting next to him. She was looking directly in his eyes, obviously speaking to him.

"Oh, uh, yeah, I'm sorry. I didn't hear you," Mason struggled to get out. "It's a story about those big dredging ships you can see out in the ocean when you're on the beach."

"Cool," the mysterious girl said.

Mason had actually shocked himself. He had been able to sound halfway articulate about the story he was reading while looking at the beautiful girl who had struck up a conversation with him. Usually, the only females who successfully got him to talk that much were his mother and a lady who he thought looked like Aunt Bea on the *Andy Griffith Show* who worked at the Carolina Beach Library. She would force him to talk by asking him questions he couldn't answer with a few words, like the time he returned a book last Friday.

"Oh, I haven't had the chance to read this one yet," she said as he handed the book to her at the desk. "What's this one about?"

Mason realized he was still staring at the girl beside him at the counter. She looked about his age, but she was definitely a petite girl. Her shoulder-length brunette hair was wind-blown, but he loved the way a few strands fell across one of her brown eyes. He even thought her nose was cute and her smile was incredible. There was a simple, natural beauty to her and Mason thought her looks and personality definitely didn't fall into the category of one of those "got rock" girls his dad talked about.

"Hey, I just noticed your T-shirt," she said, breaking Mason from his trance. "You work here?"

"Yes, ma'am. I'm on break."

She laughed. "Ma'am? Do I look that old?"

Mason's cheeks instantly grew a little pink.

"No, no way. I'm sorry. It's just a habit, the way I was raised."

"I'm just messin' with you," she said, still smiling. "I'm in the habit of doing the same thing. I'm Amy, by the way." She stuck out her hand and Mason shyly shook it.

"Hi, I'm Mason. Are you just visiting?"

"Well, yes and no," Amy said. "My parents just built a beach house here, so we're down for the summer. I actually live in Charlotte."

It was a simple introduction and was the beginning of something neither one of them realized would affect them for the rest of their lives.

Chapter Five

For a moment, Amy just smiled while Mason looked at the pretty girl still sitting beside him at the Britt's Donuts counter. He wanted to say something, anything, to impress her, but he was at a total loss for words. He realized the newspaper he was still holding was starting to shake a little so he quickly laid it flat on the counter. He was embarrassed over how he must be coming across. He was saved from the awkward silence by Amy.

"You have to admit not many people anywhere near our age read a newspaper," she said. "Unless they have an assignment or they're looking for a job, or maybe a car or something."

"Yeah, I know," Mason said.

"So, tell me, Mason, are you looking for a job; well, another one? Or a car?"

"Not really. I want to write for a newspaper."

"So, you're kind of looking for a job, huh?" Amy smiled.

For the first time since they spoke, Mason did not have to force a smile. He really liked the fast wit of the pretty girl sitting beside him. He even let out a quick laugh. He wanted to say he didn't think people anywhere near their age had her kind of wit, but he just responded to what she had said.

"I guess you're right. I am kind of studying for a job down the road."

"What in the world made you want to write for a newspaper?"

Mason sensed she was sincerely curious.

"That probably comes from my mom and dad."

"They write for a newspaper?"

"No, but I think my mom would have enjoyed writing as a career, just not for a newspaper, though; probably more for a travel magazine."

"Did she travel a lot?" Amy's curiosity still coming across very sincere.

"Not really, but when we would go on a vacation, she would write these letters to my aunt, her sister, and they would have all these details about the trip. My dad would read the letters out loud to me and he would always say, 'your mom ought to be a travel writer.' He was right. Those letters were so good they were like re-living the whole trip."

"Do you want to write travel stories for a paper?"

It took Mason a moment to answer. He had never had anybody, other than his folks, care this much about him and what his dreams are.

"I wouldn't mind writing travel stories if that would get me in the door, but not all the time."

"What would you like to write?"

"Feature stories, mainly, I guess. You know, stories about interesting people or regular people who have done something amazing."

Mason could tell Amy was listening to his every word. He wished he knew what she was thinking as she listened. He didn't know it, but Amy was fascinated a guy her age could talk about something more than cars or a video game.

"What makes you interested in those kind of stories?"

"Hmm," Mason thought for a moment. "I guess that comes from my dad. He was in Desert Storm and tells some amazing stories about people he served in the Marines with. Some of those guys are still his friends and come to see us every once in a while. A few of his other friends didn't come home."

"Does he write any?"

"I told him he should. My dad did write some memories on an old typewriter we have at the house, but he said he couldn't write an entire book. He said I should write a book for him one day."

Mason became a little distracted when he glanced at the clock on the wall of Britt's Donuts. He realized his break was quickly coming to an end.

"My break is almost over so I better get back to work. It was nice talking to you."

"But, I have some more questions," Amy said with a huge smile on her face.

"I'm not that interesting. I promise."

"I think you are. Besides, maybe ten years from now I'll write a book about the day I met a guy who went on to become a famous writer."

Mason had moved behind the counter and was getting his apron on to head back to cooking duty.

"Good luck selling any copies of a book about me," Mason said. "But, I can guarantee you'd sell two copies, to my mom and dad."

Amy laughed out loud and Mason loved the sound of it.

"I know you have to get back to work, but I have a writing assignment for you."

"Oh, really?"

"Yes, and I'll pick it up tomorrow. Write down the recipe for these donuts!"

"Ha! I work here and they won't even tell me."

"Well, my compliments to the chef anyway," Amy said, getting up from the counter to leave. "See you, Mason!"

Mason shocked and surprised himself by shouting back as she was heading to the door. "I hope so!"

Amy turned, smiled and waved.

I really do hope she comes back, Mason thought and went back to work.

Chapter Six

Mason worked at Britt's Donuts until 8:00 that night. He rode his bike home quickly knowing dinner would be waiting for him. It was one of his mom's rules. The family ate dinner together whenever possible.

At 8:01, Woody glanced at his watch and tried to sneak a snack while they waited for Mason to get home. Joy caught him and slapped his hand.

"But, I'm starvin'," Woody said.

"Oh, so much for the tough, Desert Storm Marine, huh?" Joy said.

"Hey, I fought in that war so I would have the freedom to eat when I want to."

They didn't hear Mason come in the door, but he heard the laughter from the kitchen.

"What's so funny?" Mason asked.

"Your dad is trying to use his military service to eat before dinner," Joy said.

"Again?" Mason responded.

"Okay, let's eat," Joy said, music to Woody's ears. In minutes they were all enjoying homemade lasagna and slices from a loaf of French bread. The sound of forks on plates and ice jingling in glasses of iced tea were the only sounds until Woody had a question.

"Did either of you see the story in the paper today about the three storms they're watching down in the tropics?"

"Yeah, I saw that when I was on break," Mason said.

"Did you see about the tracks? It looks like meteorologists can't agree on whether we might be affected by any of them," Woody added.

"I didn't get to read the whole story, just the headline really," Mason said. "I got into a conversation about something else."

"Oh, with Bobby?" Joy asked.

"No, ma'am, a customer."

"You don't get the chance to do that often, do you?"

"No, ma'am."

"Was it a local?"

"I don't think so. I think she's just here for vacation."

Woody had eaten quickly and was back to scanning the newspaper, but he hadn't missed the pronoun Mason used to describe the customer he was talking to at work.

"Oh, a young lady you were talking to, huh?" Woody asked.

"Yes, sir."

"Very nice," his dad said.

"Oh, leave him alone," Joy said before turning towards Mason. "Pay no attention to that man behind the paper."

Yet more laughter filled the kitchen as Mason stood to clear his plate from the table and take it to the sink.

"I'm kinda tired and have to be back to work in the morning, so I'm going to take a shower and head for bed," Mason said.

"Okay, Son, goodnight," Joy and Woody said almost in unison.

After his shower, Mason lay down and tried to read a little from a book he had checked out a few days ago from the Carolina Beach Library. He gave up trying to read when he realized he had read the same line three times. He was distracted by the same thought that would have him tossing and turning for the next hour.

I sure hope she comes in tomorrow.

Chapter Seven

Amy was a great deal quieter than usual at dinner the night after meeting Mason at the donut shop.

"You have something on your mind, honey?" her father, Paul, asked.

"I was just thinking about this guy I met on the boardwalk at that donut shop today."

"How'd you meet?"

"I asked him a question. He was reading a newspaper like he was studying for finals or something."

"A guy your age reading a newspaper? Was he looking for a job?"

Amy laughed.

"That's exactly what I asked him, but he was reading a story about dredging they are doing just off the coast with those big ships you can see from the beach. And he works at the donut shop. He was on break."

Amy's mother, Catherine, was walking back into the kitchen bringing a cake she had bought from the bakery in town.

31

"Are you making it a habit now to start talking to boys you don't know?" her mom asked.

"Nope, I just found him interesting."

"Like I told you before, you should be finding Drake Crabtree interesting. His family is old money and he can offer you a real future. He just got a new BMW for his 17th birthday, by the way."

"Mom, I told you Drake Crabtree is a smart-ass jerk."

"You watch your language around me, young lady."

Amy's dad tried to squelch a chuckle and that caught his wife's ire, too.

"Why don't you try and teach her some respect instead of encouraging her mouthing off everything that comes to her mind?"

"Well, Dear," Paul said. "In this case, I happen to agree with our daughter. Drake Crabtree is a smart-ass jerk and it got passed down from his smart-ass jerk father."

"You both don't deserve the class you live in. What kind of future is there for her talking to some boy that works in a donut shop?"

Before her dad could answer, Amy responded.

"It could be a nice future, Mom. In fact, the reason Mason was reading the paper is because he wants to write for a newspaper when he graduates."

"You even know his name already?" Catherine asked. Before Amy could answer, she went on. "You do remember I own the one of the most respected advertising agencies in the southeast and I buy ad space in newspapers all the time. Papers make a ton of money because most of them have no competition. But the reporters don't see any of that, especially not in this part of the country. If your donut boy wants a newspaper job and he's smart, which I doubt given that he's a donut boy, he'll get an MBA and forget about the news side of the news business. And if he thinks he can get any decent job fresh out of high school, he's an idiot. You know, I keep explaining this to you and I don't know why you won't believe me. This is just reality."

"Actually, WE own a respected ad agency in the southeast," Paul said.

"I'm the one that put it on the map," Catherine said. "You are from that creative side. I'm the one who knows how to sell that stuff your team comes up with."

"What's wrong with being a writer for a newspaper?" Amy asked, glad to interrupt the consistent reminder from her mother that she was the real person behind the success of the agency.

"Nothing, I guess, as long as you don't mind living below the poverty level," Catherine said.

"But, if those writers didn't write anything and if Dad and his team didn't create ads that the businesses like, what would you have to sell and where would you have the ads?"

Before Catherine could respond, Paul turned to his daughter and said, "You are wise beyond your years, beautiful daughter of mine."

Amy smiled.

"She's not wise, she's just been indoctrinated by your silly mess!" Catherine said as she marched out of the room in disgust, adding, "Like a 16-year-old knows anything about business or picking a good person to date."

Amy's smile turned into a look of a little fear on her face.

"I'm sorry, Dad. I didn't mean to cause a fight."

"Just don't bring up the boy in the donut shop around your mom. You know how she is. She wants to be in charge of everything. It's best to let her feel she is."

"Okay."

Amy went upstairs in the huge, three-story beach house her parents had just purchased a week before as a place to have an occasional getaway from their even bigger home in Charlotte. She went into her room and pulled out the device she used to distract herself from the frequent tension in her home. It was a violin and she had a reputation within the music program at her school as a prodigy. She was first chair in the school orchestra.

However, after playing through a few pages of her favorite piece, *Pictures at an Exhibition*, she stopped. She couldn't concentrate and it wasn't because of the events that just took place in the new beach house dining room. It was because she could not stop thinking about the shy boy she had met at the donut shop.

I can't wait to see him again tomorrow.

Chapter Eight

Amy had barely been awake for ten minutes when she heard the phone ringing in the house. A minute later, her mother opened Amy's bedroom door. She was carrying a cordless phone.

"Here, your aunt wants to talk to you."

"Thanks, Mom."

It never went unnoticed by Amy that her mom had little respect for her sister. Her mom never called her sister by her name and never referred to her as her sister for that matter. It was always a cold "your aunt." Amy couldn't understand that. She thought her aunt Mary was the greatest lady on the planet. Mary never had an ill word to say about anybody. Amy was always happy to see her aunt come to her home for family get togethers. She was the one that added real joy to the event. Aunt Mary loved Christmas and Amy could not imagine how drab it would be in her home if her aunt wasn't there during the holidays.

"Hey, Aunt Mary," Amy said.

"Hey, Amy. I was thinking about heading down to the mailbox this afternoon. Would you like me to come get you and go with me?"

Mary's reference to "the mailbox" was about the Kindred Spirit Mailbox located right on the beach among dunes on Bird Island, close to Sunset Beach. It wasn't an official mailbox. The U.S. Postal Service never picked up or delivered mail to the Kindred Spirit Mailbox. However, people from all over the world had made the trek to the mailbox to put letters, poems and notes inside, or write on the pads and journals placed inside for those who may not have been inspired to write anything until after they arrived to the mailbox.

The idea for the mailbox came from a girl named Claudia. She was dating a man named Frank in the late 1970s and he helped her erect the mailbox they had purchased from a hardware store. Eventually, as word of Kindred Spirit Mailbox began to spread and it became more popular, a few benches were added to the small area among dunes where the mailbox is located.

Although the relationship between Frank and Claudia came to an end, the mailbox remained and Frank became a self-appointed caretaker for the Kindred Spirit Mailbox. The more the mailbox became popular, the more volunteers began to help Frank with maintaining the mailbox and the area around it.

"I'd love to," Amy said. "But can we go kind of later in the afternoon?"

"Oh, you have plans?" Mary asked.

"Not really plans, but I met this guy yesterday. He works at Britt's Donuts and I wanted to go by and see him again."

"Why don't we go tomorrow instead. You ought to go see that boy you met. After all, if he works at Britt's, it's obvious he's sweet."

Amy laughed. She loved her aunt's sense of humor.

"Tomorrow would be great," Amy said.

"Then tomorrow it is. I'll catch the ferry over from Southport. I'll call you just before the ferry leaves to head to Fort Fisher."

"Thanks, Aunt Mary."

"You bet. Can you put your mom back on the phone?"

"Sure, just a minute."

Amy ran down the steps and found her mom sitting in an office she had put together in one of the spare bedrooms of the new beach house. She handed her the phone.

"Aunt Mary wants to talk to you."

Catherine took the phone but had no response to Amy.

"Yes," was all Catherine said into the phone.

"I'm going to catch the ferry over tomorrow and pick up Amy. She wants to go down to the Kindred Spirit Mailbox with me."

"Most people ask permission before they come pick up a child and take them somewhere," Catherine said.

"What's wrong with you, Catherine? Why do you have to be so mean?"

"It's not mean. It's direct. I run a multi-million-dollar company and don't have time for small talk or for the pie-in-the-sky romantic fantasies you live in and try to rub off on my daughter."

"She just enjoys reading the letters and journal entries people put in the box. Some of them are very moving and let people know there are still people in the world who really love and care for one another."

"Like I said, fantasy," Catherine said, sounding completely emotionless.

"Are you saying you're not going to let me come see my niece tomorrow?"

"No, come on, because I won't be able to deal with her attitude if I tell her she can't go somewhere with you. But, next time, run it by me first or she won't be coming to see you for a long time."

"Okay, see you tomorrow then," Mary said. She wanted to say more, but decided it wasn't worth it and she didn't want to risk losing a day with Amy.

Catherine didn't respond. She just hung up the phone.

Chapter Nine

About 30 minutes after her aunt Mary had called, Amy came downstairs. She was wearing a brightly colored sundress. She found her mother still in her beach house office.

"I'm going to walk down to the boardwalk," Amy said.

"Shouldn't that be, 'Mom, is it okay if I walk down to the boardwalk'?"

"Mom, I'm 16. I'm not some little kid."

"There is no age that is okay to lose respect for your mother."

"Okay, is it okay with you if I walk down to the boardwalk?"

"I guess so. But, be home by 5:30. I want to eat early tonight. And don't ruin your appetite eating those fattening donuts you always want down there."

For a moment, Amy wondered if her mom had seen her at Britt's Donut Shop the day before and she was only mentioning the donuts as her mom's way of letting her know she saw her talking to Mason. Amy brushed the thought off thinking she was getting paranoid because of the way her mother reacted to her talking about Mason the day before.

"Okay, see you at 5:30," Amy said.

As Amy walked down the steps from the porch down to the street, she didn't notice her mom had stood up from her desk and was watching her walk down the sidewalk. Amy was smiling. She was thinking about Mason. She wanted to see the shy guy who wanted to be a newspaper writer someday.

Catherine watched Amy until she turned down another sidewalk heading for the beach area and the boardwalk.

I wonder what she's smiling about, Catherine thought.

When Amy walked into Britt's Donuts, she was disappointed. There was someone else turning donuts over in the cooker. She thought Mason must not be working today. Then, she looked towards another area behind the glass in the kitchen and saw him. Today, Mason was rolling out dough and using a cutter to create the shape of the donuts. She found a seat at the counter almost directly behind Mason. She was watching him and was almost startled when a girl spoke.

"What can I get you today?" the girl working the counter asked. Her name was Patty.

"Oh, uh, how about three of them and a Coke, please."

"Sure," Patty said. "Anything else?"

"Ah, yes, please. Could you tell Mason I said hello when you get a chance?"

Patty looked surprised for a brief moment. Not many girls spoke to Mason or asked about him. He was so quiet and shy.

"I sure will."

As Patty went to grab the three hot donuts, she called out to Mason.

"Hey, Mason. Somebody at the counter wants me to say hi to you."

Mason, surprised to hear Patty call his name, looked up and then turned around towards the counter to see who was wanting to speak to him. It was exactly who he hoped it would be. Amy was smiling and waving. Mason shyly smiled and waved back. He pointed towards his watch and mouthed that he had a break in a little while. Amy nodded and smiled.

Bobby happened to see Mason waving to someone at the counter and looked to see a girl about Mason's age responding.

"Do you know that girl waving at you, Mason?"

Turning beet red, Mason stared at the dough he was working with and quietly said, "Yes, sir. Well, I kind of met her yesterday."

"Why don't you go ahead and take a break and talk to her while she's here. I'll finish this batch."

Mason looked Bobby right in the eye. He smiled and said, "Thanks."

As Mason removed his apron and started heading towards the counter, Bobby noticed it was the first time he had ever seen Mason go on break and not have a newspaper in his hand.

Amy watched Mason walk to the end of the counter and come around to the customer side. He looked unsure as whether it was okay to come up to her.

"You on break?" Amy asked down the several seats between where Mason was standing and where she was sitting.

Mason nodded.

"Come and sit beside me," Amy said.

That was the best thing Mason had heard since yesterday when he met Amy.

Chapter Ten

Mason sat down beside Amy at the counter and just smiled before looking towards the kitchen. He was very happy she had come back to the donut shop, but he was still very shy and uncomfortable. He didn't know what to say. Fortunately, Amy did.

"I wasn't sure you would be here right now because I forgot to ask when you worked yesterday," she said.

"I thought about that after you left," Mason said. "But since my shift today is 10:00 till 5:00, I just hoped you'd come during that time."

"Oh, you did, did you?" Amy said.

Mason instantly felt sheepish.

Was it okay to say that? I bet I came across as desperate or something.

"I'm sorry," he said. "I hope you don't think I'm a stalker or something. I just really liked talking to you yesterday.

"I can see right now you're going to have to get used to my warped sense of humor. I was just kidding with you. I'm glad you hoped I'd come back."

"Really?"

"Yep, really. I liked talking to you, too."

Mason hesitated a moment and then decided to tell her what he was thinking about last night.

"I was thinking about what we were talking about after I got home from work last night. I was kind of mad at myself because all I did was talk about me and what I wanted to do for work when I wanted to know more about you."

"It's not like I gave you a chance to ask since I was grilling you like a police detective or something."

Mason smiled.

"Uh, you know what I want to do, but what do you want to do?"

"Well, right this minute, I want to sit here and talk to you," Amy said.

"Oh, thanks, I was kind of meaning what you want to do after graduating."

"I know that. I was messing with you again. I've gotta stop that."

"It's okay," Mason said. "I'm glad you have a sense of humor. Most people I talk to at school don't have one, except for a friend, Don Langley. He is on the school newspaper staff with me and he has us all laughing most of the time. I guess I'm taking you too serious, huh? But, don't stop being funny on my account."

I'm talking too much, Mason thought.

"Deal, if you stop worrying about being shy around me. You said you liked my sense of humor, well I like the fact you can actually talk about real life. Most of the people I talk to in school, the guys anyway, aren't smart enough for that."

Mason was trying to take that in. It sounded like a good thing to him. She seemed to like him. He sure liked her.

"You gonna tell me?" Mason asked.

"Tell you what?"

"What you want to do, other than talk to me right now."

Amy laughed and said, "Oops, my fault, I did kind of ignore you to talk too much."

"You don't talk too much," Mason said. "I like to hear you talk."

"Oh, you do, do you?"

I did it again. Why can't I stop saying things that make me look crazy?

Amy noticed the look on Mason's face.

"I am very lucky you like to hear me talk," Amy said. "Everybody else says I talk too much."

"I don't think so, really."

"I guess that makes me a lucky girl," Amy said.

Mason had nervously kept his hands on the counter, occasionally rubbing them together while they talked. He was very sensitive as to how he came across. Right after Amy said she was lucky Mason liked to hear her talk, she reached over and grabbed one of Mason's hands for a moment. Mason tried to act completely cool about it. On the inside though, he thought it was the greatest thing he had ever had happen to him.

"I'm not 100 percent sure what I want to do, maybe something in music, like be a music teacher or something," Amy said.

"Do you sing or play an instrument?"

"I've played violin since I was 11."

"Wow, that sounds amazing."

"You haven't heard me play," Amy said, her sense of humor kicking in again.

"I bet you sound great. I'd like to hear you play sometime."

"Maybe one day. I don't want to scare you away. We just met."

Amy might not want to play the violin for him yet, but everything she said sounded like music to his ears. If she was being serious with him, she sounded like she really liked him, and he liked that.

"I bet you'd make a great teacher," Mason said. "Your students would love you cause you make people feel at ease around you."

"Do I make you feel at ease?" Amy asked.

"Oh, yeah. Do you know how you say everybody says you talk too much? Everybody says I don't say anything. I've said more to you the past five minutes than I have to any girl at school."

"Then I'm honored," Amy said. She grabbed his hand for a moment again.

Loving it, but embarrassed again, Mason happened to glance at the clock. He was sad that his break was ending in two minutes.

"Doggone it, my break is almost over," he said.

Amy gave a giggle and said, "Doggone it? I haven't heard that in a while."

"I know, I sound like a wierdo."

"Not to me. You sound like a great guy."

Mason turned so red he wanted to turn away.

"You are being nice, but I appreciate it," he got out.

"Nope, I'm just being honest, the only way I know how to be. Oh, what time you get off from work?"

"At 5:00."

"Would you like to go walk around the boardwalk and maybe on the beach a little while after you get off?"

"Yeah, I'd like that a lot."

"See you then," she said before she briefly grabbed his hand one more time and left.

Wow, was all Mason could think. He looked at the clock again. It was almost 2:00 o'clock. He knew the next three hours were going to be a long time. He also knew his heart sure was beating fast.

Chapter Eleven

Mason was thankful things got very busy at Britt's Donuts just a few minutes after Amy left. A YMCA daycare program had brought two busloads of kids down for a day at the beach. They took a break from enjoying the surf and had lined up in force along the counter. It had the whole staff hopping to meet the demand.

Being busy made the time seem to pass faster, but Mason still glanced at his watch frequently waiting for 5:00 o'clock to come around. Just as the crowd of YMCA kids were starting to thin out, Mason took another look at his watch. It was just a few minutes until 5:00. He looked towards the counter. Standing just inside the entrance to the shop stood Amy. She saw him looking in her direction, so she smiled and waved. He shyly smiled back.

Just a few minutes after Mason and Amy exchanged smiles and waves, Mason appeared from the back of Britt's Donuts. He was out of his apron. He made his way in Amy's direction and she spoke first.

"Hey! You want to go for that walk?"

"Sure," Mason said.

They had barely walked away from Britt's Donuts when Amy stopped.

"Hey, where's your newspaper today?" She was smiling.

"Oh, I accidently left it at home."

"You? The future Pulitzer Prize winner forgot your newspaper?"

"Yeah, I did. Hey, you know about the Pulitzer Prizes?"

"I do," Amy said. "In the 8th grade my English teacher made us choose a book to read from a list she had. I looked down the list and saw the cover of her copy of "To Kill a Mockingbird" had an emblem on it that said the book had won a Pulitzer Prize. I thought that must mean something important. It really did, because that is one powerful book."

"It really is," Mason said. He didn't say what else he was thinking, which was this girl was like none other he had ever met.

"Wait a minute," Amy said. "You got me distracted from what I was talking about. How in the world did you, of all people, forget your daily newspaper to read on break?"

"Umm, I was, ah, thinking about you maybe coming by today, so I forgot."

"Wow! That makes me feel pretty special to beat out a newspaper with you."

Mason smiled and turned a little red. Amy reached up and put her hand on Mason's arm just above his elbow and they started walking again. That made Mason feel a lot more special than a newspaper, too.

When they approached one of the access ramps from the boardwalk to the beach, Amy guided them in the direction of the ocean. When the ramp reached the top of the dune, the steady breeze off of the Atlantic was immediately noticeable. Mason glanced in Amy's direction. He liked the way the wind was gently tossing her hair around her shoulders.

For the next fifteen minutes, Amy and Mason just walked along the shoreline. Amy finally broke the silence.

"Isn't it funny how sometimes you don't have to talk to get to know somebody?"

"Yes, it is," Mason said.

Amy's hand then slid down Mason's arm to his hand. They intertwined their fingers and kept walking, hand in hand.

This is not your typical guy, Amy thought.

Wow, Mason thought. Holding hands with Amy was the best feeling he had ever experienced.

Mark Grady

Chapter Twelve

When Mason's dad came in from work, he walked into the kitchen and noticed the table was only set for two.

"Did Mason have to work over?"

"No," Joy said. "He called on break this afternoon and said he had a date tonight. Except he called it 'kind of a date.'"

"Really? Is it the same girl he said he was talking to at the shop?"

"I'm not sure, but he said her name was Amy."

"That doesn't sound like any of the girls from school. Must be her. Did he say where they were going? He didn't borrow the car."

Joy smiled at Woody's curiosity. He was sounding more like her these days.

"He said they were probably just going for a walk. I assume that meant on the beach."

"Oh, no," Woody said.

"Why do you say that?"

"I remember a couple of people who went for a walk on a beach and it got them both in years of trouble."

Joy laughed. "Trouble? That's what you call being with me? Trouble?"

"In a good way, of course," Woody said as he pulled Joy to him and gave her a hug and a kiss.

Amy and Mason had walked about a mile down the shore when they turned around and started heading back towards the boardwalk. They were getting close to the pier on the northern extension and that meant they were running out of beach to walk on without crossing over to Freeman Park which was usually noisy and crowded with campers and cars during the summer months. It was the only place on the beach where cars and overnight camping were allowed.

Their walk had again drifted into a contented silence. As they headed back, Amy eventually started telling a few stories about funny things that happened at her school last year. Since he usually was more interested in listening than talking, Amy was surprised and glad when Mason shared a few stories of his own from his school.

A little over an hour-and-a-half into their walk, Amy's mother left her home office in the new beach house and found her husband outside. He was watering some plants in the back yard.

"Where's Amy?" she asked.

"She said she was going walking around the boardwalk."

"I know that, but where is she now?"

"I guess she's still walking around the boardwalk."

"Go get her."

"Why? Is there an emergency?"

"No, I just think she's been gone long enough."

"She's not 10 years old anymore, Catherine, and she has never done anything to make us not trust her. Don't keep the reins so tight or you'll run her off when she is 18."

"She's too dependent on my money to run off."

"Your money? We both own the company, Catherine."

"It would be nothing if it weren't for me and you know it."

Paul turned off the hose, set it down and started walking away.

"Where are you going?" Catherine shouted his way.

"I need to go for a walk, too."

Catherine sighed in disgust and went to the street-legal golf cart in the carport under their stilted house. She drove off in it heading for the boardwalk area.

After getting to the boardwalk, Catherine began walking around looking for Amy. She was not seeing her anywhere which was making her angrier by the minute. Finally, she spotted Amy and Mason crossing over the ramp from the beach to the boardwalk. She made a beeline for them.

"Where have you been, Amy?"

"I've been walking on the beach, why?"

"Because it's time for you to come home."

"Mason, this is my mom."

"Hi, ma'am. Nice to meet you," Mason said. He held out his hand, but it was ignored.

"Mom, this is Mason."

"I know who he is," Catherine said and then turned towards Mason.

"I don't appreciate you taking my daughter off somewhere without asking my permission. You are no longer allowed to see her."

"Mom! You're being ridiculous! Mason did nothing wrong."

Ignoring Amy, Catherine continued. "Besides, my daughter is not interested in getting involved with or dating someone who works in a little donut shop and whose only dream is to work for a newspaper making a living in near-poverty."

Mason was visibly uncomfortable and embarrassed. It was easy for Amy to see it.

"Mason, I'm so sorry. Please don't listen to her. I'll be back to see you tomorrow."

"We'll just see about that," her mom said.

"I'm sorry, Amy," Mason said. "I didn't mean to cause you any trouble."

"You didn't, Mason," Amy said as her mom took her arm and dragged her to the golf cart.

Mason stood still on the ramp for a long time. He was in shock. He had met the first girl who ever gave him much more than a nod and now he wondered if he would ever see her again. Mostly, he worried about Amy.

How can she live with a mom like that? I hope she's not in trouble because of me.

Chapter Thirteen

Amy did not say a word on the ride back home with her mom at the controls of the golf cart. The look on Amy's face was all the communication she needed. It spoke volumes of disgust, anger and humiliation. When they came to a stop light, Catherine looked over at her daughter.

"You can be mad at me all you want, but I will always look out for your best interests. That boy is not in your best interests."

"How would you know? You didn't give him a chance to say more than three or four words," Amy said.

"You can be disrespectful all you want. One day, you'll thank me for keeping you on track with what's important."

"What's that, being rude to people?"

"No, focusing on your future and getting into Juilliard. You don't need any distractions from that."

"You know, Mom, people can have work, dreams and someone to love; even a family. You did it."

"And some of that has been a distraction to my business."

"Don't you mean you and Dad's business?"

"It would be nothing without me. I'm tired of talking about this."

Amy and her mother drove the rest of the way home and sat through dinner in silence. When Amy got up from the table, Catherine broke the silence.

"You going upstairs to practice?"

"No, I'm going to bed."

When Mason walked in the door of his home, it was still light outside. He was home quicker than his parents expected him, considering he had plans with a girl.

"Hey, son. Everything go well with your date?" Woody asked.

"It wasn't really a date. It was more of disaster."

Joy looked up from her book.

"Oh, no. What happened, honey?"

"Um, everything was actually going great. We took a long walk on the beach after I got off work. But, when we got back to the boardwalk, her mom was waiting for her. She said something about Amy not being interested in anybody like me or anybody who wanted to work for a newspaper. She said something else about me living in poverty."

"Wow," Woody said. "She sounds like a first class . . ."

"Don't say it," Joy interrupted. "But, her mom doesn't sound like a very nice lady. She doesn't even know anything about you. She has no business judging you or anyone she doesn't know. Her daughter would be very lucky to have a guy like you."

It was obvious from the expression on Mason's face he was beyond disappointed on how the evening ended up.

"Thanks, Mom, but I guess that's not going to happen."

"Maybe her mom will come to her senses. Anyway, I saved a few burgers we cooked on the grill for you. I'll go heat them up for you."

"No, thanks. I'm not really hungry."

"You want to watch a little TV with us?"

"No, ma'am. I just want to go to bed."

Joy and Woody glanced in each other's direction. They were concerned about Mason and how he was taking the terrible treatment he had suffered by Amy's mother.

Mason went into his room and laid down on his bed, staring at the ceiling. He wasn't sleepy at all, but he didn't want to stay awake either. His mind was filled with Amy. He thought he had met the best girl he had ever known. Now, it all was over with a few hateful words from her mother. Despite trying his best attempt to resist getting too upset, a tear ran down his cheek.

In an expensive home in a more ritzy neighborhood on the island, Amy was staring at the ceiling in her room. She couldn't sleep either.

I can't believe what Mom did to Mason, she thought. *He will probably never speak to me again. The best guy I've ever met and it's all ruined. Thanks, Mom. Just because you don't love anybody doesn't mean I can't.*

Amy turned over on her side and cried herself to sleep.

Chapter Fourteen

The next morning, Joy hoped to lift Mason's spirits by making him his favorite breakfast, pancakes and bacon, before he headed off to work. Her efforts did help a little.

"Thanks, Mom," Mason said. "That was really good."

Only the parent of a teenager could relate to Joy's feelings after hearing her son's compliment. She was proud of him and held back a tear. How many teenagers would still be thankful and considerate the morning after getting embarrassed and heartbroken on the same night at the same moment.

I have an incredible son, Joy thought. *That girl's mother is crazy.*

Less than a minute after Mason left for work, the phone rang. Joy knew who was calling before she answered the phone. Woody had to leave early that morning to make the drive to the lumber yard in Wilmington to buy treated lumber for a deck he was building at Kure Beach. Joy knew he would be concerned about how Mason was doing when he got up.

"How was he this morning?" Woody asked.

"He was okay, I guess. But, I could see in his eyes that what happened last night was still bothering him."

Woody was quiet for a moment, thinking, before he said, "I know every parent thinks their kids are great. But, that woman could not find a better guy to take her daughter out. She sounds like a piece of work."

"Piece of work is a lot nicer than what I called her when nobody could hear me this morning."

Woody laughed. "I think I will be in the mood for Britt's Donuts after lunch."

"Come get me before you go," Joy said.

They both really wanted to check on Mason.

Amy had stayed in her room all morning. She didn't want to come downstairs for breakfast and have to endure another lecture from her mother. Just the thought of it eliminated any appetite she had. She sat by her bedroom window looking out over the Atlantic, pondering the same thing she had on her mind when she went to sleep last night.

I hope Mason doesn't hate me. He's the most amazing guy I've ever met and Mom had to go screw everything up. She's a control freak. Why?

Amy's thoughts were interrupted with the only pleasant thing she had heard since talking with Mason the day before. It was the voice of her aunt, Mary. She was there to pick Amy up for a visit for a few days to her home at Sunset Beach.

Knowing her mom wouldn't try and start a major disagreement in front of her sister, Amy wandered downstairs and into the kitchen still wearing the oversized T-shirt she usually wore to bed. Mary made a beeline to give her niece a hug.

"How is my beautiful niece this morning?"

As she hugged Amy, Mary could sense the tension in the room between Amy and her mother. As usual, Mary kept her upbeat demeanor knowing it was obvious it was not a good time to ask any questions.

"What's this?" Mary asked Amy. "You not excited about our visit?"

"Of course, I am," Amy said. "Why would you say that?"

"Well, you are still in your PJs."

"Oh!" Amy laughed. "Won't take me but a minute."

Amy darted up the stairs to change clothes and place a few things for her visit in a tote bag. While she was upstairs, her mom was stoic around Mary.

"Is something wrong?" Mary asked.

"Why would something be wrong? The only thing wrong is you taking my daughter for two days and putting some of your silly thoughts about life in her head."

Before Mary could even respond, Catherine walked out of the kitchen and down the hall to her office. It was just a few seconds later when Amy appeared and said, "I'm ready when you are."

Amy and Mary left the house. It didn't go unnoticed by Mary that Amy didn't say goodbye to her mom.

Chapter Fifteen

They had barely pulled out of the driveway at Amy's beach house when Mary couldn't take it any longer.

"All right, niece of mine, you do know I've been around about a thousand blocks in my life. Something is up. What is wrong, honey?"

"Mom," was all Amy said.

"What has she done this time?"

"Really, it's not Mom I'm worried about as much as I am about Mason."

"Who's Mason?"

"The guy I went for a walk with on the beach last night."

"Oh, yes, the guy you were telling me about that you met at the donut shop. Did he do something wrong?"

"No, ma'am, he did everything right. He's the nicest guy I've ever met. When we got back to the boardwalk after our walk on the beach, Mom was waiting for us and she made Mason feel like crap." Amy went on to fill her aunt in on the details.

Mary had checked the Southport-Fort
Fisher Ferry schedule before she had left her
house by calling a toll-free number. The
recording said one of the two drive-on ferries
used on the route was down for maintenance.
She decided rather than wait a full hour for a
ferry, she would rather take that time to go
ahead and make the trip by way of driving up
to Wilmington, take the bridge across the Cape
Fear River, and then drive Highway 421 South.

Amy was finishing up the quick story of how
her mom had treated Mason as Mary was
driving across the Snow's Cut Bridge, leaving
the Carolina Beach town limits. Mary merged
into the left-hand turn lane just after she
crossed the bridge. Amy wondered why her
aunt was taking a different route.

"Are you trying to take River Road up to
Wilmington?"

"No, I'm going back to the beach for a little
bit."

"Did you forget something?"

"Nope. I all the sudden have a hankering for
some Britt's Donuts."

Amy felt her heart skip a beat.

As Mary pulled into the public parking lot
near the boardwalk, Amy's heart began to beat
harder.

"Aunt Mary? I don't know if it's such a good
idea for me to go into Britt's right now. Maybe
I better wait in the car. Mason probably hates
me."

Mary sighed and smiled. "Honey, there is one thing I do know and I haven't even met the boy. He does not hate you over something your mother did. If he hates anybody, he probably hates himself for being the reason your mom embarrassed you like that."

Reluctantly, Amy opened her car door, got out, and began walking towards the boardwalk with her aunt.

It was a weekday afternoon so there were only about six customers in the donut shop when they walked in. Amy immediately caught a glimpse of Mason, or at least the back of him, as he stood over the cooker, flipping a batch of donuts.

Amy and Mary grabbed a couple of stools near the end of the counter. Just as they were sitting down, Mason glanced over his shoulder and saw Amy with a lady who looked like she was in her 60s. His cheeks turned red and he quickly turned back to face the cooker. Amy didn't see Mason's response, but Mary did and she immediately realized who Mason was. About the same time, Bobby, the donut shop owner, appeared from around the corner.

"Hi, Mary, how in the world are you?" Bobby asked. "And you, too, Amy?"

Amy was surprised Bobby knew her name.

"We're doing well," Mary said. "How about you and your family?"

"Doing fine, just staying busy as usual during the summer months."

Mary laughed and said, "Yeah, but at least you get to take most of the winter months off to make up for all that summer work."

"I plead the fifth on that one," Bobby said.

While Mary laughed, Amy barely heard the exchange. She was still distracted by Mason being so nearby.

"What can I get you two?" Bobby asked.

"Wow, waited on by management," Mary said. "I feel special. Give us a few apiece to eat here and then we'll get a dozen to take with us. Amy's coming to spend a few days with me down at Sunset Beach."

"How many do you consider a few?" Bobby asked.

Mary laughed and said, "Normally, I consider a few to be two, but here I consider it a half dozen."

"Okay," Bobby smiled. "Anything to drink?"

"Oh, yes. I almost forgot. Could we get a couple of large Pepsis?"

"Absolutely. That it?"

"Just one more thing," Mary said. "Would you ask that young man back there cooking those good donuts to come out here when he gets a chance?"

Amy almost gasped.

"I sure will," Bobby said.

Chapter Sixteen

Bobby went to relieve Mason of his duties at the cooker.

"There is a great customer that's asked to speak with you," Bobby said, pointing in the direction of the woman sitting next to Amy. This time it was Mason's heart that skipped a beat.

Oh, no, Mason thought. *Now there's even more of her family after me.* He approached Amy and the lady very sheepishly.

"Hi, Mason," Amy said, sounding a lot less confident than the first time she had spoken with him just a few days ago. She sounded almost embarrassed and that made him even more uncomfortable.

"Hey, Amy," Mason said very quietly. "I'm really sorry about causing you so much trouble last night. I didn't mean . . ."

Mary jumped right in, interrupting.

"Hi, Mason. I'm Amy's aunt. My name is Mary and it's so nice to meet you. I'm sorry for interrupting, but I just can't sit here and let you take the blame for something you didn't do.

The only trouble caused last night was caused by my sister. So, I'm the one that's sorry for what you went through."

"It's okay, ma'am, but I don't think Amy's mom likes me very much."

"Psst, she wouldn't like Prince William, or anybody else, if they showed an interest in her daughter," Mary said. "Don't you let that bother you. From what Amy tells me and from what I can tell, and I'm a good judge of character, you seem like a mighty fine young man to me."

"Thank you, ma'am." Mason blushed.

He looked at Amy who was now wearing one of her famous smiles on her face. He finally felt comfortable enough to speak to her more. "Sounds fun, going to Sunset Beach. I've never been there."

"It's a really neat place. Aunt Mary and I love to walk down to the Kindred Spirit Mailbox and read what's inside."

"Kindred Spirit Mailbox?"

"You've never heard of it?"

"No, I haven't."

"It's really cool. There are notebooks, pens and pencils in the mailbox right on the beach. People come from all over the place to write messages and letters and put them in the mailbox for anyone to read."

"Wow," Mason said. "How did it get there?"

Amy remembered hearing the story some time ago, so she passed the question along to her aunt.

"Wasn't it some couple that put the mailbox there?" Amy asked Mary.

"That's right," Mary said. "They were dating at the time. She came up with the idea, but he was the one who put the post in the ground and installed the mailbox."

Mason was fascinated by the story.

"What happens to all the stuff people write down and put in the mailbox?"

"Usually, it just stays in the mailbox for people to read. Most of the messages in the notebooks and letters people put in it are mainly to remember special moments or get things off their chest," Mary said.

"That's why Aunt Mary and I like to walk down and see what's in the mailbox," Amy added. "We've sat down there for hours reading what people have written."

"Yes, we have," Mary said. "When the mailbox gets too full, volunteers come and clean it out and make sure there are enough blank pages in the notebook for people to write on."

"What happens to the stuff they clean out?" Mason asked.

"Amy said you wanted to be a newspaper reporter. Well, you're going to make a good one. That's a great question. I need to ask about that myself. I know they don't throw it away, but I'm not sure if they have a place in the library where they keep it or if some of the volunteers store it at their houses. I'm definitely going to ask my friend, Carol, who is one of those volunteers, and I'll let you know."

Before Mason could respond, he noticed some other people headed his way to see him. It was his mom and dad.

Chapter Seventeen

When Woody and Joy first walked into the donut shop, they scanned the area where the donuts are rolled out as dough, cut and placed in the cooker before being dipped in glaze. They didn't see Mason working.

"Oh, there he is," Joy said, pointing towards the end of the counter where Mason was talking to a lady and a girl who looked to be about Mason's age.

Mason was in the middle of answering a question Amy's aunt had asked him about what kind of writing he wanted to do for newspapers. He lost his train of thought when he glanced up.

"Oh, it's my folks," he said.

"Son, have they got you doing customer relations now?" his dad asked, smiling as he approached.

"Hi, Dad, this is Amy."

"Hi Amy," Woody and Joy said, almost in unison. They were a little surprised to meet Amy and see her in the donut shop talking with Mason considering the story they had heard last night. Before Mason could introduce Amy's aunt, Woody said, "Hi, you must be Amy's mom."

"Oh, no, I'm just her aunt," Mary said. "I'm not responsible for the actions of my sister towards your son last night. That's why I wanted to bring Amy down and talk to him. And I figured I'd load up on some Britt's Donuts in the process."

Everybody laughed.

"They do have a way of putting things in perspective," Woody said. "It's nice to meet you both."

"Speaking of donuts, I better get back to work," Mason said.

"Just one second," Mary said to Mason. She grabbed a napkin, quickly gathered a pen from her purse, and wrote a telephone number on the napkin. She handed it to Mason and said, "Don't lose that. It's the number to my house at Sunset Beach. Amy will be with me the next few days, at least, and you better call at least once a day. No, make that twice a day. If we've stepped out, I've got one of those answering machines, so you can leave a message and Amy will call you the moment we get back in."

"Thank you, ma'am," Mason said.

As he took the napkin and carefully put it in his pocket, Joy leaned towards Amy and whispered, "Your aunt is a hoot."

"She sure is," Amy said, smiling.

As Mason walked away to head back to his duties, Mary said to Woody and Joy, "You folks sit down and join us."

"Thanks," Joy said. "We can't come in here and not get at least a few donuts."

"You've got that right," Mary said.

It is common knowledge to anyone who has ever been to Britt's Donuts that they are like no other donuts anywhere. They are so light you wonder if they'll float away and they melt in your mouth.

Joy and Woody joined Amy and Mary. They enjoyed a few donuts and talked for almost 30 minutes. Frequently, Mason would glance in their direction and Amy would see him and smile. He smiled back and thought about how lucky he was for the turn of events after the nightmare he had experienced the night before. He was thinking about an important promise he had to keep when he got off work that evening. He had a telephone number in his pocket he needed to call.

Chapter Eighteen

The atmosphere in Mary's car was very upbeat during the drive from the Carolina Beach boardwalk to Sunset Beach. It was definitely different than the mood Amy was in when her aunt picked her up that morning and as Amy relayed the story of how her sister had treated Mason after their walk on the beach the night before.

Mary and Amy talked about their plans during the visit, including their walks to the Kindred Spirit Mailbox and places to eat dinner. Then, Mary brought up the subject of Mason.

"I sure like Mason," she said. "He seems like a really good fella."

"See? I told you, Aunt Mary. I wish Mom could see that."

"Your mom hasn't been around anybody but people she lets be around her. That's not a criticism, it just means she hasn't been around enough folks to know how to judge them. You've heard that saying, 'I've been around the block a few times?'"

"Yes, ma'am."

"Well, I've been around the block about a thousand times."

"I know. You say that all the time," Amy said as she laughed and instantly thought about Mason's mom saying her aunt was "a hoot."

"And I'll tell you something else," Mary continued. "You know why he's such a good guy?"

"Why's that?"

"Look at his parents. I could tell the minute they sat down with us at the donut shop they were good people, too. Not only that, look at the way his mother and father treated each other. Now, that's a couple still in love after being with each other a long time. You know what that tells me don't you?"

"What's that?" Amy asked. She was sincerely interested in her aunt's opinions of the parents of the guy she could not stop thinking about.

"It tells me Mason has been raised in a home where his mom and dad have not just told him, but have shown him, how people are supposed to treat each other. That's a powerful way to grow up."

It was quiet in Mary's car for the next ten miles of their drive to Sunset Beach. Amy was thinking about everything her aunt had just told her. It made her feel confident her first impression of Mason was a good one since her aunt felt the same way. In the meantime, Mary was pondering the frustration she had with her sister's actions the night before. She knew Catherine could do some serious damage to the relationship with her daughter.

That sister of mine is going to mess around and have her own daughter despise her if she isn't careful. But, I better be careful talking too much about her mother. I don't want to be the one to cause even more dissension. I'm going to have to have a talk with Catherine when I bring Amy back home.

"Aunt Mary?" Amy said, breaking the silence. "How am I going to get Mom to see in Mason what I see in him?"

Since Mary was just thinking about the situation, she wanted to be careful in her answer. She didn't want to make things worse.

"Um, the good thing is you're young and you don't have to be in a hurry," Mary responded. "So, I wouldn't push too hard to try and change your mom's mind. Give her a little while to think about it. What happened last night is probably as fresh on her mind as it is on your's and Mason's. That's why our trip is good timing, don't you think?"

"Yes, ma'am, it is. But, Mom's so used to controlling everything, I don't know if it will ever blow over as far as she is concerned."

"I know it's hard to see it, but your mother thought she was looking after you. She just had a way of showing it that wasn't a good one."

"You've got that right," Amy said. "I mean, if she didn't want me to see Mason, why didn't she just tell me that when we were at home? Why did she have to make a scene and belittle Mason in front of me?"

"I'm so sorry that happened, honey. I think she kind of got that from our mother. She died when you were little, so you didn't get to know her, but she could sometimes be a little, oh, I don't know how to describe it . . ."

"Controlling?" Amy asked.

"Well, maybe a little brash."

Mary was becoming uncomfortable about the direction their conversation was taking, but she knew Amy was no longer a little girl. Mary knew nothing ever got fixed by sweeping it under the rug or doing what she called "playing ostrich by sticking your head in the ground and pretending it doesn't exist."

"Well, like all couples do, I think, our dad learned what triggered our mother and vice-versa, so they kind of avoided subjects that they knew would cause trouble. Plus, since Daddy was very successful when he started their business, Mother didn't want to upset the apple cart too much with him. She had become very used to the lifestyle. So, your mother, James and I became the ones who she tried to control the most."

Mary stopped herself. She knew she was getting too close to having to explain the details of what had happened to Amy's grandfather, who she never knew.

"I probably shouldn't have told you all that," Mary continued, "but maybe it will help you understand why your mom is like she is. It's not all her fault."

"How come you are completely opposite, Aunt Mary?"

"I don't know. I guess people always process things differently. While your mom was very impressed with the money and the lifestyle, and the business, I didn't really want anything to do with all of it. I just wanted a simple life."

"Is that why Mom inherited the ad agency instead of you?"

Mary hesitated. She didn't know if she should go down that road. But, it was the truth.

"Um, actually I did. But, all I saw was a business that kept everybody so busy they never had time for family. I didn't want that. So, I worked a deal with your mom that she would give me her half of the beach house we inherited, the one I live in now, and she could have the whole business."

"Wow." Amy said. "But, isn't the business worth a lot more than one house?"

"Not to me, it isn't." Mary said.

"Sounds like you and I are more alike than Mom and I are."

"You are also old enough to know that your dad was the one who kept the agency from dying."

"What? Mom always says it is nothing without her, that she is the one who made it successful."

Mary found herself hesitating again. She wanted to give Paul a complement and not make her sister look all bad in front of her daughter.

"Catherine definitely has a business mind, but the advertising business is based on a lot of creativity. She focused too much on the numbers and the creative staff started going to work for other agencies. Your dad came along and was the most creative person any of us had ever known. He had even drawn cartoons for newspapers while he was doing a stint in the Army."

"I guess I don't know as much about my parents as I thought I did," Amy said.

"Most of us don't know much about our parents. Anyway, your mom offered your dad a partnership if he would run the creative side of things. All the advertisers loved his work and it put the agency back on top again."

"I sure wish Mom would give Mason the same chance she gave Dad."

Hearing her niece suffering over her mother's reaction to a genuinely good guy bothered Mary a great deal. She wanted to help.

"I'll tell you what, as far as this thing with Mason and your mother, I'll have a one-on-one talk with Catherine when we come back to bring you home. In the meantime, let's talk about what kind of notes we might find in that mailbox tomorrow."

That had become a game Amy and Mary played every time they planned to make the walk down to the mailbox. Whoever guessed the most stories or kinds of messages they would find correctly did not have to wash the dishes that day.

"Oh, okay," Amy said. "I bet there is a letter in there to a girl from a guy who still loves her after they have had a big fight."

"Good one," Mary said. "I bet there is a letter in there from a girl who wants to convince her parents to like her boyfriend as much as she does."

Amy burst out laughing. "Hey, I might have to write that one myself and put it in there tomorrow."

"I've got another one," Amy said. "I bet there is a story in there from somebody who hasn't seen someone in a long time, but still loves them."

"Ah, the proverbial one that got away," Mary said.

The conversation with her aunt made the drive go by quickly. They were already crossing the bridge onto Sunset Beach.

Chapter Nineteen

Mason got off work a little over two hours after Amy, her aunt, and his mom and dad, had left the donut shop. Because of the very nice surprise visit from them all to the shop, he had been in very good spirits the rest of his shift. Mason focused on a phone call he would be making later that evening.

Because of what had happened between Amy, her mom and him the night before, Mason had walked to work that morning, hoping it would clear his mind a little. Now, walking home, he was in an entirely different mood. He had a smile on his face as he thought about how lucky he was considering the 180-degree turn of events the day had brought his way.

Mason glanced at his watch the fifth time during his walk home, this time as he was walking up the five steps of his front porch. It was almost 5:30 in the afternoon. He guessed that Amy and her aunt had arrived in Sunset Beach about 15 minutes ago. He wanted to call right now but decided he would wait a few hours to give Amy and Mary a chance to eat dinner and visit a while before he interrupted their time together.

The moment Mason walked in the front door, his mom popped into the living room from the kitchen and his dad jumped out of his favorite chair in front of the TV. They both said, almost in unison, "We really like Amy."

Mason laughed and said, "So do I."

"I can see why you like her," Joy said. "And her aunt sure is a feisty lady. I really like her, too."

"Me, too," Woody said.

"I should have thanked her aunt for bringing Amy by today," Mason said. "If she answers when I call Amy tonight I can tell her then."

"That's nice of you to think to thank her," Woody said. "Proud of you, Son."

"Thanks, Dad. I think I'll go take a shower. I smell like dough and donuts."

"Isn't that a good thing?" Joy asked.

As Mason left the room, Joy and Woody looked at each other. They didn't have to say a word. They knew they both were thinking the same thing. They were very glad their son was in much better shape than he was when he got home the night before. They both thought they needed to thank Mary, too.

Chapter Twenty

"Are you hungry?" Mary asked Amy a few minutes after they arrived at her aunt's house on Sunset Beach.

"Not yet. I think I ate one too many donuts," Amy said.

"You can never eat too many Britt's Donuts."

Amy laughed and Mary added, "But, I'm not hungry either. When we are we can head out and get some seafood."

"Sounds good to me," Amy said.

Mary changed the subject.

"It just hit me that I didn't see you bring your violin. Did you forget it?"

"No, ma'am. I need a break from it. I was hoping you'd let me play your keyboard some while I'm here."

"Hope you can play it? You know you're welcome to anything in my home anytime. As much as you've been playing the violin lately, I thought you wouldn't want to be away from it long."

Amy's expression changed. She looked down.

"Oh, Lord, I must've said something I shouldn't have. I'm sorry, honey," Mary said, reaching out and putting her arm around her niece.

"You didn't say anything wrong at all, Aunt Mary. It's just this fight with Mom about Mason has me thinking about a lot of different things . . . even the violin."

"You mean you're thinking about giving up music?"

"No, ma'am, not at all. It's not about music, it's about what I'm playing. It's not that I don't like the violin," Amy said as she sat down in a chair in Mary's breakfast nook. To her aunt, it looked like a sign Amy needed to talk, so she sat down across from her niece.

"The violin has never been my passion. It was Mom's passion for me. I probably never told you this, but you are the reason I fell in love with music. When we came over when I was little, my favorite times were when we sat down and you played those funny songs on the old piano you used to have."

"Gosh, you must have only been between three and six when we did that. You still remember?

"Yes, ma'am, like yesterday. You'd play *Three Little Fishes* and *Mary Had A Little Lamb* and add really funny verses you'd make up. I laughed till I cried. Mom even laughed. I saw how happy music could make people and I wanted to be just like you."

Amy noticed a little tear form in the corner of one of her aunt's eyes.

"Oh, no. I'm the one saying something I shouldn't have," Amy said.

"No, no, not at all," Mary said. "It just means so much to me to know I had that kind of effect on you. I just can't believe how grown up and mature you sound these days."

"It's all true," Amy said. "I loved those times. After you'd play those funny songs you'd start playing songs like *Maple Leaf Rag* and I loved it."

"I sure wish I could still play some of those old ragtime and boogie woogie tunes, but this blasted arthritis I inherited from my dad makes that kind of a challenge these days. I can't tell you how honored I am to hear you say I somehow inspired you to want to play music. You are a natural. You didn't need me to help."

"Well, you did, more than you'll ever know. I always wanted to play the piano because of you. The violin wasn't my choice, it was Mom's. When I told her I wanted to be a musician and play the piano, she said, 'Everybody plays the piano. If you want to be a musician, that's fine, but you're going to play something that makes you stand out like a real musician, like the violin.'"

Amy paused a moment and then continued.

"The next day after she said that, Mom took me to a music store in the mall in Charlotte and bought me the most expensive violin they had in the store. I kept looking at the beautiful pianos and the new fancy, high-tech keyboards they had in there. Mom ignored all that. She had made up her mind and I knew I couldn't change it. I never said anything because I didn't want her to think I didn't appreciate what she had just bought me, especially with what it cost."

It was quiet for a moment around Mary's small, quaint breakfast nook table. They were both thinking about the story Amy had just shared. Amy finally broke the silence when she asked, "Why is Mom like that?"

Mary smiled and sighed. She had already promised herself on the drive down that she was going to be very careful not to make a bad situation worse by piling on any more negative opinions about her sister. Mary decided just to let the question hang in the air. She changed the subject.

"I don't know about you, pretty niece of mine, but now I am hungry. What you say we head over to that seafood place where we ate the last time you were here."

Mary noticed Amy glance over at the phone in the kitchen before she answered.

"You think maybe we could get it to go," Amy asked. "It's been awhile since I've been down, so I'd kind of like to spend as much time as I can here at your house tonight."

Like Mary had said many times, she had been around the block a thousand times. She immediately knew the motivation behind Amy's request. She was waiting for a special call from a special guy at Carolina Beach.

"You know what? Now that you mention it, all that driving today kind of wore me out. Why don't I call and order a pizza delivered here tonight and we'll do seafood tomorrow."

"Sounds perfect," Amy said.

Mary called her favorite pizza place on Sunset Beach and ordered a large, Italian-style pepperoni pizza to be delivered to her house. The moment she placed her phone back in the cradle, it started ringing. Mary picked it right up.

"Hello."

A smile spread across Mary's face and she looked at Amy who had had a look of hope on her face.

"Well, hi Mason! It's good to hear from you."

Mary listened for a moment as Mason spoke on the other end.

"Oh, you don't have to thank me. I wanted to bring her by to see you, but you are certainly welcome. Amy's right here. Let me put her on."

Chapter Twenty-One

Amy and Mason talked on the phone for almost two hours. About 30 minutes into their conversation, the pizza was delivered. Amy said, "Aunt Mary ordered us a pizza and it just got here so I guess I better go."

Mary heard what Amy told Mason, so she said, "Nonsense, you don't have to hang up. You keep talking to Mason. I'll bring you a Coke and your pizza."

"Thanks, Aunt Mary."

Mason heard the exchange on his end. "Your aunt is really something."

"That, she is." They went back to talking about all kinds of subjects. They just enjoyed hearing each other's voice.

All of their conversation was upbeat. Nobody had to compare what had happened the night before with what had transpired today. However, Mason was still worried things may change when Amy returned home and under her mother's roof. The more they talked, the more Mason hoped this was just the beginning of many more nights they would spend talking.

The more they talked, the more he also worried about Amy's mom. He hoped this great day would not be a short-lived event when Amy returned to Carolina Beach. It was obvious to Mason her mom was not impressed with him at all.

Mason was having a debate with himself as he and Amy talked. He wondered if he should tell Amy about his concern. Then, he remembered something his mom had told him more than once – "You should never be afraid to tell someone if something is bothering you." He decided to take his mother's advice.

"Can I ask you something?"

"Always," Amy replied.

"Do you think your mom will try and keep you from talking to me or seeing me when you get back?"

"I've got some good news about that."

"Really? You mean she's okay about everything now?"

"Not yet, I don't think, but Aunt Mary said she's going to have a talk with Mom about us when we get back. If anyone can get through to Mom, it's Aunt Mary."

"That is good news," Mason said, feeling very relieved.

"And even if she doesn't listen to Aunt Mary, we will make it work out."

Mason liked the sound of that, especially the "we" part.

At Amy's beach house, her mom was getting madder by the minute. She had been trying to call her sister's house at Sunset Beach for almost two hours. She had been trying every two or three minutes and each time she only heard a busy signal. Catherine was not only mad about not being able to get through, she was also angry her sister had never taken her advice about getting call waiting added to her home phone service.

"It's just two dollars a month," Catherine had said when they argued about it.

"I don't care if it's free," Mary had responded. "I think it's rude to interrupt someone in the middle of a call."

"What if it's an emergency?" Catherine asked.

"If it's that much of an emergency, call the police and send them over to tell me. Besides, most of the people trying to get through are probably those blasted people trying to sell you something on the phone."

Reliving that conversation in her mind, Catherine tried calling Mary's phone again. Still busy. Catherine started walking through the house trying to vent off some of her frustration. When she walked through the kitchen, she noticed her husband was sitting at the table working on today's *New York Times* crossword puzzle. He looked up and saw the look on her face.

"What's wrong with you?" he asked.

"I've been trying to get through to Mary's house for two hours and keep getting a busy signal. I can't even find out if they made it there all right."

"If you're getting a busy signal, wouldn't that mean they made it? Mary doesn't have anybody else living there that would be on the phone."

"Oh, you sound like Mary with all her Wayne Dyer positive thinking crap. And why are you doing something such a waste of time as doing a crossword puzzle?"

"It's the way I like to relax," he said. "You know that. I like them."

Catherine sighed as deliberately loudly as she could before she stormed out of the room. She was just about to try Mary's number again when her phone rang and Catherine answered it. It was her sister on the other end. Mary had decided it was best to talk to her sister about Amy and Mason now instead of waiting until she brought Amy back home.

Chapter Twenty-Two

"It's about time," Catherine said when she heard her sister's voice on the other end of the line.

"About time for what?" Mary asked.

"You know for what. About time I hear from you or Amy. I've been trying to get through for over two hours. I told you to get call waiting."

"I'm glad I don't have it because it sounded like Amy was having a very pleasant conversation."

"Who was she talking to?"

"To a really nice boy I met today named Mason."

"What?!?!" Catherine had obviously hit the roof. "Did she call him?"

Mary remained calm. "No, I gave Mason my number and told him to call Amy while she is here visiting."

"I made it clear to both of them I did not want them in any kind of relationship and that includes talking on the phone. So, while you may not have known that until now, now you do. So, if he calls again you are to tell him to never call back."

"I'll do nothing of the sort," Mary said.

"I will not have you disrespecting me and interfering in my rules for my daughter. Go tell Amy to have her things ready. I'm leaving here in ten minutes to come get her."

"If you do something silly like that, I'll put her in my car before you get here and we'll go spend the night in a motel in Myrtle Beach."

"You are going to force me to call the police on my own sister," Catherine said. She had a bite in her voice.

"Will you just hush a minute and listen to me for a change? You are going to make your daughter despise you if you aren't careful. Have you forgotten she will be 18 in less than a year? If you try to control everything in her life, especially trying to keep her from going on a date with a boy she likes, which is normal by the way, you're going to make her leave and never look back."

"That's ridiculous," Catherine shot back. "She knows I'm keeping her on track to do the right thing."

"What's wrong with her having a boyfriend?" Mary asked.

"Because it's distracting her from focusing on her violin practice so she is assured her spot at Juilliard."

"Is that the right thing for her, or for you?"

"I don't even know why I'm having this conversation with you. Amy is my daughter and, quite frankly, this is none of your business."

"You're my sister and Amy is my niece. It is very much my business if you two end up miserable and estranged from each other."

"That's silly," Catherine said.

"You mean silly like our brother?"

Mary's words brought the conversation to an abrupt halt. Catherine was now speechless. Mary knew she had hit a nerve with her sister and hoped it made her point, so she let the silence just hang there for a moment.

"Think about it, Catherine. Please. Didn't our mother do the same thing to James? Didn't she try to over-control every aspect of his life? She had his best interests at heart, too. But she pushed and pushed until she ended up spending most of her life hardly ever seeing her only son. I don't want that to happen to you and Amy."

There was more silence on Catherine's end of the line. Mary just waited, hoping.

"Well, I'll let this mess go on for a little while," Catherine finally said. "It will probably be over when she goes back to school in Charlotte anyway. But, if she ends up in any kind of trouble with that boy, I'm holding you personally responsible. You're the one encouraging this."

"Fair enough," Mary said. "But I hope you'll ease up or you'll lose a great daughter."

Catherine hung up. Mary smiled. She knew she had made an important comparison when she brought up their brother and mother. Catherine and Mary's mom was very much like Catherine, insisting on being in control of everything.

When James became interested in a girl their mom said was "from the bad part of town," she shipped her son almost a thousand miles away to a boarding school. Two years later, on his 18th birthday, James walked off the boarding school campus and moved across the country to Placerville, California. He opened a woodworking shop, mainly making cabinets.

Since their mother had spent most of James' life prepping him for law school, she was incensed at his decision. But, after what she had done to him and the girl he liked, he never wanted anything to do with the subject of law ever again. Even when he decided to create an LLC for his business, he did the work online instead of walking into a lawyer's office.

When James moved away, the family rarely saw him after that. He returned home for their mother's funeral and left the next morning.

Catherine had been thinking about her brother ever since she had hung up on her sister. She definitely did not want to repeat the story of James and their mother when it came to Amy. However, instead of simply letting an innocent high school summer romance happen between her daughter and Mason, she decided she just needed another way to keep them apart without her being the bad guy.

Catherine's mind started concocting a plan.

You want a boyfriend, Amy? Fine. I'll get you a boyfriend worth having.

Catherine walked down the hall to her office at the beach house and sat down at her desk. She thumbed through her Rolodex until she found the telephone number of Dr. Wilson Crabtree, one of Charlotte, North Carolina's most prominent physicians. He happened to be their neighbor in Charlotte.

The Crabtrees' son, Drake, was on the road to follow in his father's footsteps and go to medical school. Catherine also knew, by occasionally listening in on conversations between Amy and her friends when they were over, that Drake had told all her friends how pretty he thought Amy is.

"Hello."

"Hi, Wilson, this is your neighbor, Catherine. You're just the one I hoped to talk to."

Chapter Twenty-Three

After a few minutes of neighborly small talk, Catherine eased into the real purpose of her call.

"Yes, we really are enjoying our first summer in the new beach house, but I have been a little concerned about Amy."

"Oh, is she okay?" Dr. Crabtree asked.

"She's fine. It's just she hasn't been able to make many friends here since most people are here at the beach for just a few days at a time. That's one of the reasons I'm calling."

"How can we help?"

"Well, I thought it would be nice if I could surprise her by bringing a little of Charlotte here by having a long-time friend come down for a visit. Do you think Drake would enjoy a week at the beach? Of course, he'd have his own room with a private bath."

"That sure sounds like a nice offer knowing how Drake feels about Amy. I'm sure he'd love to see her, but I don't know what his plans are for the next few weeks. It's been so busy at the practice he and I haven't had much time to catch up. Let me get him to the phone."

"Thanks, Wilson, I appreciate that."

In less than a minute, Drake Crabtree picked up the phone. Catherine had no problem selling him on the idea of coming down to spend some time with Amy and spend a week at the beach. He was talking to some guys at the country club earlier in the afternoon and they were arguing about who the hottest girl at school was.

"I think Amy is hot," Drake had said.

"No way," Jeff Harriott, son of a famous Charlotte architect, said. "She's kind of weird. Always has her face in a book or playing a violin. Kind of geeky if you ask me."

"You'd forget all about her geeky side if you saw her in a bikini at her pool. It's the advantage I have living next door to her and being able to see their pool from my room upstairs."

"Sounds like a sick stalker," Jeff said.

"Oh, shut up," Drake said.

It wasn't lost on Drake that Amy's mother's invitation had happened the very day he had been in that discussion with his friends.

"Thanks, Mrs. Cole, I really appreciate the invitation. I can't wait to see Amy again. Is she there? I'd love to talk to her."

"She's not here right now, Drake. She's at Sunset Beach with my sister for a few days. And I was hoping we could make your visit a surprise. If you don't mind, could we keep this our secret? You could just plan on being here on Monday afternoon to surprise her."

"Oh, sure, absolutely. Sounds good to me. Thanks."

"No, thank *you*, Drake. I appreciate you coming down to see her. Drive carefully on your way down Monday."

"I will. See you and Amy on Monday."

Catherine hung up and smiled. She knew her sister was right. If she pushed too hard to keep Amy away from Mason, it could backfire and have the opposite effect. However, having a visit from a very wealthy boy who shows up driving a very expensive car would just have to be a distraction. She smiled even more when she thought how Mason would react seeing Amy riding around with a very handsome boy in a convertible BMW.

After Amy and Mason talked earlier, Amy had gone upstairs to take a shower and that was when Mary had taken advantage of the time to have her confidential call with her sister. Amy came back downstairs in her oversized T-shirt and sat down beside her aunt just a few minutes after Catherine and Mary had finished their talk.

Mary and Amy started talking about Mason and his parents again. Mary was singing their praises.

"You can just tell they're good people."

"I think so, too," Amy said. "And thank you for everything today, Aunt Mary. I don't know what I'd do without you."

"Anything in the world for my wonderful niece. I know I'm changing the subject, but what time do you want to head down to the mailbox tomorrow?"

"Mason said he has to be at work tomorrow morning at 10:00, so could we wait until after that time in case he decides to call before he goes to work?

"Of course, we can," Mary said. "That gives me a little time to sleep in. After 10:00 works perfect for me."

Chapter Twenty-Four

After their talk, Amy and Mary headed to their bedrooms to settle in for the evening. Amy had always had her own room at her aunt's house as long as she could remember.

Amy was about to get into bed and realized she was still too excited thinking about Mason and the support of her aunt to even think about going to sleep right now. Plus, bringing up her memories about the songs Mary had played for her on the piano when she was a little girl got her thinking about that keyboard downstairs. She decided she could unwind by going to play it a while. To keep from waking her aunt, she grabbed some headphones from her tote and took them downstairs and plugged them into the keyboard.

When she lifted the piano stool at the keyboard, Amy found all kinds of sheet music and they were almost all songs she remembered Mary playing. She sat down and started playing. Each song brought back happy memories. She remembered how her aunt would play a song and then show her some simple chords so she could play along, too.

Amy played a lot longer than she intended to because she loved every minute. Playing the keyboard just added to what had turned out to be a great night. When she looked at the clock, it was almost 1:30 in the morning, so she decided she better get some sleep.

Despite her late night, Amy was up by 8:00 the next morning. She was hoping she would get a call from Mason and she wasn't disappointed. At 8:45, Mary's phone rang and Amy answered it.

"I'm not calling too early, am I?" Mason asked Amy.

"Not at all. I've been staring at the phone all morning hoping you'd call."

That made Mason feel great.

"It was all I could do to wait this long to call. I got up at 6:30 and I've been waiting for a time that I hoped wouldn't wake you or your aunt. I should have asked when would be a good time to call when we were talking last night."

"That's okay. I love to hear from you anytime."

They picked up where they left off on their call last night. There was never a lull in the conversation when they talked. It was obvious they had been cut from the same cloth when it came to things that interested them and being able to talk easily.

Just as Amy had gotten lost in time while playing her aunt's keyboard last night, they both experienced the same thing during their morning telephone call until Mason happened to glance at his watch.

"Oh, no. I've got to be at work in 20 minutes. I guess I better get going."

"We've been on the phone that long? Wow. Sure doesn't seem like it," Amy said. "I better let you go. Have fun at work and eat a donut for me."

Mason laughed and said, "I need to stop eating so many of those things. Oh, you going to that mailbox you were telling me about today?"

"We sure are. We'll probably be heading out in just a little bit."

"Is it okay if I call back tonight so I can hear about what kind of stories you find in there?"

"Did you just ask me if it was okay if you call tonight? It's more than okay. I'd be sad if you didn't call."

"Me, too," Mason said. "Talk to you tonight."

Just as Amy and Mason were exchanging their goodbyes, Mary walked into the kitchen.

"Can I lay a thousand dollar bet on who that was on the phone?" Mary asked.

"No, ma'am, cause I don't have a thousand dollars to give you and I know you know who that was."

"Well, doggone it, I was hoping to win some money for a cruise."

They both laughed.

"You ready to eat a quick breakfast and hike on down to the Kindred Spirit Mailbox?" Mary asked.

"Yes, ma'am."

"Good. Let's have a completely unhealthy breakfast. I'm going to take some of those donuts we brought home out of the freezer and heat 'em up in the microwave. We'll get all sugared-up for our walk."

"Sounds good to me," Amy said.

Although they were separated by many miles along the North Carolina coast, as Mason walked to work and as Amy strolled with her aunt down Sunset Beach, headed to the mailbox, they both shared a very warm and content feeling. It was something neither of them would ever be able to adequately express with words.

Not far from the Kindred Spirit Mailbox, Amy had decided she knew what this amazing feeling she was having was all about.

I know what this is. I'm falling in love.

Chapter Twenty-Five

A mild cold front had passed through the area in the overnight. It had brought the usually almost unbearable summer humidity in eastern North Carolina down to a decent level. It was 87 degrees, but it felt a lot better than the mid-to-upper 90s the coast had endured for over a week. It made Amy and Mary's walk down to the Kindred Spirit Mailbox a pleasant one.

Mary was a little winded from the slightly-over-a-mile walk, so she sat down on one of the wooden benches built by volunteers beside the mailbox.

Amy reached inside the mailbox and pulled out a notebook and a few of the envelopes from inside. She sat down beside her aunt and handed her some of the stack. They started reading.

While Amy was opening some of the unsealed envelopes and reading what was inside, Mary was scanning some of the contributions in the notebook. It was almost completely filled with new notes, comments and stories.

They both were engrossed in their reading until Amy opened an envelope and began reading the letter inside. It was obvious it had been written on an old typewriter that could use a new ribbon.

"Oh, no."

Mary looked up from the notebook. "What is it, honey?"

"Read this one," Amy said, handing the letter to her aunt.

Mary noticed a tear forming in one of Amy's eyes. The more Mary read the letter, the more tear drops began to hit the paper she was reading.

Dear Debbie,

It has taken me over a year to be able to write you this letter. I remember the day your best friend, Lisa, told you about this mailbox on the beach she discovered when her family came here for vacation. You said you wanted to see the mailbox someday.

I have cried every day because I never brought you here. I drove from our house in

Memphis all night to leave you this letter here. I prayed the entire trip that angels would let you know the letter is here for you to read.

When we lost your mom to cancer, you were only 11. I worried every day if I would be able to take on being dad and mom for you. We ended up okay as a team, didn't we? I am so proud of the girl you became.

Whenever you brought home a report card and every time I watched you play your favorite sport, tennis, I was so proud. And I'll never forget it being so hard to hold back tears when you came down the steps wearing the gown you had picked out and we had bought at the mall the week before.

You looked so beautiful when you walked out the door to go to your junior-senior prom with that nice young man who asked you to be your date. As you got into his car, I thought about how fast time had gone by. It was hard to believe that one year from that night, you would be graduating from high school.

If only I had known the night of that prom would be the last time I would ever see you. I would have told you a million times more how much I loved you and how proud I was to be the man you called your dad.

Over the past year, I ask myself every day why the girl driving that other car thought it was okay to be driving so fast and texting her friends at the same time. Why did it have to be you, or anybody, taken by such a selfish, terrible act. I also ask every day for the strength to get through one more day.

Losing you and your mom proved two things to me. First, no one should ever take a single day for granted. The second thing is that it is true what many have said, that only the good die young.

I hope you and your mom are loving your days of spending forever together.

I love you both and I think about you both every minute.

-    Dad

Amy sat quietly as her aunt read the letter. She couldn't bring herself to read something else while she was waiting. The letter had hit her straight in the heart. When Mary finished reading, she reached into her purse and retrieved a Kleenex so she could dab her eyes.

"That poor man and that poor girl," Mary said. "Please promise me you will always drive carefully and keep your eyes out watching what everybody else is doing while they are driving."

"I promise, Aunt Mary."

For another hour, Amy and Mary read more letters, notes and stories placed in the Kindred Spirit Mailbox from people across the country and even from overseas. There were some happy stories about meeting soul mates and other heartbreaking stories, including a few written as tributes to spouses who had passed away. All of the stories and letters moved Amy, but she still could not forget the letter written by a dad who had lost his daughter in a car accident the night of her school prom. She was still thinking about the sad letter as they walked back to Mary's house from the mailbox.

"You think that man will be okay? The one who wrote the letter to his daughter who died in that wreck?" Amy asked.

"We're not supposed to bury our children," Mary said. "He'll never completely get over it, but I get the feeling that writing the letter and driving all the way over here from western

Tennessee was good therapy for him. It helped him say what he was thinking."

"He sure loved his daughter."

"Yes, he did," Mary said. She was also still moved by the power of the letter.

About five minutes flowed by as Amy and Mary walked along the shore listening to the surf and the seagulls. They enjoyed the refreshing breeze coming ashore from the Atlantic. Mary was obviously still thinking about the same letter Amy was.

"Even though people don't always show it, there is something special between good fathers and their daughters. I can't imagine how heartbroken he was after losing his wife and his daughter."

Amy just nodded. Mary was still thinking about the loss.

"And, you know, it's not always death that tears dads and daughters apart. It makes me so mad when couples get a divorce and then use their children as pawns. I hate to admit it, but that's when it's women who can be evil. They know they usually end up with custody and then they do everything they can to keep children from spending time with their dads. Just because the mom wants to move on from her ex doesn't mean that's a good thing for children."

"Yes, ma'am," was all Amy said. Her own family never spoke much about their history, but Amy sensed her aunt's observations on dads and children came from some personal experience. Amy's grandmother, the mother of her mom and her aunt, had died years ago. She had never heard either of them speak of their father.

When Amy was in middle school, she brought up the subject of her grandfather after meeting the grandfather of one of her friends.

"Where is my grandfather? Amy had asked. "Is he dead?"

Amy's mother responded by just walking out of the room as if she had not heard the question. Her dad simply said, "He was a good man." The subject never came up again.

Several more minutes passed in silence before Amy and Mary began approaching her aunt's house. Amy thought of the moving letter they had read one more time.

It's so sad families get torn apart like that. And to think it happens when people are still living is just as sad. Maybe if people would read that dad's letter they'd think twice about the way they treat each other.

Amy and Mary were walking up the steps to the porch when they both heard the phone in the house begin ringing.

"You better run and get that," Mary said, smiling. "I bet it's for you."

Chapter Twenty-Six

Like the night before, Amy and Mason eased into a comfortable, easy conversation. Amy told Mason about the visit to the Kindred Spirit Mailbox, especially about the letter that moved her.

"Wow, that's so sad," Mason said.

"It really is," Amy said. "On a happier note, you know what I like about talking to you?"

"What's that?"

"It's like we've known each other a really long time. You're so easy to talk to."

"That's funny," Mason said. "I was thinking the same thing after we got off the phone last night."

"Actually, I have to take that back," Amy said. "I don't like talking to you."

"Huh?"

"I love talking to you."

"I think you love giving me little mini-heart attacks, don't you?"

"Hey, gotta keep you on your toes."

Mason laughed and said, "I guess I need to be kept on my toes. Oh, by the way."

"What's up?"

"I love talking to you, too."

Amy and Mason continued talking for another hour before Amy happened to glance at a clock.

"I bet Aunt Mary is getting really hungry. I promised her we'd go to the seafood place tonight."

"Guess I better let you go."

"Only after you make me a promise," Amy said.

"What's that?"

"We'll only be gone about an hour or so, so you need to promise you'll call back around 8:30."

"I promise, but you and your aunt are going to get tired of hearing from me."

Amy smiled and said, "Not a chance."

At the seafood restaurant, Amy ordered a combo of crab legs and flounder. Mary asked the waitress for a large popcorn shrimp platter.

After the waitress left their booth to go put their order in, Amy said, "I thought you said the doctor told you to stop eating so much fried food, especially shrimp."

"Oh, to heck with him," Mary said. "What kind of doctor tries to keep his patients from having a good quality of life."

Amy laughed.

The waitress returned quickly with their drink order, two sweet teas. They both took a sip and Mary said, "They have the best tea on the beach."

"It is really good," Amy said before changing the subject. "Um, I think Mom is really upset with me."

"Why do you say that?"

"She hasn't called since I've been down here."

"Actually, she tried last night while you were on the phone with Mason. I know because I called her after you guys got off the phone."

"Oh."

"I meant to tell you, but I got distracted by our walk to the mailbox and by that letter from the dad to his daughter. That letter has bothered me all day."

"I thought about it, too, and even told Mason about it," Amy said. "Did Mom sound mad?"

"Oh, she was just a little aggravated because she had tried to call a few times and kept getting a busy signal. She can be a little impatient sometimes."

Amy laughed and said, "You think?"

"Anyway, I decided to have that talk with her about you and Mason."

Amy tensed up. Since her aunt had not brought up the call until now, she worried Mary was delaying giving her some bad news.

"How did it go?"

"I think I actually got through to her."

"Really?" Amy asked, relaxing a little.

"Yep. I reminded her you weren't twelve years old anymore and I didn't want you two to have a bad relationship because of her not understanding it was normal for someone your age to have a boyfriend."

"What did she say to that?"

"Nothing. That's how I know I got through."

Amy felt relieved and hopeful. They spent the rest of their dinner together talking more about the letters, notes and stories they read at the Kindred Spirit Mailbox earlier in the day.

After they ate, the waitress brought the check and Mary paid for dinner and left a generous tip.

"Thanks, Aunt Mary," Amy said.

"This is a very tiny price to pay to spend some time with my favorite niece."

Amy laughed and said, "I'm your only niece, but thanks for dinner and for talking to Mom about Mason."

"You're very welcome, honey."

"I knew if anybody could get through to Mom it would be you."

Mary had made her points to Catherine, but not in the way she and Amy hoped. Mary had only convinced her sister that it was her method and not the goal that was not the right thing to do. To Catherine, her sister's point that pushing Amy to end any contact with Mason could backfire and damage their relationship for a long time was a valid one. However, Mary had not changed Catherine's mind about Mason being a bad match for her daughter. After she spoke with her sister, Catherine simply decided she needed a plan B to end the silliness between her daughter and "that boy at the donut shop." Catherine smiled knowing her plan B would be arriving to Carolina Beach on Monday driving a BMW convertible.

Chapter Twenty-Seven

The next few days went by quickly during Amy's visit with her aunt. On Sunday morning, a slow-moving warm front moved in from the west and decided to hang around a while blanketing all of the Carolina coast in a steady rain.

Amy spent most of the afternoon on the phone with Mason. He had the day off.

At one point during the call, Amy said, "I'm in a really happy mood."

"You are?" Mason asked.

"Yep, because I get to come home tomorrow and actually see you instead of just talking on the phone."

"Well, that's not fair," Mason said.

"Why do you say that?"

"Because that is exactly what I had planned on saying to you today."

Amy laughed. "I guess that just makes us like the mailbox – kindred spirits."

"Sounds good to me," Mason said.

At Carolina Beach, Catherine had gone through the house several times making sure everything was in its proper place and doing the closest thing to a white glove inspection her husband had ever seen her do. Since Catherine had hired a cleaning service to go through the beach house three times a week, her husband wondered what all the fuss was about.

"Have you got something on your mind?" he finally asked.

"What are you talking about?" Catherine responded.

"You've been going back and forth all afternoon cleaning and straightening over-and-over again. Since we pay enough to that cleaning service to keep the entire company afloat, I was just wondering if I should call them and cancel the service if they're doing that bad of a job."

"They're doing a fine job. I guess you forgot Amy comes home tomorrow."

"Of course I haven't forgotten that she comes home tomorrow. But, do you actually think she'll care about the house being in some kind of museum condition?"

"She's not the only one coming tomorrow. We have company coming, too."

"That's the first I've heard of it. Who's coming?

"It's Wilson Crabtree's son."

"You mean that Drake boy?"

"Why do you say his name like that?"

"He's a little too stuck on himself for my taste."

Catherine sighed. "That's what you say about anybody who has been raised with any class."

"What did he do, invite himself down for a free beach trip?"

"No, I invited him down to spend a week."

Amy's dad spent a moment pondering what his wife had just told him. It didn't take long to see through Catherine's actions.

"I know exactly what you're doing inviting that boy down here. You should be ashamed of yourself." He walked out the front door and went for a walk.

Catherine was glad her husband had left the house. It gave her privacy so she could make sure her plan was still in play. She called the Crabtree residence in Charlotte hoping Drake would answer the phone. She wasn't interested in any neighborly small talk with the doctor or his wife right now. Drake was the one who answered.

"Hi, Drake. I just wanted to make sure you were still coming tomorrow."

"Oh, yes ma'am. I'm packing up right now."

"Do you have an idea what time you might be getting here?"

"I think I should get there sometime around 2:00."

"Sounds perfect, Drake. Oh, I know I told you I wanted your visit to be a surprise for

Amy. I would like for you to do me one more favor."

"Yes, ma'am."

"I don't want you to tell Amy I invited you down. I want her to think a Charlotte friend missed her enough to come see her on their own."

"Of course. I won't say a word."

"Good, Drake. See you tomorrow."

Catherine hung up the phone and instantly picked it back up. She dialed the number to her sister's house. It made her angry to get yet another busy signal. It looked like it was going to be a repeat of the first night of Amy's visit to her aunt's. This time it took three hours to get through.

Amy had barely hung up the phone after talking with Mason when her aunt's phone rang. Since she had just spent a long time on the phone with Mason, she knew it was very unlikely it was him calling back, so she let her aunt answer the call.

"Hello."

As usual, Catherine had no interest in anything other than getting right to business.

"When do you plan on bringing my daughter home tomorrow?"

"I guess whenever Amy's ready to leave," Mary said.

"You need to be on your way no later than noon. I have plans tomorrow afternoon."

"Okay, I'll pass that along to Amy. Better yet, she's in the kitchen because of the rain, so let me put her on so you can tell her yourself."

"That's not necessary. I'm very busy right now. Just call me when you are leaving tomorrow."

Catherine hung up. She was pleased with herself. Everything was falling into place very nicely.

Chapter Twenty-Eight

Monday dawned as a beautiful day. The warm front from the day before had finally passed through leaving a clear blue morning sky behind.

Mary slept in an extra hour. When she got up and made her way into the kitchen, she found Amy on the phone with Mason. Amy waved and smiled. Mary returned the smile and went to work preparing bacon and eggs for breakfast.

"What time do you get off work today?" Amy asked Mason.

"I'm supposed to get off at 7:00, but since it's Monday it probably won't be too busy, so I bet Bobby will ask me if I want to leave at 5:00 when Garrison comes in."

"Do you think you might be up for another walk on the beach when you get wrapped up there? Or, will you be too tired?"

"Trust me, knowing you're coming back today is giving me enough energy to walk to Wilmington and back. I was hoping you'd want to do something this evening."

"Of course," Amy said. "Aunt Mary's making us breakfast so I better get off this thing so we can eat, get ready and start heading that way."

"Can't wait to see you," Mason said.

"You know I feel the same way about seeing you."

Since Amy knew the earliest Mason would be able to get off work was not until 5:00 that afternoon, she took her time getting ready to go home. She hoped that would make the time go by quicker. She was very excited about seeing Mason, but somewhat apprehensive about being around her mom, despite Mary having her talk.

Over breakfast, Amy and Mary talked about planning another visit together before Amy had to return to Charlotte for school.

"I was just thinking," Mary said. "I wonder what those great folks of Mason's would think about me inviting him down for a visit the next time we come down. Maybe you guys could walk down to Bird Island and show him the mailbox we were telling him about."

"That would be really great, Aunt Mary."

Mary did a few chores around the house while Amy ventured upstairs to take a shower and get her stuff together to head home. About 12:45, the phone rang. Mary answered to discover her sister on the other end.

"You mean you haven't left yet?" Catherine said.

"Very observant, sister. No, we had a late breakfast and Amy is upstairs taking a shower and getting ready."

"Were you not listening to me when I told you I had plans this afternoon? I want Amy to be here."

"Oh, don't go and get all bowed up," Mary said. "We'll be leaving in about an hour. But, don't run a stopwatch on us because I want to take her by Britt's for a few donuts before I bring her home. Mason is working today."

Catherine took a deep breath. She was about to release her full fury on her sister, but her mind stopped her.

This might actually be a good thing. This ought to time out for Drake to get here right about the time they are at the donut shop. I'll just send Drake right over there. That will be a big surprise for Amy and Mason.

"Are you still there?" Mary asked.

"Yes, I guess that will be fine. Just tell Amy I'll see her when she gets home. And don't tell her I said anything about any plans. That might change."

"Okay," Mary said and Catherine hung up.

Plan B is coming together even better than I thought, Amy's mother thought.

Chapter Twenty-Nine

Amy came downstairs after getting ready. She was carrying her tote bag with her.

"Can I do one thing really quick before we go?" Amy asked her aunt.

"Absolutely, take your time. Your mother called while you were in the shower. We can take our time heading back."

"Great," Amy said. She ventured into the family room of her aunt's house and played a few songs on the keyboard. She placed the sheet music back in the piano stool and went back to the kitchen.

"Sorry, I had to get just a few minutes more in before I head back to the violin."

"Don't be sorry at all. You play that thing a lot better than I ever could."

"I don't think so," Amy said.

"Well, I DO think so."

During the drive back to Carolina Beach to take Amy back, Mary said, "I bet you are pretty excited about getting back to see a particular fella that wants to be a newspaper writer."

Amy laughed. "You bet I am!"

"Do you two have any plans to be able to see each other today?

"Yes, ma'am. He's getting off sometime between 5:00 and 7:00 and we're going for a walk on the beach."

Mary smiled and said, "Kind of a do-over, huh?"

"Yes, ma'am, and hopefully with a happier ending than our first try."

"Hopefully so!" Mary said and added, "Well, I've got a surprise for you. I want to see him, too, so we're going to stop in at Britt's for a few donuts before I take you home."

"You sure about that? Mom will probably blow a gasket if we do that."

"No, she won't. I already told her we were going to do that when I talked to her on the phone."

"Wow, you really did get through to her."

The closer Amy and Mary got to Carolina Beach the more excited Amy became. By the time they were driving across the bridge at Snow's Cut, Amy was uncharacteristically fidgety. Mary noticed and laughed.

"We're almost there, honey, so you can relax."

"I'm sorry, Aunt Mary. I just really miss him."

"No reason to be sorry for a thing. I know you miss him and I don't blame you. I'm sure he misses you, too. I can't wait to see the look on his face when he sees us walk into the donut shop; especially since he doesn't think he's seeing you until he gets off work. This is going to be fun."

"I see how it is," Amy said. "I'm just here for your entertainment."

"Exactly. I'm just reliving the love life of my youth vicariously through you."

They both laughed.

Mary was not disappointed when she saw the look on Mason's face the moment he noticed them walking into Britt's Donut Shop.

"Told you," Mary whispered to Amy. "Look at him. You'd think he just won the lottery."

Amy and Mary ventured back to what had become their usual seats near the end of the counter. When Bobby saw them, he walked up to Mason who was flipping donuts in the cooker.

"I think this looks like a good time for your break," Bobby said.

"Thanks!" Mason said.

Mason took off his apron, ran to the back to store it and made a beeline to Amy. He was surprised, in a very happy way, when she jumped up and gave him a big hug. Then, they both were surprised because Mary was standing behind them waiting to give Mason a hug, too.

"This niece of mine couldn't wait to see you," Mary said.

"Thank you for bringing her. I couldn't wait to see her either."

Mason sat down beside Amy and they began to fill each other in on the details of everything that had transpired since their phone call that morning. Mason had some big news to share.

"After we talked this morning, I got a call from the *Star-News* in Wilmington. They accepted my application to be an intern in the newsroom in the afternoons after school."

"Mason, that's fantastic!" Amy said and hugged him again. "That's such great news," she said in Mason's ear.

Before Mason could even say thank you, their moment was interrupted.

"What's this? I let you out of my sight for just a few weeks over the summer and I find you hugging on another guy?"

It was the voice of Drake Crabtree.

Chapter Thirty

Amy's back was to Drake Crabtree when he spoke. Mason and Amy were still hugging tightly, but Mason felt Amy tense up at the sound of Drake's voice. She slowly turned around.

"What are you doing here, Drake?" Amy asked.

"I was missing seeing my favorite girl, so I decided to come for a visit. Your mom said you would be here."

Mary frowned when she heard Catherine had told Drake that Amy would be at the donut shop. Mary also noticed how uncomfortable Mason had quickly become.

"Hello, Drake, remember me?" Mary asked.

"Yeah, Miss Mary, right?"

"Yes, and this fella here is Mason. He's Amy's boyfriend."

Drake didn't acknowledge Mason's existence. Instead, he turned towards Amy.

"Boyfriend? What are you doing? Is this some summer fling thing?"

Drake didn't wait for Amy to even respond. He turned right to Mason.

"Where you from, man?"

"I live here," Mason said.

"Here at Carolina Beach?"

"Yep."

"Oh, okay, so you're just summer break guy. You do know Amy lives in Charlotte, right?"

"I know where Amy lives."

Drake looked at Mason like he was subhuman. He didn't want to talk to Mason anymore, so he turned back towards Amy.

"Why'd your folks get a beach house at this place? Don't they know Wrightsville Beach is where the classy people go? Everybody knows that anybody who is anybody has a place at Wrightsville, not at this redneck place.

Mary had heard enough.

"Young man, some of the nicest people I've ever met in my life live at Carolina Beach. The man and his wife who own this place you're standing in are just two examples. Amy's boyfriend and his parents are the classiest people I know."

"So, Mason," Drake said. "You live in one of those big, three-story places down here?"

Mary didn't give Mason a chance to respond.

"Drake, what kind of question is that? Sounds to me like you've never been taught the real meaning of what classy is. I've met people in old, tiny houses who are as classy as they come and I've known people who live in huge mansions, like the one you live in, that are jackasses."

Amy and Mason laughed. Drake got visibly angry.

"Whoa, lady. Wow, Amy, when did your aunt become such a bitch?"

No one knew that Bobby had been walking up to say hello to Mary and Amy, so he had heard the last few exchanges. Mason had clinched his fists and was moving towards Drake, but before he got close Drake almost fell backwards. Bobby had grabbed him by the back of the collar and was pulling him to the door. When he had him outside, Bobby turned Drake around and grabbed him by the front of his shirt.

"I don't tolerate your kind of behavior in my shop. And I don't tolerate anybody being disrespectful to someone as honorable as Mary. Don't you ever come back in here."

When Bobby turned around to come back into the donut shop, Amy, Mason and Mary saw Drake glare at Mason and give him the finger.

After the moment of shock subsided with everybody, Mason asked, "Who is that guy?"

"It's Drake Crabtree," Amy said.

"Is he your boyfriend in Charlotte?" Mason asked.

"Hah! No way. He has always thought he was."

Mary jumped in. "I can tell you who he is. He's a spoiled-brat, little jerk."

"You've got that right," Amy said.

Mason was relieved to hear Amy was not somehow involved with Drake. Mary was disgusted with Drake's behavior and Amy was embarrassed that she was the one Drake had come into Britt's to see in the first place.

There was one thing left unsaid but was on all three of their minds. They wondered why Drake had come to Carolina Beach and they all felt like trouble was brewing.

Chapter Thirty-One

Before Amy and Mary left Britt's Donuts, Mason checked with Bobby about what time he would be getting off work. Bobby said 6:00 would be a good time to plan on.

Just a few minutes before 6:00, Amy walked into the donut shop. Mason saw her when she came in and noticed she looked very bothered by something.

Drake, Mason thought. He clocked out and found Amy sitting in her usual spot when she came to visit him at work.

"Hey, you want a few donuts before we go for a walk?" Mason asked.

"Can we just go ahead and go for the walk?"

"Absolutely," Mason said.

The moment they walked out of Britt's, Amy took Mason's hand. That gesture made Mason happy, but it was very obvious to him that something was wrong. Amy was way too quiet.

Back at Amy's family beach house, Drake and Catherine were talking.

"You sure it's okay for me to stay?" Drake asked Amy's mom.

"Of course, why wouldn't it be?"

Catherine had noticed Amy seemed shocked to discover Drake was staying at their house for a few days, but she was asking in the event something else was going on. When Mary brought Amy home, no one said anything about what had happened at the donut shop a little earlier. When Amy left to go see Mason and Mary had left to return to Sunset Beach, Drake brought up the incident.

"Ah, there was a little trouble with this guy that works at that donut place where Amy was," Drake said.

"What kind of trouble?"

"He acted like Amy was his girl or something. He even tried to come at me, so I had to leave."

"I guess that explains why Amy left when my sister went out to her car to leave. But, don't you let that boy run you off. You're my guest. Amy just needs time to see you are much better suited for her to go out with."

Amy and Mason walked along the beach in silence. Mason knew Amy was very upset about what had happened that afternoon, but something was telling him she wasn't ready to talk about it. They quietly strolled, sometimes arm-in-arm and other times holding hands. They were walking along the edge of the surf.

At least a half-hour went by before Amy spoke. She sounded very reserved.

"I'm sorry about what happened."

"You don't have any reason at all to be sorry. You didn't do anything. But, just who is that guy to you?"

"He's a jerk, that's who he is. He's my neighbor in Charlotte. His dad is a rich doctor in town and he gets anything he wants."

"The way he talked, I thought you had dated him or something."

"Never," Amy said. "That's what gets on my nerves. He goes around school and the neighborhood telling everyone I'm 'his girl.' He's so used to getting what he wants he thinks he can just stake a claim to me or something. I think he sees me as some kind of challenge since I'm the only girl around there who isn't impressed with his car or his money."

Now, Mason was quiet. He was thinking about Amy's neighbors obviously being rich. This meant she lived in a ritzy neighborhood. He was hoping she was being honest about not being impressed over money and cars because, right now, he didn't have either. What money he was making at the donut shop he was trying to save for a used car. If he needed to drive now, he had to borrow his mother's car or his dad's work truck. Neither would impress someone with big money.

For the second time since meeting Amy, Mason was worried about whether he would be able to hold on to the greatest, most beautiful girl he had ever known. He wondered if he would ever be able to compete with any guy who could keep her in the lifestyle she was accustomed to.

Chapter Thirty-Two

Considering the marathon talks Amy and Mason usually had, whether they were together or talking on the phone, their walk on the beach that evening was strangely quiet. However, they enjoyed being together, holding hands, watching children playing in the sand and surfers riding a few more waves during the last hour before the sun set.

After an hour walking towards the northern extension of Carolina Beach, they turned around and began heading back towards the boardwalk. Amy finally felt like talking.

"Mason?"

"Yes, ma'am."

Amy smiled for the first time that afternoon and evening. "There you go with that 'ma'am' stuff again."

"Habit and respect," Mason said.

"Are we okay?"

"I sure hope so."

"I mean, this thing with Drake showing up out of the blue is not going to change anything between us, will it?"

Mason thought for a moment and then answered, "Not with me."

"He doesn't mean anything to me."

"I do worry about it a little bit," Mason confessed.

"Why?"

"Um, it's kind of obvious he has a lot of money. I just worry when you get back to Charlotte for school that you'll realize he'll be able to give you a lot more than I might ever be able to give."

Amy stopped and stepped in front of Mason to stop him from walking, too. She grabbed his arms.

"Mason, please don't ever think that. I really don't care about stuff or how much money somebody has. That doesn't mean anything to me. I grew up with wealthy parents and that means they hung around other rich people. Most of them, like Drake, are selfish and are never satisfied. They always want more. I'm not like that. Being around rich people made me not want to be like them."

"You never wanted to be rich?" Mason asked.

"No, I never wanted to be a self-centered jerk."

"But, maybe that's because you've never known what it's like to not be able to get what you want."

Amy squeezed Mason's arms a little tighter.

"You know what I want?" she asked.

"What's that?"

"You, Mason."

Amy took her right hand off of Mason's arm and moved it up to his cheek.

"I don't want to scare you away because I say this too fast," Amy said. "But, I realized while I was at Aunt Mary's that I love you."

Mason felt himself get a little weak in the knees. He steadied himself and hoped he was not just dreaming the words he just heard. It took a few seconds before he could speak.

"I love you, too, Amy."

They moved into each other's arms. Mason leaned back enough to take Amy's face in his hands. They both moved towards each other at the same time and began kissing. The beach around them was still filled with people, but they didn't care. It was a moment when they felt like they were the only ones on the entire coast.

Chapter Thirty-Three

Amy's mother had long ago set her a weeknight curfew of 9:00 p.m. and Amy did not want to sling gas on a fire by ignoring it.

Mason walked her home. It was the first time he had actually seen her family's beach house. He studied the three-story waterfront mansion with a large sunbathing deck on top of the home accessible by a spiral staircase.

Parked in front of the house were three cars, a Lexus, a Lincoln and a convertible BMW. It was obvious which car was Drake's.

Speak of the devil, Mason was giving Amy a goodnight kiss in front of the house when they heard the same irritating voice that had interrupted their hug at the donut shop that afternoon.

"Okay, donut boy, it's time for her to come in and get back to reality."

"Drake, shut up," Amy said before she refocused on Mason. "I can't wait to see you tomorrow."

"Sounds great," Mason said.

Amy walked past Drake like he wasn't even there. As she walked up the steps to her front porch, Drake stopped following her and looked back at Mason.

"Hey, man, see my car? Pretty cool, huh?"

Mason just stood there. Drake tried to get under his skin again.

"Oh, that's right. I forgot. I heard you don't have a car."

"Not yet," Mason said. "I'm saving to buy my own car instead of having to have one given to me."

Drake wanted to pound Mason in the face. He decided getting in trouble in front of Amy's house was not a good idea. He knew "donut boy" would not always have Amy around to stand up for him.

Mason began his walk home. It had been a special afternoon and evening he and Amy had shared. He trusted her and believed her when she told him she loved him. Even thinking about her saying those words made him very happy, but that didn't change the fact he didn't like Drake staying in the same house she was in right now.

Amy walked into her house and headed for the kitchen where she found her mother standing at the counter drinking a cup of hot tea.

"Hey, honey. Isn't it nice of Drake to come all the way down from Charlotte just to see you?"

"No, it's not nice, Mom. He's a jerk. The owner of the donut shop had to kick him out. You should have heard what he called Aunt Mary."

"I heard it was that boy you're infatuated with and your aunt that were the ones who were rude to him. If he did say something, it sounds like he was provoked."

"Mom, you're crazy if you believe that."

"See? You are being rude and disrespectful to me right now. Did you learn that from that boy and your aunt? If that's the way you all treated Drake today, no wonder he was forced to defend himself."

"Mom, are you the one who invited Drake to come down here and stay in our house?"

"Doctor Crabtree is our best neighbor, so when his son said he wanted to come see you, I decided to treat him as the neighbor he is and told him he could stay in our guest room."

"Why would you do that without even asking me if I was comfortable with that?"

"This is my home and I don't need to ask you for permission to host a neighbor for a visit."

Amy and Catherine were unaware that they were not the only ones hearing their conversation until they heard somebody speak up. It was Amy's dad walking into the kitchen.

"Catherine, Amy is exactly right. You should not have invited someone of the opposite sex her age into this house without talking to both of us about it. You don't have any idea how he treats Amy at school or anywhere else for that matter."

"You can stand up for your disrespectful and unappreciative daughter all you want. I could ask you the same thing about that boy at the donut shop. Aren't you concerned about her hanging out with him? Have you not noticed she never talked to me this way until she met him?"

"I heard Mary talk about Mason and his parents. They sound like good people to me."

Catherine had reached her limit in being challenged by her husband and her daughter.

"Both of you just get out of here so I can enjoy my tea without listening to this ridiculous mess."

Amy and her father walked out of the kitchen. They both knew Catherine was too stubborn to ever change her mind.

There was another problem. Amy, her mom and her dad had no idea they were not the only ones privy to the discussion held in the kitchen. Drake, standing in the hall near another entrance to the kitchen, had heard everything.

He concluded that since Amy and her dad had done exactly what her mom told them to do when she told them to get out, it was obvious to him who ruled the roost in Amy's house. It was obvious her mom was the boss and that she liked him and wanted him to be the one with Amy, not donut boy.

Drake felt a surge of confidence.

Chapter Thirty-Four

Amy went upstairs, took a shower and headed to her room. She used her hidden key to open her desk and pulled out her journal. She began to write down the events of the day, especially the one she never wanted to forget.

I told Mason I love him today and he said he loves me, too! One of the best days of my life!

The run-in with Drake at the donut shop was something she deliberately left out. She only wanted to remember the good parts of the day.

Amy heard the phone ring. She was hoping it was Mason calling. When no one called for her to pick up the phone, she was disappointed and guessed it was another business call for her mom. Actually, it was Mason calling and her mom had answered the phone.

"Hello."

"Hi, Mrs. Cole, this is Mason. Could I speak to Amy, please? That is if she's there."

"She is," Catherine said without a fraction of friendliness in her voice. "I think you know she has company down from Charlotte right now, so it's not a good time to be calling. As a matter of fact, since he is down for the rest of the week, it's not a good week to be calling."

"Oh, okay," Mason said. "Will you please tell her I said hello?"

Catherine hung up the phone and ignored his request.

Mason had used the phone in the kitchen at his house to try and call Amy. His mom was washing the dishes.

"Wow," Mason said as he placed the phone back in the cradle.

"What's wrong?" Joy asked.

"Amy's mom. She just hung up on me."

"She definitely doesn't sound like the warm and fuzzy type."

"No, ma'am, she's not."

Joy tossed the towel she was using to dry the dishes beside the sink and sat down at the kitchen table with Mason.

"I wouldn't let her bother you and I definitely wouldn't let her scare you away from Amy. You guys aren't ten years old. In fact, think about it this way, if her mom is like that all the time then Amy needs someone like you in her life."

Mason pondered what his mom said for a moment and then said, "I didn't think about it like that. I just hope Amy's mom doesn't try and make it hard for us to stay in touch, especially when she has to go back to Charlotte for school."

"Maybe you should find a nice way to tell Amy about what happened. Tell her if she is not hearing from you it certainly isn't because you aren't trying to reach her. And you can tell her she is more than welcome to call here anytime. When she is back in Charlotte, she can call collect."

"Thanks, Mom. That's a good idea."

Since it was obvious Amy's mom was not going to let her take a call from him tonight, he hoped she would come into the donut shop tomorrow.

Amy had just returned her journal to her desk and locked the drawer when she heard a knock at the door. Expecting it to be her mother with another lecture to deliver, she was surprised to see Drake standing there.

"You wanna go for a ride? I'll put the top down on the Beemer."

"No thanks. I'm tired," Amy said.

"Oh, well we'll go tomorrow then."

"No, we won't," Amy said and shut the door.

About ten minutes later, there was another knock at the door. Amy sighed, tossed the book she was reading down on the bed beside her and went to the door. Expecting Drake to be back to bother her, she swung the door open ready to deliver a terse leave-me-alone speech. This time, it was her mother at the door.

"We have to talk," Catherine said.

"Does it have to be tonight, Mom? I'm really tired."

"Yes. We have to talk now."

Amy walked away from the door and sat on the edge of her bed. Her mom came in and shut the door.

"I don't like the way you are treating Drake," Catherine said. "He is our guest."

"Then, I guess we're even," Amy said. "I don't like the way he treated Mason and Aunt Mary."

"Umph, the way I understand it, it was Drake that was treated poorly by you, Mary and Bobby."

"Mom, are you going to believe Drake or your own sister and daughter?"

"It's hard to trust you because of your attitude since you took an interest in that boy," Catherine said. She sounded curt, as usual.

"'That boy' has a name. It's Mason."

"See there. Being disrespectful again. And as far as my sister goes, she has always let you get away with anything. I ought to prohibit your visits with her."

"Mom, you do realize I will be 18 in just months and I can see my aunt anytime I want to then."

Catherine's eyes narrowed as she said, "As long as you live in a house I own or as long as I am financing your education, you will respect me and do what I say. But, this discussion is not about that. It's about you being rude to Drake and your silly infatuation with Martin, or whatever his name is."

"It's Mason and why is it silly?" Amy asked.

"With the grades you get, I'm surprised I have to tell you," Catherine said. "He does not fit in with the class of people we have always associated with. You may think now, when you get everything you want, that you don't need the lifestyle you have been raised in. Just imagine having to barely make it on some newspaper reporter's salary. And if you get yourself in that mess, don't expect me to come to your rescue."

"I don't need anybody to come rescue me, Mom. I will be working, too, if I'm lucky enough to have Mason in my life."

"Ha! Lucky? The person you'd be lucky enough to have in your life is a guest in our house right now."

"Oh, please, Mom. I want someone who really knows how to love somebody, not someone who loves themselves to the point of being narcissistic and obnoxious. Drake doesn't love anybody but himself."

"That's your age speaking. When you get older and wiser, you'll understand that the love you think exists does not."

Amy just looked into her mother's eyes for a moment and almost felt sorry for her.

"Well, Mom, if real love doesn't exist, then what's worth living for?"

"Lifestyle, and that's something Drake can give you and that boy at the donut shop can't. I'm just trying to keep you from making a huge mistake."

Amy sighed and said, "I really want to stop talking about this. I'm going to bed."

Amy jumped off her bed and walked to the door of her bedroom and opened it. Her mom walked out and Amy shut the door. She was disturbed by the conversation she just had and knew she would not be able to go to sleep for a long while. In addition to being aggravated with her mother and with Drake, she was wondering why Mason had not called her tonight.

Mason was at home in his room unsuccessfully trying to concentrate on a book he was reading. He was wondering why Amy had not returned his call.

Chapter Thirty-Five

The next morning, Mason's dad drove him to the boardwalk for work. A front had stalled along the Carolina coast and it had been raining most of the night. It wasn't just showers, it was a hard, steady rain.

Mason was completely quiet on the short drive. When his dad pulled his truck as close to the back entrance to Britt's Donuts that he could get, he turned to his son and asked, "Is everything okay?"

"I guess so," Mason said. "It's just that I called Amy last night and left a message for her to call me back and she never did."

"Did you leave a message on an answering machine? Maybe she didn't hear it."

"No, sir, her mom answered the phone and I left a message with her."

"I probably shouldn't say this, but her mother sounds like the type who just might selectively forget to tell her," Woody said.

"Yeah, you're probably right," Mason said.

Mason hopped out of the truck and ran into the donut shop. Normally, rain didn't bother

Mason, but it did today. He knew it likely meant Amy would not be venturing out to see him at work. It also meant they would not be as busy as usual at the shop. Time would go by very slowly.

Amy woke up still concerned why Mason had not called her last night. When she went downstairs to find something for breakfast, she noticed the driving rain when she looked out of the double glass doors leading to the back deck from the dining room. It was raining so hard she could not see the ocean.

Great, Amy thought. She had decided the moment she walked out of her room she was going to go to the donut shop to see if everything was okay with Mason. Despite the rain, she knew she was going anyway. She quickly ate a muffin, drank some orange juice and got dressed. She grabbed a hooded jacket from her closet, went back downstairs and was headed for the front door when her mom saw her.

"Where are you going?"

"Down to the boardwalk," Amy said.

"Why don't you just say where you're really going, to that donut shop?"

"Because, Mom, I don't want to hear another lecture about Mason."

Ignoring Amy's response, Catherine said, "You do see it's pouring rain outside. Drake is in the den. Why don't you ask him to drive you over there?"

Amy sighed, pulled the hood over her head and ran out into the rain.

Chapter Thirty-Six

Just as Mason had predicted, the rain had inspired most beachgoers to stay inside. The busiest business on the island was the pizza place that made home deliveries. The entire time Mason had been at work, he guessed only a dozen customers had been in for donuts. They were the die-hard, heavily-addicted-to-Britt's Donuts crowd.

Moments ago, Bobby went through the shop asking if any of the staff wanted the afternoon off. The forecast was calling for the rain to keep falling hard until the wee hours of the morning. While most of the crew took the boss up on his offer, Mason decided he would rather stay at least a little busy rather than sitting around the house wondering why Amy never called him back. With most of the staff now gone, it left Bobby, his daughter and Mason as the whole crew for the rest of the day.

About twenty minutes later, Mason was standing at the cooker, flipping one small batch of donuts, when Bobby walked up to him.

"Well, it looks like at least one person in here is popular enough to bring someone out in the rain to see us," Bobby said.

"Sir?" Mason asked, but then caught a glimpse over Bobby's shoulder discovering what his boss was talking about. Standing just inside the shop, with a jacket dripping wet from the hood to the bottom of it, stood Amy.

"Go ahead. I'll finish this batch up," Bobby said."

"Thank you, sir," Mason said as he pulled his apron over his head and walked up to Amy.

Just as he approached her, Amy said, "I want to hug you so bad I can't stand it, but I don't want to get you wet."

"I don't care," Mason said, and he grabbed Amy in his arms and hugged her tight. He whispered in her ear, "I am so glad to see you. I've been worried all night and all day since you didn't return my call last night."

Amy leaned back and looked Mason right in the eye. "Return your call? You called last night?"

"Yes, your mom answered the phone and said you were busy, so I left a message."

Amy looked angry and said, "She didn't tell me about the message."

"That's okay," Mason said and smiled. "You're here now. I was just hoping you hadn't decided to go out with Drake."

Mocking being mad, Amy said, "You listen to me, Mason James. There is a big, huge difference between you and Drake. I can't stand being around him, but I can't stand being away from you. I love you and don't you forget it!"

"I never get tired of hearing that," Mason said.

Amy smiled. "You know what today is?"

Mason glanced outside. "Uh, the day we need to start building an ark?"

"Well, that, too, but it's our anniversary. We met in here two weeks ago today," Amy said.

"Wow," Mason said. "It seems like yesterday."

"I know, but it kind of makes me sad," Amy said.

"Why?"

"Because it means it's two weeks closer to the end of the best summer of my life and when I have to go back to Charlotte."

"Now, you've got me sad," Mason said. "How about we make ourselves a promise to not talk about that, or even think about it. I just want every day we have together to be happy memories."

"You've got a deal," Amy said.

Bobby had just completed the latest batch of donuts and had dipped them in glaze. He walked up to Amy and Mason with a dozen of them in a bag, still nice and hot.

"The rain is keeping everybody away," Bobby said. "You guys better eat these up. It would be a shame for them to go to waste, especially since I double-dipped them.'

"Mr. Bobby, you're going to make me gain about 50 pounds this summer!" Amy said.

Bobby smiled and said, "Ah, but they'll be happy pounds."

Amy and Mason laughed.

"Besides," Bobby added. "This is health food."

"How can this be health food?" Amy asked, laughing as she was pulling a donut out of the bag.

"It's mental health food," Bobby said.

Amy laughed again and said, "Now that's very true."

Mason laughed, too, but he was thinking, *I wish I could hear that laugh for the rest of my life.*

Chapter Thirty-Seven

Not long after Amy had dashed out into the rain to go see Mason, Drake Crabtree walked into the kitchen of Amy's family's beach house. Catherine was standing at glass double doors that led to large back deck. She was looking out over the beach, watching it rain while she was drinking a cup of coffee.

"Hey, Mrs. Cole."

Catherine turned around and said, "Good morning, Drake. The rain is really coming down."

"Yes, ma'am, it is," Drake said, using the on-demand charm he had learned to harvest when it was to his advantage. "Is Amy still asleep?"

"No, she left."

"In this?" Drake said as he tilted his head towards the rain coming down outside.

"Yes, it's silly, but she went to see that boy at the donut shop."

Drake had no come back, at least none he could say in front of Amy's mom, so he just kept staring at the rain. After a few moments, Catherine turned towards Drake.

"If you like Amy, you should be patient. I doubt this thing she has for the donut boy lasts when we all get back to Charlotte for school to start. I've never believed that absence makes the heart grow fonder, no matter what they say."

"Thanks, Mrs. Cole. I do like Amy, a lot. She is definitely different from most girls I know. I mean that in a good way."

"I know you do," Catherine said, placing her coffee cup in the sink. "Make yourself at home, Drake. I have to get a few things done back in my office. Just because I'm at the beach doesn't mean I don't have a business I still have to run."

"Yes, ma'am. Thanks."

Drake decided to venture back upstairs and watch some TV in the guest room Catherine had put him in for his visit. He was walking by Amy's room and noticed the door was slightly cracked. He looked over his shoulder, making sure no one was around. It was obvious he was the only one in the upstairs portion of the house. He slowly pushed the door to Amy's room open and walked inside, carefully pushing the door almost shut.

At first, Drake just stood behind the door looking around the room. He noticed some photos on the wall, mostly of Amy and her friends. He saw a stack of music books on the window ledge with a violin case beside them. He walked over to Amy's desk and tried to open the top, center drawer. It was locked. He tried one of the side drawers, the one at the top, and it opened. Inside was only one item – a photo album. Drake sat down in the chair at Amy's desk and started thumbing through the pages.

The first photos looked like they were taken when Amy was maybe nine or ten years old, but as he perused the album, he noticed the photos became more recent. When he hit a collection of pictures taken within the last year or two the more interested he became in what he was seeing. The last page with photos in it were of Amy and her friends at the beach. One of the photos stopped Drake from scanning any more. It was a picture of Amy taken on the back deck of the beach house. She was smiling, looking right into the camera, holding a glass of iced tea in her hand. She was lying back in a recliner wearing a bikini.

"Damn," Drake whispered to himself. "She looks hotter in a bikini than I even remembered seeing her at the pool. I have to have some of that whether donut boy likes it or not."

Chapter Thirty-Eight

Amy and Mason talked as they devoured the special batch of donuts Bobby had made for them. It was just about time for Mason to get off break and get back to work when Bobby walked up to them.

"Mason, I don't think it's going to get any busier with that monsoon going on out there. My daughter and I can handle things here if you want to go ahead and head out to spend some time with Amy."

Mason called home and his mom offered to come pick him and Amy up. While Mason and Amy waited under the awning of Britt's Donuts, Bobby's daughter approached her dad.

"Look at you, you old softie. You're playing Mister Matchmaker aren't you?"

"What if I am?" Bobby said, smiling and putting his arm around his daughter. "Look at them. I like 'em both and I think they are made for each other."

"Like I said, old softie."

Mason's mom pulled up to the back of the donut shop and tapped her horn. Mason and Amy took a breath and ran down the small alleyway beside the shop and hopped in the car. The rain was coming down so hard even the short dash had left them soaking wet.

"Oh, no, Mrs. James? I'm getting your back seat all wet," Amy said.

"Don't worry about that," Joy said. "A little water never hurt anything."

"Thanks for coming to get us, Mom," Mason said. "I think we'd be covered in more than just a little water if we had tried to walk."

"Glad to do it, Son. Amy, do I have to take you home or can you come for a visit?"

"Mason and I had planned on spending the afternoon and evening together, but I don't want to invite myself over."

"You are always welcome," Joy said, smiling at Amy by looking into the rearview mirror. "In fact, this looks like a movie kind of night to me. Why don't I drive to the house and you can let me out and use the car to go to a movie or dinner."

"That would be great, Mom. Thanks a lot."

"Yeah, thanks, Mrs. James," Amy added.

"You guys are very welcome. Just be very careful driving in this rain."

Joy pulled into the driveway, jumped out and made a beeline for the front door. She turned to quickly wave to Amy and Mason before she went inside. Mason and Amy hopped into the driver and front passenger seats. Mason was just about to restart the car, but he stopped.

"What would you like to do?" Mason asked.

"Seeing a movie sounds nice, but there is just one problem with that."

"Oh, will it be keeping you out too late to get home in time?"

"No, not at all. It's just we can't talk in a movie."

"Very true," Mason said, smiling. "Would you rather go out to eat?"

"If you're hungry we can certainly do that, but after all those donuts Bobby gave us, I don't think I could even eat a kernel of popcorn right now."

"Me either," Mason said and laughed.

"Is there a place we could go and just talk? Just the two of us?"

"I know just the place," Mason said as he started the car. He pulled out of the driveway and started heading south towards Fort Fisher.

Chapter Thirty-Nine

Mason and Amy drove south on Highway 421 through Kure Beach. There were not many others on the road. Most people had obviously found someplace they wanted to stay, avoiding the rain. Within a few more minutes Amy and Mason were approaching two large columns, one on each side of the road. "Fort Fisher" was painted on each of the columns.

"I heard about this place," Amy said. "This is where they had one of the battles of the Civil War, right?"

"Yep," Mason said. "They have a neat museum here and you can actually hike around the mounds of the actual battlefield. There also used to be an Air Force radar installation here years ago, but they shut it down and turned the base into a place where people in the Air Force can come down and rent a house for vacation. They were the houses where the people who ran the radar installation used to live."

Within a minute, they were driving by the former Air Force base and then the museum. After a few more curves, Amy spotted a sign at the entrance to the Southport-Fort Fisher Ferry.

"So that's where the ferry is," Amy said. "My Aunt Mary said she was going to take me on that ferry the next time I go visit her at Sunset Beach. Since I always came to visit her from Charlotte before Mom and Dad built the beach house this year, I never went on the ferry."

"It's really cool. It's about a 45-minute ride and you drive your car right onto the ferry. You get off in Southport, which is a neat little town. They have some great seafood restaurants over there."

"Are you asking me on a date to eat seafood?"

Mason laughed. "I'd go on a date with you anywhere you want to go."

Amy noticed Mason's cheeks turned a little red. He had obviously shocked himself by saying something he had never said before. Amy leaned over and placed her head lightly on Mason's shoulder, careful not to interfere with his driving.

Just past the ferry entrance, Highway 421 came to an end. There was a mostly dirt parking area with a boat access ramp. Because of the weather, there were no other cars in the lot. Mason found a space that gave them a great view of the water, even in the rain. He put the car in park and turned it off.

"This is a really neat place," Mason said. "It's hard to see it in the rain, but there is the walkway built out in the water with rocks and asphalt that goes from here to an island called Zeke's Island. The walkway is called the Rocks. They started putting rocks out there in the 1870s to close the New Inlet so that sand from the Atlantic wouldn't keep getting into the Cape Fear River. Then, I think it was in the 1930s, they put a layer of concrete on top of the rocks making a walkway out to the island. They eventually added another layer of concrete, but I can't remember exactly when they did that."

"This isn't just a date, it's a history lesson with a great tour guide."

Embarrassed, Mason said, "I'm sorry. I'm turning into my dad. He knows every bit of history around here."

"Don't be sorry at all! I love it." Amy said as she reached over to hold Mason's hand. Mason turned towards Amy. For a moment, they just looked each other in the eyes. Then, they both moved closer and Mason kissed Amy gently.

"I love that even more," Amy said.

Mason adjusted the driver's seat to a little more reclined position. Amy placed her head on his shoulder. That's the position they stayed in, occasionally stroking each other's hair and face while listening to the rain falling on the car. Mason eventually glanced at his watch, shocked at how much time had seemed to float by.

"Oh, no! Your mom and dad are going to kill me."

"For what?" Amy asked, coming out of the peaceful trance they were in,

"I can't believe it, but it's 9:30."

"But, I don't want to go home," Amy said, snuggling closer to Mason.

"I don't want to take you home, but there's another good reason to head back."

"What's that?"

"When the tide comes in, most of this parking lot gets flooded. In fact, when my mom and dad were dating, they came down here one night to make out. They were so into each other, they didn't realize the bottom of my dad's car was almost under water until he turned on the headlights to leave."

"That's a funny story. So, are you saying that by leaving now you are saving me from drowning?"

"Of course," Mason said. "But, I'm also being kind of selfish trying to save myself from the wrath of your mom. I don't want her to have any reason to try and keep you from seeing me."

"You know what, Mason?"

"What's that?"

"You are one of a kind. I didn't think guys like you existed."

"That makes us even," Mason said. "I sure didn't think I'd ever meet anybody like you."

For a moment, Amy remained still with her head still on Mason's shoulder. She leaned up and said, "You know what this means, don't you? That we're made for each other."

Mason shocked himself again by responding, "That would be a dream come true."

During the drive back to Carolina Beach, Amy and Mason held hands, not saying a word. They were both thinking the same thing, how incredible it was to be so close to someone that you didn't have to speak to know you were falling head over heels in love.

During the ride back to her beach house, Amy was basking in the feeling of falling in love. She had no idea what waited for her later that night. It would be a complete nightmare, created by Drake Crabtree.

Chapter Forty

When they pulled up in front of Amy's beach house, neither one of them wanted to end the evening. They sat in the car, held hands, and talked some more. Mason knew he would have to be the one to wrap up their date. He didn't want Amy's mother having any excuse to keep them apart.

"I don't want to go, but I don't want your mom mad at me and try and keep us from going out again."

"That's not going to happen," Amy said. "No matter what she says, I'll find a way to see you. She forgets I'll be 18 in ten months and I'll be able to see who I want, when I want."

"You don't know how great that makes me feel, but I don't want to make things harder than they have to be. Ten months is a long time and I don't want to have to wait until then to see you."

"I know. You're right. I love you, Mason."

"I love you, too."

With that, they exchanged a quick kiss and Amy hopped out of the car. Mason wanted to walk her to the door, but Amy had already said that would only catch the attention of her mother, who was likely watching the front porch from the security cameras she had placed all around the house.

Mason stayed parked out front and watched to make sure she got into the house okay. Just before she opened the front door, he saw her turn around, smile and throw him a kiss.

He started the car and headed home, the entire time thinking how incredibly lucky he was to have found Amy, or that she had found him.

The moment Amy walked in the door the first thing she saw was her mother sitting in a chair in the living room facing in her direction.

"Playing it a little close on curfew time, aren't you?"

"Just on time, actually."

"Don't get smart with me, young lady," Catherine shot back. "Would you prefer I make curfew time earlier?"

Amy remembered what Mason had said about not provoking her mother. So, she toned it down a bit.

"No, ma'am, but I am home at the right time." Amy changed the subject. "I noticed Drake's car isn't out front. Did he go back to Charlotte?"

"I wouldn't blame him if he did," Catherine said. "He's just gone out for a drive around the beach. I gave him a key so he could get back in when he returns."

"Mom? You gave him a key to our house?"

"Of course. He is our guest and he is a good boy with a good upbringing."

Amy was about to challenge her mom, but she didn't have to. Her dad walked into the living room and beat her to it.

"I asked the same thing. I don't think it is wise to be passing out keys to our home."

Catherine sighed and said, "You two get some kind of kick out of always talking back to me. I'm going to bed."

When Catherine left the room, Amy's dad asked her how the evening had gone with Mason.

"We had a great time, Dad. Mason is incredible. You'd be amazed at the things he knows. He was even telling me about Fort Fisher and the Rocks down past the ferry.

"So, that's what young people talk about on dates these days."

Amy laughed. "I know, it's not usual date night stuff, but we talked about all kinds of things."

"Sounds like you two have no problem carrying on a good conversation."

"No, sir, we sure don't. I guess I better head off to bed."

"Okay, sleep well, Kiddo."

Amy gave her dad a quick kiss on the cheek and started heading up the steps.

Why can't Mom say things like "sleep well," Amy thought.

No one in the house at the time had any idea that sleeping well was something Amy would not do that night. Drake Crabtree had not gone on a long drive. He had driven directly to a bar where he had produced a fake I.D. he had bought from a guy in Charlotte. He paid dearly for it. Actually, his parents had paid dearly for it through the high weekly allowance they gave him.

It didn't take long for Drake to have enough drinks to feel emboldened. Now, the only thing on his mind was the picture of Amy in a bikini he had seen in her album.

It's time for me to have that, Drake thought as he staggered back to his BMW.

Chapter Forty-One

Amy was too excited, reflecting on how perfect her night with Mason was, to go right to sleep. She wrote in her diary awhile and then locked it back up in the center drawer of her desk. After reading a few chapters in a novel she had checked out from the Carolina Beach branch of the New Hanover County Library, she finally started getting drowsy, She turned off the lamp on her night stand and peacefully drifted off to sleep.

Less than an hour later, Amy was jolted out of sleep. She felt herself being touched and as she became more awake she realized someone was fondling her right breast. She jerked herself up and turned on her lamp. Drake Crabtree was laying beside her. He was wearing nothing but his underwear.

"What are you all jumpy about?" Drake slurred as he placed his hand over Amy's mouth. "You know you want it as much as I do. There is not a girl at school who wouldn't want this body. Donut boy isn't up to the task, but you can close your eyes and pretend it's him if you want to."

The booze on Drake's breath almost made Amy sick as he talked into her ear. She tried to push his hand away from her mouth, but he was much stronger than she was, even when he was sloshed.

Drake took his free hand and lifted the T-shirt Amy wore to bed. He started to pull down on her panties. He took his underwear completely off.

Amy realized she had to use her brain. She couldn't just physically overpower him. She thought just a few seconds and made her decision. As Drake started to move on top of her, she quickly brought her right leg up and kicked him as hard as she could between the legs. He took his hand off of her mouth to grab himself in pain. She kicked him again, this time in the face. She screamed as hard as she could. Blood began to pour from Drake's nose.

"You stupid bitch!" Drake shouted as he steadied himself and lifted his fist over his head to hit Amy.

In all the commotion, Amy and Drake did not know they were now not alone in the room. Before Drake could strike Amy, his arm was grabbed from behind. It was Amy's dad. He pulled Drake's arm back so hard he almost broke it. Drake felt himself being pulled off the bed. He then felt a hand on his throat as he was slammed into the bedroom wall.

"Look, old man, your daughter wants me to screw her," Drake said, still slurring his words. "Let go of me or I'll have to kick your ass."

Amy's dad said nothing. He was too enraged to talk. Instead, he kneed Drake in the groin and repeated the process four more times. Drake slumped onto his knees as Catherine came flying into the room.

"What are you doing to Drake?!?!"

"Drake was trying to rape Amy and you're asking me what I'm doing to Drake?"

Hearing Catherine come to his defense emboldened Drake. With blood still streaming from his nose and still on his knees in pain from the repeated assaults between his legs, he changed his persona for Amy's mom.

"Don't believe 'em, Miss Catherine. She was coming on to me. She screamed because she said it hurt at first."

"You mean hurt like this?" Paul said before he stomped on Drake's private parts with his right foot. Drake fell on his side in even more pain.

"Why are you taking it all out on him?" Catherine asked Paul in anger. "You heard him say she instigated all of this."

Amy had never shouted at her mother in her life. Both Paul and Catherine were shocked to hear Amy scream out, "Mom! If you believe him, then GET OUT OF MY ROOM! JUST GET OUT!"

Catherine's eyebrows furrowed with more anger. "Don't you ever raise your . . ."

She was interrupted by Paul before she could complete her sentence.

"Catherine, that's enough! Now, get out of here and let me handle this."

Catherine stomped out of Amy's room and headed downstairs. Paul pulled Drake up by his arm and then pulled the arm behind Drake's back, holding it up as high as he could. Drake was moaning in more pain.

Paul was attempting to maneuver Drake to the door when Drake was able to spin around. He pulled his fist up to hit Paul, but he never got far before he was knocked against the bedroom wall by a punch thrown by Paul that landed directly on Drake's already bleeding nose.

"Where in the hell did you learn to fight, old man?" Drake spit out.

"In the United States Army, you piece of shit. Now, you're getting out of my house."

"I gotta get my stuff!"

"Nope, no stuff. You're just getting out."

"But, I don't have any clothes on."

"That's your damn problem," Paul shot back.

Amy watched all of this in shock. She had never seen her father mad and had certainly never seen him get violent. It just proved what he was willing to do to protect her.

Paul pulled Drake by the arm and drug him downstairs where he threw him out onto the porch.

"Give me my keys!" Drake shouted from the porch.

As Paul was shutting the door, he said, "Don't worry, I have a limo coming to pick you up."

After he locked the door, Paul walked into the kitchen and picked up the phone. Catherine had just walked into the kitchen behind him.

"Who are you calling?"

"The police, Catherine."

Catherine put her finger on the phone cradle, preventing Paul from making the call.

"Take your finger off the phone or that punk that tried to rape Amy will not be the only one I throw out of the house tonight," Paul said, and the look on his face made it clear he was serious.

As Paul was dialing and waiting for the police to answer, Catherine got in one more swipe.

"You're going to ruin our reputation with the most important family in our Charlotte neighborhood."

"Go watch your DVD of *Gone With the Wind*, Catherine," Paul said.

"See, you're crazy," she said. "What does that have to do with anything?"

"Just fast forward it to the part where Clark Gable says, 'I don't give a damn.'"

Chapter Forty-Two

Paul tried to remain as calm as possible while he was on the phone with the dispatcher for the Carolina Beach Police Department, but he still sounded a little shaky.

"Just come to my house as soon as you can. You will find a teenaged boy on my porch or nearby. He is naked because I threw him out with no clothes on after he tried to sexually assault my daughter."

After a few questions from the dispatcher, she told Paul the police were on the way. He hung up the phone and went back upstairs to check on Amy. She nervously told him the whole story of what happened when she woke up to find Drake trying to rape her.

"I never liked that guy in the first place," Paul said. He was trying to remain as calm as possible, not wanting to make Amy more upset than she already was. "I'm sorry I didn't put my foot down when your mother invited him down here in the first place."

Amy moved closer to her dad who had sat down on the edge of her bed. "It's not your fault,

Dad. I'm just glad you heard me. I've never seen you angry before, but I'm glad you did what you did to him."

"That's what happens when my daughter is in trouble."

For the first time since she last thought of Mason before she drifted off to sleep, Amy smiled. "I'm just sorry I was the cause of you and Mom getting into it."

"Don't worry about that at all. I didn't mean for that to happen in front of you, but I had to stop it. She isn't thinking clearly over that . . ." Paul paused to keep from spurting out anymore profanity about Drake. "ah, idiot."

"Idiot is being too kind," Amy said.

"You've got that right. I'm trying to contain myself. Are you going to be okay staying in your room tonight?"

"I will be now." Paul's gentleness with his daughter had helped Amy relax a little after the nightmare.

They both heard the doorbell ring. Paul stood up and went to look out of Amy's bedroom window. He could see down on the street that the police had arrived.

"The police are here," he told Amy. "I'll go down and talk to them. They are going to want to talk to you at some point."

"That's fine, but I would kind of just like to sit here until I have to come down, if that's okay."

"Take all the time you need," Paul said before he leaned over and gave his daughter a gentle kiss on the top of her head. Then, he headed downstairs,

As her dad closed the bedroom door behind him, Amy's thoughts turned to Mason.

Should I call Mason and tell him what happened? What if he thinks like Mom, that I had anything to do with it? I don't want to upset him. What if he wants to stop seeing me now?

In the middle of a thousand worries running through her mind, Amy jumped when she heard a knock on her bedroom door. Her dad opened the door slowly and said, "Honey, I know this won't be easy, but the police need to talk to you."

Her voice sounded nervous when she said, "Okay, I'll be down in a minute."

While Amy and her dad were talking minutes earlier, they didn't notice the phone was ringing, but Catherine did and answered it on the second ring. It was Mason asking to speak with Amy. He apologized for calling so late and said his dad had heard police dispatched to their house on his scanner and wanted to make sure everything was okay.

"It's fine and she's not available right now."

"Would you please tell her I called?" Mason asked.

Catherine hung up the phone without responding. As usual, she ignored his request.

Chapter Forty-Three

Amy came downstairs and walked into the living room to find two uniformed Carolina Beach police officers talking with her dad. Standing with the officers was a lady wearing jeans and a simple blouse. Amy wondered who she was until she noticed she was wearing a gun. A plainclothes officer, she thought.

Seeing Amy walk into the room, the lady officer approached her and placed a hand on her shoulder.

"Hi, Amy, I'm Sgt. Debbie Miller. Are you okay with you and me finding a quiet place where we could talk?"

Seeing police made Amy nervous. It made everything that had happened earlier more real than the surreal feeling she had been experiencing. Barely above a whisper, Amy answered Sgt. Miller by saying, "Yes, ma'am. I think so."

Amy led Sgt. Miller into a breakfast nook near the back of the house. When Amy sat down, Debbie Miller sat down across from her.

"I'm just here to listen, Amy. You don't have to tell me anything you don't want to. In fact, you don't have to tell me anything at all. But, you have to realize I am a police officer and I want to hold people accountable when they do something bad. I just need to tell you that."

Amy immediately sensed a sincerity and genuine concern from the police lady sitting across from her. She liked Sgt. Miller. The reality of what had happened to her at the hands of Drake Crabtree was now affecting her. Amy tried to fight the emotion she was feeling, but she couldn't stop a tear from streaming down her cheek. Debbie reached over and placed a hand on top of Amy's hand.

"Do you want to be alone for a little while?"

Immediately, Amy said, "No, please stay here. You want to know what's really bothering me right now?"

"Yes, I do."

"It's my boyfriend. I don't even believe boyfriend is the best word to use. He's more than that. He's the greatest guy I've ever met."

"Obviously, the guy involved in the assault tonight is not your boyfriend," Debbie said.

"Absolutely not. He has never, and would never, treat me with anything but respect."

"He does sound like a great guy. May I ask his name?"

"It's Mason James."

"You mean Joy and Woody's son?"

"Yes, ma'am."

"I've known them ever since I joined the department. They are really nice people. But, why is Mason bothering you?

"He's not really bothering me, it's just bothering me what he might think when he finds out what happened. I want to tell him, but I'm scared it will change the way he feels about me. Should I tell him?"

Debbie leaned back in her chair, looking uncomfortable over Amy's question.

"Um, the policy of the police department is that I'm not supposed to answer personal questions not directly related to investigating a case."

"Oh, I'm sorry," Amy said.

"Don't be," Debbie said and smiled. "A policy isn't law. When I think about a question like that, I try and turn the situation around. Would I want to know if something happened to someone I cared a lot for? Knowing the Jameses, I bet they would want to know because they care, not because they would want to judge you in any way."

"I would want to be there for him, no matter what happened," Amy added.

"I think you have your answer."

Debbie saw a few tears begin to slowly slide down Amy's face.

"I wish I could talk to him now," Amy said, with a shakiness in her voice.

"Do you want to go call him?"

"Not with Mom in the house. She doesn't like Mason because she doesn't think his family is rich enough. To her, it's all about money."

Debbie took a moment to study Amy's face. She saw someone who desperately needed someone to talk to that she trusted and cared for. Debbie stood up and said, "Please come with me."

Amy followed Sgt. Miller into the living room where they found her parents still speaking with the other officers.

"I have to take Amy down to the station to conduct some more of my investigation," Debbie said.

"Won't that put her close to that S.O.B. that attacked her?" Amy's dad asked.

"No. sir. He has been taken to the county jail in Wilmington. She'll be going with me to the Carolina Beach P.D. station. There's no way the suspect could be bailed out before tomorrow."

"You okay with going with her?" Amy's dad asked her.

"Yes, Dad. She's helping me a lot."

Amy went upstairs to quickly change clothes. When she come back down, Debbie led Amy to her a car that looked nothing like a police car. It was an older model Jeep Cherokee. Debbie noticed the look on Amy's face.

"Oh, my car. This is my personal car. I was at home when I got the call to come to your house. I'm always on call when there are assaults involving women or girls."

"I'm sorry you had to come back to work on my account," Amy said.

"I'm not," Debbie said and smiled. "I want to be here to help."

"Do I have to go the station to write a statement or identify Drake with pictures or something?"

"Yes, I do need a statement. It shouldn't take too long."

On the drive to the Carolina Beach police station, Amy mentioned Mason two more times. Hearing her obvious attachment to him, Sgt. Miller decided on a change of plans. The moment they arrived at the station, she led Amy into an interview room and told her she would be right back. She went to her desk in another area of the station and made a telephone call.

"Hello."

"Mr. James, I'm very sorry for calling you after midnight. This is Debbie Miller at the police department."

"That's okay, Debbie. Don't tell me. Has someone stole some of our construction material again?"

"No, sir, but I think I could use Mason's help. His girlfriend, Amy, has had a bad night."

"Oh, no," Woody said. "I'm sure Mason wants to do anything he can to help. He thinks the world of her and we do, too."

"I can certainly tell Amy feels the same way about Mason. It is okay if I bring her over this late?"

"Absolutely, I'll get Mason up right now."

Sgt. Miller went back to the interview room where Amy was waiting.

"Amy, for the second time tonight, I have decided to break protocol. I would like you to come with me."

"Yes, ma'am. Can I ask where we are going?

"You'll see in just a moment."

Chapter Forty-Four

When Woody slowly opened the door to Mason's room, he was surprised to see Mason was still awake. Mason had been reading for quite a while trying to relax enough to go to sleep. He read several lines in the book two or three times. He was distracted thinking about his great evening with Amy and was worried about why police had been dispatched to her house. The fact Amy had never returned his call to tell him everything was okay made it hard for him to concentrate on what he was reading. Seeing his dad walk into his room surprised him and the look on his dad's face made him worry.

"Son, I think you better get up and get dressed really quick."

"What's wrong, Dad?"

"I'm not quite sure, but Debbie Miller at the police department is bringing Amy over."

Mason instantly jumped up and got dressed. Within a minute he was walking back and forth in the living room. They all heard the light knock at the front door. Woody, Joy and Mason all came to the door and found Sgt, Miller and Amy on the front porch.

The moment they walked into the house, Amy flew into Mason's arms and started to cry. Debbie and his parents walked into the dining room to leave them alone for a while.

"Amy, what's wrong?" Mason asked, his voice becoming unsteady. "Please tell me you're okay."

He could feel Amy's heart pounding and realized his was, too. He just held her tight, patiently waiting for her to feel like talking.

Amy broke into tears. The shock she was in had vanished when she saw Mason. Now, the reality of what had happened to her had filled her with a range of emotions. She was angry, hurt and scared about how Mason would react. Mason kept his arms wrapped around her. His mind was filled with all kind of scenarios about what may have made Amy so upset to the point that police were involved.

Did something happen between her and her mom? Is her dad okay? It never crossed his mind what Amy was about to tell him as she slowly gained some composure.

"Please tell me you will still love me?" Amy began.

"Of course, I will. You know I will. Always."

Amy pulled together the strength to look Mason in the eyes.

"Drake tried to rape me tonight."

Mason became instantly enraged. He wanted to shout out what an S.O.B. Drake was, and he wanted to go find him, but he quickly composed himself. He knew that right now it was not about him or his anger. It was all about Amy. He didn't want to say anything that would upset her even more than she already was.

Mason's silence scared Amy.

"You aren't mad at me are you?" she asked. "You're not saying anything."

He held Amy even tighter and said, "Of course I'm not mad at you. I just didn't want to say anything that might make you more upset. What I wanted to say is he is the first guy I ever met who I hated the minute I laid eyes on him and heard him talk. I have never been in a fight, but I can't promise you I wouldn't do anything to him if he was here right now."

Amy did not want any more violence tonight, but Mason's words actually made her feel better. She knew he wanted to protect her. She knew he was not the type to go looking for trouble, so his anger meant one thing – he really did love her.

"Where is he?" Mason asked.

"In jail in Wilmington."

"Good, that's where he belongs."

Amy lifted her head from Mason's shoulder. It pained him to see her red eyes and the remnants of fear on her face. He wished he could do anything to stop her pain.

"Can we just go sit on the porch a little while?" Amy asked.

"Of course," Mason said, gentle as always.

Mason's mom and dad were in the dining room talking with Sgt. Debbie Miller. They stopped talking when they saw Mason and Amy walk into the room.

"Amy would like for her and me to sit on the porch for awhile," Mason said.

"Is that okay?" Amy asked, directing the question to Sgt. Miller.

"Of course, it is," Debbie said as she smiled. "I'm on your schedule tonight.

Chapter Forty-Five

Mason and Amy sat in the swing on the front porch. Mason had his arm around her and she was holding his free hand with both of hers. For a long time, they just sat and rocked gently in the swing.

"Mason?" Amy broke the silence.

"Yes."

"You will never know how much I love you."

"I think that's the other way around."

Amy leaned up so she could look Mason in the eye.

"I'm serious. I've read stories about guys dumping their girlfriend after they have been attacked."

"Why would I want to do that? I love you."

"The stories said some guys feel like the girl may have done something to encourage the attack and some others feel like they don't want to have anything to do with damaged goods."

"Neither one of those things ever crossed my mind," Mason said, reaching up and gently running his hand down Amy's face.

Mason's gentle responses calmed Amy down. She felt like she could now tell him anything.

"You should have seen my mom. She was actually standing up for Drake! I couldn't believe it."

"Why would she do that?"

"I didn't understand Mom for many years. Now, I see she is one of those people who is impressed only by money. Since Drake's dad is this rich, supposedly highly-respected doctor in Charlotte, Mom has always wanted to be in their inner circle. I think she thought getting Drake and me together would help her get there."

"So, she was willing to stand up for a guy who tried to . . ." Mason stopped for a moment. He didn't want to use the word rape. "I'm sorry. I shouldn't be talking about your mother."

"Why not? I am. But, my dad was a whole different story. You should've seen him. He decked Drake and kneed him so many times I don't think he'll be in any condition to do anything to another girl for a while."

"Good for your dad."

"He likes you a lot. He always asks about you."

"I'm glad at least one of your parents likes me," Mason said and smiled.

"I wouldn't worry about Mom," Amy said. "I don't think she likes anybody."

Mason and Amy grew silent again. She laid her head on his shoulder and they went back to gently rocking in the swing.

The phone began ringing at Amy's house. Catherine answered. Dr. Crabtree was on the phone, calling from his car phone.

"Catherine, could you tell me what is going on? I just got a call from Drake to call our lawyer. I'm on my way to Wilmington. He said Amy accused him of trying to rape her."

"I'm so sorry, Doctor. I don't know what is going on, really. I'm hoping it's just all a big misunderstanding."

"Did Amy tell you Drake tried to rape her?"

Catherine delayed her response. She knew the question led to no-win answers.

"She said he was in her room with no clothes on."

"Did Amy have *her* clothes on?"

"I don't know. I'm still waiting on some answers, too. And Amy is not here. A woman police officer has taken her down to the police station here at the beach."

"I guess it would be best if we talked again after we have some more answers."

"Of course, Doctor. I hope some simple dispute between our children doesn't damage our relationship as neighbors."

"I don't think accusing someone of rape is a simple dispute, Catherine."

The doctor's phone went dead.

Damn, Amy, Catherine thought as she hung up the phone. *I was going to ask Doctor Crabtree to write you a letter of recommendation for Juilliard. I hope you haven't ruined everything.*

Chapter Forty-Six

The front door opened at Mason's house and Sgt. Miller stepped out onto the porch.

"Amy, I really hate to bother you and Mason, but I have to let you know I just got a call from the station that your mother called there looking for you. They told her you were with me, but she was pretty insistent in coming to get you."

The news changed the entire mood between Mason and Amy.

"I guess I better go," Amy said. She kissed Mason.

"Will you please call me tomorrow and let me know how you are?" Mason asked.

"Call you? I'm coming to see you no matter what."

Woody and Joy stepped out on the porch.

"Amy, please let us know if there is anything we can do, and I'm serious about that," Joy said.

"Just letting me come to see Mason this late means more than you know," Amy said.

"You're always welcome here," Woody said. "Anytime."

"Thanks," Amy said. Next to her Aunt Mary, Mason and his parents had become her favorite people. She felt loved around them all.

Amy gave Mason another hug and got into Debbie's car.

"I guess we better head to the station," Debbie said.

"Yes, ma'am," Amy said.

During the short drive to the station, Amy said, "I'm sorry my situation is keeping you away from your family tonight."

"I'm here for you, Amy. That's my job. And I don't have a family, yet anyway. I was engaged a few years back, but that fell through."

"I'm sorry to hear that," Amy said.

"Don't be. I'm glad I found out before it was too late that he is kind of like that Drake guy, a jerk."

For the first time since Amy's encounter with Drake, a slight smile formed on her face. She knew she could trust Sgt. Miller.

As Debbie pulled into the parking lot of the Carolina Beach Police Department, Amy couldn't believe what she was seeing.

"You've got to be kidding me," Amy said.

"What is it?" Debbie asked.

Amy pointed to a new dark blue Lexus in the parking lot. "Mom's here."

The Lexus was empty, so Debbie took Amy inside the station. Standing inside the lobby, talking to another officer, was Catherine. When she saw Debbie and Amy walk in, she made a beeline to Debbie.

"Where have you been with my daughter?" Catherine demanded.

"Mrs. Cole, this is an active investigation of a major crime. I have been talking with your daughter in a safe place."

"And just where is this safe place?"

"Mrs. Cole, I'm sorry, but I can't tell you that. Like I said, this is an investigation about a major crime that has taken place."

"I don't call some spat between a couple of teenagers a 'major crime,'" Catherine said, using her fingers to insinuate quotation marks around "major crime."

Debbie felt the back of her neck turn red.

"Mrs. Cole, I can hardly stand here and listen to you call attempted rape a spat. Your daughter needs your support and understanding, not this."

About ten minutes after Catherine had left the house on the way to the police station, Paul went looking in the house for her. When he realized she was gone, he knew she was headed for one of two places, either to the station or to Wilmington to try and bail out Drake. He was livid and hopped into his car.

Before Catherine could respond to Sgt. Debbie Miller's last comment, the door to the police department opened. Amy's dad walked in.

"Catherine, what are you doing?"

"I'm here to pick up Amy."

"Did the police ask you to? I didn't hear the phone ring at the house." Paul pushed on the subject.

"No, and I don't need permission from anyone to be able to pick up my own daughter."

Paul turned to Sgt. Debbie Miller and asked, "Are you finished with the investigation?"

"No, sir, I am not," Debbie said.

"Then, in that case, it's good I'm here," Catherine said. "You should know there may be questions about how all of this started."

The look on Paul's face turned from frustration to anger. He took Catherine's arm and said, "Come outside with me just a moment."

Once they were outside, Paul raised his voice. "What the hell are you doing?"

"I already answered that question," Catherine said.

"This time, I'm asking you what are you doing trying to interfere with the police and, even more importantly, trying to convince the police to question the attempted rape of your own daughter?"

"The police have a right to hear Drake's side of the story."

"Then, that's an issue Drake and his parents will have to handle, not you. Now, go home."

Catherine gasped in disgust. "I'm getting sick of this disrespect."

"You're doing better than me," Paul said. "I'm already sick of it."

Since Paul was standing between her and the door of the Carolina Beach Police Department, Catherine said, "Get out of my way."

Paul didn't move.

"If you go back in there, I will be at the lawyer's office first thing in the morning to file for divorce."

"Fine with me," Catherine said.

"Don't jump so fast, Catherine. I will also ask for full custody of Amy. She's 17 years old. That means if they put her on the stand and ask where she wants to live, what do you think she'll say?"

Catherine's eyes narrowed. She turned around, stormed to her car and squealed tires pulling out of the parking lot.

Chapter Forty-Seven

At Mason's house, everyone was still awake. They were sitting around the table. Mason was filling his parents in on what Amy had told him.

"No wonder Amy looked so upset," Joy said.

"It's bad enough what Drake did, but her mom's making it worse," Mason said.

"How so, Son?" Woody asked.

"Drake made up some lie about Amy coming onto him first and her mom was standing up for him, believing what he said."

"What kind of mom doesn't want to stand by her daughter when she says she's been almost raped?" Joy asked.

"Not much of one," Woody said.

Joy and Mason looked at each other. Woody would often give an opinion on a subject, but rarely said anything negative about a person, until now.

At the Carolina Beach Police Department, Amy's father asked Sgt. Miller if he should wait at the station to take Amy home, or if he should go home until she called for him to come get her.

"I would like to get a statement on tape, if Amy is up to it, so I'd be glad to bring her home when we are through."

"I'm okay with that," Amy said. She felt safe with Debbie and believed she was looking out for her best interests.

Paul gave Amy a hug and said he would wait up until she got home. Amy was very glad to hear that. She didn't want to walk in and have to confront her mother alone after what had just happened.

Catherine had returned to the beach house and walked the halls. Her mind was reeling between what had just transpired at the police department and the obvious anger of Dr. Crabtree when she spoke with him on the phone earlier. Mostly, she was mad.

Paul Cole is crazy if he thinks I'm going to EVER allow him to walk out of here with my daughter. And, it's obvious Amy isn't thinking clearly at all. Maybe Drake went in there to tell her goodnight and since she was half asleep, she didn't realize she was letting things get out of hand before she woke up completely. I've got to get clever here and take back control of all of this.

Within a few minutes, she had formulated a plan. She was glad she was able to think through it all that fast because she heard the door open and Paul walk in.

"Just go to bed, Catherine. I'm waiting up for Amy. They are going to bring her home."

"I will wait up, too," Catherine said. Her tone was completely different than at the police station.

"Just go to bed, you have already upset Amy enough after all she has been through tonight."

"I know that," Catherine said. "I realize that now. I'm sorry about the way I handled things with Amy and with you. I'd like to be here to tell her how sorry I am."

Paul was shocked at the 180-degree change in his wife. He said nothing and sat down in a recliner in the living room. Catherine sat on the couch and picked up a magazine to begin thumbing through while they both waited for their daughter to get home from what had begun as the best night of her life only to turn into the worst experience of her life.

About a half hour after Amy's parents had sat down in the living room to wait, she arrived home. Sgt. Debbie Miller had walked her to the door. The moment she walked into the house, her parents stood up.

"How are you holding up, honey?" Paul asked her.

"I'm feeling very tired now. I'm going to go ahead and try and get some sleep."

She turned to head to the steps but was stopped by her mother.

"I need to speak with you just a moment," Catherine said.

Amy cringed.

"Mom, can it please wait until the morning?"

"Just one moment, please."

Amy reluctantly turned around and came to the door of the living room.

"I have already apologized to your father and I am apologizing to you, too. I should have listened to you tonight. I was just trying to make something good out of a bad situation, but I wasn't thinking clearly in all of the commotion. I'm sorry. You can go on to bed now."

Amy exchanged glances with her dad before she said, "Okay. Thanks, Mom."

Back in her room, Amy realized that despite being very tired, she was too wound up to just lay down and try to go to sleep. She unlocked her top desk drawer and pulled out her diary. With her pillow against her backboard, she sat in bed and started to write.

How does one night go from one of the greatest nights of my life to the worst and then back to good again? That's what happened to me tonight. It started with a date with Mason.

We drove to Fort Fisher and just parked in the rain and talked. I love him so much.

After I got home, I was almost raped in my own room by Drake Crabtree. I have never liked him and now I hate him.

I was so scared after it happened that Mason would end our relationship. It was the opposite. Thanks to his mom and dad, and a great lady cop, I was able to talk to Mason and tell him everything. He was so gentle and loving about everything. I'm the luckiest girl on the planet to have Mason.

Thinking about Mason calmed Amy. She knew she could get some sleep now. She was glad everything about Drake Crabtree was over. At least, that's what she hoped.

Chapter Forty-Eight

At 9:30 the next morning, two sheriff deputies from the New Hanover County Jail escorted Drake Crabtree into court. The nameplate on the judge's stand read Judge Albert Yates. He had not yet entered the room.

As Drake entered the courtroom, he looked to see who was there. His dad was sitting behind the defense table in the spectator section. Their family attorney, who he had only seen at dinners, was seated at the table. He had followed Dr. Crabtree down from Charlotte very early in the morning.

At the table across from that one was a man in a suit and a woman cop. They were an assistant district attorney, Bill Vinson, and Sgt. Debbie Miller. Seated behind them was only one person, Amy's father. When Drake made eye contact with him, Paul glared.

Dr. Crabtree stood when his son approached the table and was close enough to talk. Drake leaned towards his dad. "Where's Mom?"

"She didn't come."

The deputies turned Drake towards the table and his lawyer pointed for him to sit down. Before the lawyer had a chance to speak with Drake, the bailiff walked into the room.

"All rise."

Judge Yates entered and sat down as he looked at the parties in the courtroom.

"Mr. Vinson, you may proceed."

Assistant D.A. Bill Vinson stood.

"Your honor, this is the case of the state versus Drake Crabtree. Mr. Crabtree is 17 years old and is charged with the sexual assault and attempted rape of a young lady his same age. Mr. Drake was a guest in the home of the young lady and returned to that home last night after using a fake I.D. to buy alcohol. That was when the assault occurred."

The Crabtree family attorney was also standing.

"Your honor, I'm David Dobson of the Charlotte bar. The defense would like to request the matter be transferred to juvenile court since the defendant is under 18 years of age."

"We object, your honor," Bill Vinson said. "The defendant is old enough to know his actions. Considering the seriousness of the crime and the fact he used a fake I.D. to purchase alcohol that was a factor in the assault, we request he be tried as an adult. Since the defendant thought he was above the law, he should be tried in this court."

"I agree," Judge Yates said. "I've read Sgt. Miller's detailed report. I'll set bail at $200,000 and, if the bond is met, I order the defendant to remain within the state, specifically in Charlotte or here in Wilmington, to appear in court. I'm also issuing a no-contact order. The defendant is not to call, contact or be within 50 feet of the young lady involved."

Drake stood up and blurted out, "That's not fair! I have summer tennis tournaments to play in. They'll kick me off the team!"

His attorney pulled Drake back into his seat and the judge's tone changed.

"Mr. Crabtree, one more outburst like that and I'll have you held without bond. You should have thought about your team when you used a fake I.D. to buy alcohol. While the matter of the assault has yet to be tried, Sgt. Miller's report proves to me you had a phony driver's license in your possession. In fact, here it is." The judge held up the fake I.D..

During the exchange between the judge and Drake, Assistant D.A. Vinson, Sgt. Miller and Amy's dad all kept a stoic game face on. However, they were all thinking the same thing Paul was. *Keep it up, asshole, you're making the case for us.*

"Anything else?" Judge Yates asked.

The Crabtrees' attorney, Bill Vinson, had planned on challenging the amount of the bond and to make a few other motions, but he knew

Drake had just screwed that all up. It would have been a waste of breath.

The deputies took Drake back to jail and everyone left the courtroom. In the lobby, Dr. Crabtree walked up to Paul when he noticed he was alone.

"I think we should talk," he said to Paul.

"I think we should not," Paul said and walked away.

Dr. Crabtree went back to his attorney and they went to bail Drake out and drive to Charlotte. They had Drake's BMW towed back to Charlotte.

Chapter Forty-Nine

About the same time Drake's dad met the requirements for bonding his son out of jail and they had hit the road back to Charlotte, Amy came down the steps. She had slept in. Her mom was in the kitchen drinking a cup of coffee.

"I was about to come up and check on you. I've never seen you sleep this late," Catherine said.

"It was a long, rough night," Amy said.

"Yes, it was. Would you like me to make you some breakfast?"

Amy was again shocked over the change in her mother's demeanor.

"No, ma'am, but thanks. I think I'll just drink some orange juice and walk down to the boardwalk to say hello to Mason."

"Oh, I thought you'd be through with guys for a while after last night."

"Mason is not some guy, Mom. He is really great and if you'd give him a chance, you'd see that, too."

Catherine bit her tongue, reminding herself to stay focused on her new plan. She was saved from responding by the phone ringing.

"That's a call I'm expecting from the office."

Amy drank a glass of orange juice on the back deck while looking out over the ocean. She knew nothing about what had happened in court today and that was what her dad wanted. He knew she needed a break.

The phone call Catherine had walked back into her beach home office to take was not the one she was expecting, it was Mason asking to speak to Amy.

"She's upstairs getting ready to come see you," Catherine said.

"Oh, that's great. Please tell her I'll see her in a little while. Thanks, Mrs. Cole."

Some habits are hard to kill. She said nothing, hung up and ignored Mason's request to tell Amy he had called.

Dr. Crabtree spoke briefly with Drake on a visit to the jail. Since they knew most jailhouse visits are monitored, Drake's dad only said he was going to go put up property to meet the bond and get him out of jail. He wanted to wait until he was away from law enforcement eyes and ears to have any real talk.

When the bond conditions were met and Drake and his dad were headed back to

Charlotte, it was uncomfortably quiet in the car for the first hour.

"Tell me exactly what happened, and don't B.S. me," Dr. Crabtree finally said.

"It's like I told Amy's mom. We started making out and it kept going. She wanted it all, but when it came time to go all the way, she just freaked and started screaming. That's when her dad came in and kicked my ass."

"Back it up," Drake's dad said. "Let's start with that fake I.D. thing. Where'd you get it?"

"A guy at school knows this dude who is really good at making them."

"Who is the guy at school?"

"If I tell you and he finds out, I'm dead. The guy who makes them is in a gang."

"If he's so dangerous, why did you want to have anything to do with him in the first place?"

"I don't know."

"Well, I do. It's because you want what you want and don't care about anybody else. That is also how the district attorney will play it to the jury if this rape accusation goes to trial."

Drake just sat there.

"Actually, this is my fault," Dr. Crabtree said. "Since I have to work all the time at the hospital, I wanted to make up for the time I wasn't with you by making sure you had nice things, like that car. All I did was spoil you and teach you not to appreciate what it takes to earn that money. Those days are over. I'm going to have the car locked in the garage. You will have to find a job and earn it back, that is if they don't put you in prison."

His dad's message didn't get through. Drake didn't take responsibility for anything. All he could think was, *Damn you, Amy!*

Chapter Fifty

Mason walked into the kitchen already dressed for work. His mom was sitting at the table.

"Hey, Son. Have you heard anything from Amy?"

"No, ma'am, but she said she was going to drop by the donut shop today."

"That's good. I can't imagine what she went through last night."

"Me, either. I guess it's good I didn't see Drake around last night or I would probably be in jail."

"I understand the anger, but don't get into a stink match with a skunk. They always win. From what I could see of Debbie Miller, she is really watching out for Amy."

"She really is. Amy respects her a lot."

"Good. And I have some good news for you."

"What's that, Mom?" Mason asked as he poured himself a bowl of cereal.

"I was watching the local news on TV this morning. Drake's arrest made the news. They even had his mug shot on TV."

"They didn't mention Amy, did they? That would really bother her."

"No, most news outlets don't use the name of a sexual assault victim."

Mason relaxed. "Thank goodness."

Amy walked into Britt's Donuts about ten minutes after they opened. Mason wasn't scheduled to come into work for another 50 minutes. Bobby saw her come in and walked to the counter where she was sitting.

"Hi, Amy. How are you doing?"

"Okay, I guess. Long night."

"Sorry to hear that. Mason doesn't come on duty until 11:00, but he should be in a little before that."

"Mr. Bobby, I hope it doesn't bother you that I come in here to see him. I don't want to get him in trouble on the job."

Bobby sat down on the stool beside Amy.

"See, that right there is why it doesn't bother me a bit. You care enough to ask. Mason is a good worker and I've never seen you being here distract him from his work. You are welcome in here anytime. Besides, I wouldn't want your Aunt Mary to ever be upset with me. She is one of my favorites."

Amy laughed and said, "She does have a way with people, doesn't she?"

Having Bobby bring up Mary reminded Amy that her aunt had probably not heard what had happened unless her mom had called her. Since they didn't speak much, she doubted Mary knew anything.

I need to call Aunt Mary, Amy thought just as she felt a hand on her shoulder. She turned around. It was Mason.

"Wow, you're in early," Amy said as she hugged him. "Bobby said you were not scheduled for about another 45 minutes."

"Yep. But, I was hoping you would be here."

Amy and Mason talked right up until it was time for him to go on duty. As he stood up to head to the back, he said, "Any chance we can get together after I'm off?"

"What time is that?"

"At 4:30."

"I'll be here," Amy said and gave him a quick kiss. As she made it to the door, she turned around and threw him another one.

As Mason was preparing to take over the job of cutting out the donuts in the dough, it struck him that in the almost 45 minutes he and Amy had talked this morning, one subject was never brought up – Drake Crabtree. He hoped he would never have to hear that name again, unless it was in the news that he was in prison.

Chapter Fifty-One

"Hello, Amy! It sure is good to hear your voice. I've called twice this week and you were out. I bet you've been spending time with Mason," Mary said, excited that Amy had called.

"You called twice?" Amy asked.

"I sure did. I left a message with your mother for you to call me."

"You know Mom. She never writes down a message."

"That sister of mine. I don't know what in the world gets into her. Sometimes I wonder if one of us was switched at the hospital."

Amy laughed and her aunt joined in.

"I guess Mom didn't call you today."

"No, not today. She rarely calls any day."

"I have something to tell you."

"Oh, my. The sound of your voice scares me."

Amy told Mary the entire story of what had transpired last night with Drake Crabtree. Amy had never heard her aunt cuss until now.

"That damn boy! He's nothing but a worthless spoiled brat and his parents are just self-centered jerks. I didn't like them the first time I met them. How did he get in the house?"

"Mom gave him a key."

"What?!?!"

"Yes, ma'am. She actually invited him down to spend the week and gave him the key so he could get back in if he stayed out late."

"You put her on the phone right now. I'm going to give her a piece of my mind."

"She's not here right now, Aunt Mary. That's why I called you. She said she had to run some errands. And you won't believe this, but she told me last night that she was sorry for asking Drake to come down and for not believing me at first about what happened."

"She actually apologized?"

"Yes, ma'am."

"Well, I better hang up and go get my affairs in order. These are the last days."

"This is one of the reasons I love you, Aunt Mary. You can always make me laugh no matter what is going on."

"Sometimes, niece, I have to find a little humor in a situation or I'm afraid I'd go on a killin' spree."

Amy laughed again.

"Let me change the subject," Mary said. "When are you and Mason coming down to see me?"

"That's actually one of the reasons I called, other than to tell you what happened. Mason has to work most of the day for the rest of the week and he suggested I spend some time with you. He thought I could use a break from being in the house where everything happened."

"How old did you say Mason is?"

"Same as me, 17."

"That's hard to believe. He has to be the most unselfish, thoughtful guy his age I've ever known."

"He really is, Aunt Mary. I just wish Mom could see that."

"You want me to come pick you up in the morning?"

"That would be great."

"See you then," Mary said.

Within five minutes of hanging up with her aunt, the phone rang at Amy's house. She answered it.

"I'm lucky this time," Mason said. "Usually your mom answers."

"She's out running some errands and Dad went down to the Kure Beach Pier for a while, so it's just me here. Are you off of work early?"

"Nah, just on break," Mason said. "But, I was missing you."

"Do you know when I miss you most?" Amy asked.

"When is that?"

"Anytime when you're not around."

Hearing that made Mason feel as good inside as he ever had felt in his life. He was euphoric at knowing he loved someone who really loved him back.

While they were talking, Catherine walked into the house. She had a folder in one hand and waved through the kitchen door with the other one. She walked down to her office and shut the door.

"I talked with Aunt Mary a few minutes ago and she is coming to pick me up in the morning," Amy filled Mason in.

"I know you will enjoy the visit and she will, too. How many days are you going to be gone?"

"I'll be coming back in the evening the day after tomorrow."

"Your aunt only has a few days?"

"No, Mason James, I can't take it being away from you so long."

In her office, Catherine cringed. She had picked up the phone quietly and was listening in on Mason and Amy's conversation.

So, she's going to my sister's for a few days. I'm sure she'll feed Amy with more of her junk about Mason being good for her, but I have to stay focused on the plan. Amy being gone will give me a chance to get everything in order. It's actually good timing.

Catherine opened the folder she had returned home with. It was a real estate contract. It was for the sale of the beach house. She had arranged it without the knowledge of Paul or Amy. She was reviewing the contract while she waited for Amy to hang up the phone. As soon as she heard Amy heading upstairs, Catherine made a call to her hand-picked CPA for the advertising agency. She needed to go over the details of another plan she putting into action to take complete control of the business.

"Hello, Catherine, how are you?"

The voice on the other end of the line was David Wallace, CPA. Without her husband's knowledge four weeks ago, Catherine had fired the long time CPA for their company and signed a contract with Wallace. She knew Paul wouldn't approve because Wallace had just regained his CPA privileges after his license was suspended for violating state rules. She was his first client after reopening. She liked having people she could hold things over if she needed to.

"Are you where we can speak confidentially?" Catherine said.

"Yes. I'm in my office with the door shut. Is something wrong?"

"Not as far as you're concerned. But, I have an offer for you. How would you like to own 25 percent of the ad agency?"

Chapter Fifty-Two

The moment Mason got off work, Amy was there to meet him at Britt's Donuts. They went for a walk along the beach, holding hands and talking about all kinds of subjects, except for Drake Crabtree, of course.

"I just got the schedule and Bobby has me off on Friday. Since that's the day you get back from your aunt's, would you like to spend the afternoon and evening doing something together?"

"Like you even have to ask."

Mason smiled and Amy leaned over to kiss him on the cheek while they walked.

Close to dinner time, Paul returned home from his afternoon strolling around Kure Beach and walking out on the pier. Catherine was waiting for him when he walked in. She had a disturbed look on her face.

"What's wrong? Is Amy okay?"

"Yes, it's not about Amy, she's out with that boy from the donut shop."

"His name is Mason."

"I got a fax from the CPA this afternoon and it's not good."

"What do you mean it's not good. Last month's report you sent to the management team showed we had the best month ever."

"That was then. This is another month."

Catherine handed him the fax. The first thing Paul noticed was the letterhead.

"Who is David Wallace?"

"I switched CPAs a few weeks ago. You never listen to me when I tell you important things. Besides, it's because of him that this serious problem was found.

"I would remember something as important as changing CPAs, Catherine."

"Would you just concentrate on this right now," she said, pointing at the fax in Paul's hand. He kept reading.

MEMO/CONFIDENTIAL
To: Paul and Catherine Cole
Ref: Yearly Audit Report

While I have not completed all aspects of the audit, I just discovered some serious discrepancies in the financials of the advertising agency. It appears to me someone within the agency is embezzling large sums of money and using accounting tricks to hide it.

I don't want to unnecessarily alarm you and I know you are enjoying your first summer in your fine beach home. However, I do believe the matter is serious enough for you to return to Charlotte as soon as possible.

- David Wallace

"Do you have any idea what this is about?" Paul asked.

"Not a clue," Catherine said. "I think it's best we head back to Charlotte within the next few days. Amy is going to Mary's until Friday afternoon. That will give us time to get everything together to head home."

"My God," Paul said. "What else is going to go wrong this summer?"

Catherine just stood there as Paul was shaking his head, exasperated over what he had just read from the CPA. He was also mad about his wife switching CPAs without his knowledge, but that was another battle for another day. His frustration over the news was interrupted when he thought about Amy.

"Wait a minute. It just hit me that Crabtree bailed out his son and they are back home in Charlotte. I don't want to take Amy back there right now. Maybe you better head back and just keep me informed what you find out."

Catherine did not plan on Paul's response. She thought fast.

"You don't have to worry about Drake. Doris Barkley told me this morning they had taken Drake to their mountain place in Asheville. I guess they didn't want to deal with any neighborhood gossip."

After telling that lie, Catherine began to cry, putting on a performance worthy of an Academy Award.

"Besides, I can't handle all of this by myself. I need you there."

Paul had not heard words like that in ten years.

Chapter Fifty-Three

Amy came downstairs at 8:30, ready to eat something quick for breakfast before Mary arrived, but Mary was already there, sitting in the dining room with Catherine and Paul. They had said nothing about having to return to Charlotte on Friday.

"Well, good morning beautiful niece of mine," Mary said.

"Hey, Aunt Mary. You're early. I guess I could just eat a Pop Tart or something on the way."

"I actually have breakfast plans for us. That's why I came early."

"Oh? Where are we eating?"

"It's a secret."

Amy went upstairs and grabbed the tote bag she had packed the night before. Within five minutes, Amy and Mary were pulling out of the driveway.

"What is this about a secret breakfast?" Amy asked.

"It just so happens I have a hankerin' for some donuts."

Amy laughed, "Aunt Mary, you are something."

"I am, aren't I?"

When Amy and Mary walked into Britt's Donuts, Bobby made a beeline to see them both.

"Mary, when am I going to convince you to leave Sunset Beach and move here?" Bobby asked.

"There's no way," Mary said. "If I moved here I'd be eating these donuts of yours every day and I wouldn't meet the weight requirement to drive over that bridge anymore."

Everyone within earshot laughed.

"Mary, you sure are something," Bobby said.

"I just told her the same thing not five minutes ago," Amy said.

"Amy, Mason just ran out to run a quick errand for me to the bank. He should be back any minute and that should be a good time for his break."

Amy smiled and, right on cue, Mason walked in carrying a paper bag with a bank pouch hidden inside. He saw Amy and a huge smile spread across his face.

"I was just telling Amy you would be right back and that it would be your break time," Bobby said.

"You sure?" Mason said.

"Of course. I'll go get Amy and Mary some donuts."

Bobby took the bank bag and Mason sat down with Mary and Amy.

"This is a good surprise to see both of you," Mason said.

"It's good to see you again, too, Mason; and it's good to see those donuts heading our way," Mary said.

They all laughed and Mason said, "You are really something Miss Mary."

"Everyone seems to be saying that today," Amy said.

Bobby walked up and placed a white bag with a dozen donuts on the counter in front of Amy, Mary and Mason. Right behind him was his daughter bringing soft drinks. Mary started to open her purse.

"Nope, no ma'am," Bobby said. "These are on the house. Just call it a perk of knowing one of our best employees."

"Mason, I'm glad I know people in high places," Mary said.

They all pleasantly chatted while they ate the donuts.

"We should let Mason get back to work and we should hit the road," Mary said.

"We still on for Friday?" Amy asked Mason.

"Like you even have to ask," Mason said.

"You using my words back at me?"

"Of course."

On the drive to Sunset Beach, Amy was glad Mary did not want to hear any details about Drake Crabtree. She wished the whole incident would just go away. Plus, she knew she would have to deal with it again when his trial came up, so she would rather forget it until then.

"Sounds like you and Mason have a big day planned on Friday," Mary said. "I'm not keeping you from having that today, am I?"

"No, ma'am, not at all. He has to work every day until then, so this is a great time for our visit."

"Oh, that's right, you did say he had to work a lot this week. See there? I'm gettin' old and senile."

"You are not old and you are the smartest lady I know," Amy said.

"I need you around as a cheerleader."

They laughed.

"You have anything special planned on your Friday date?"

"Not that I know of, but Mason has a way of always having some special surprise he just seems to think up when we get together."

"The more I hear about that fella, the more I like him and the more I like it that you two met."

"Me, too, Aunt Mary."

Amy began wondering what surprise Mason may have in store on Friday. She didn't know the only surprise she would experience involved her being in a car headed back home to Charlotte at the very time she and Mason were supposed to meet for their date.

Chapter Fifty-Four

On Thursday afternoon, Mason was wrapping up his duties at the donut shop and thinking of tomorrow, the day he would be spending with Amy. Bobby noticed the content look on Mason's face.

"You obviously must be thinking of Amy, considering the look on your face,"

"Is it really that obvious?" Mason asked.

"It is. Have you got a big day planned tomorrow with her?"

"Yes, sir. I thought about it a lot the past couple of days and thought she might like to take the ferry over to Southport. Right after we met, she mentioned she almost rode on it to go see her aunt but found out it was very busy that day and had cars waiting for the next two runs. I think she would like roaming around Southport and eating some seafood there."

"Now, that sounds like a great date. She'd probably think Fishy, Fishy is a neat restaurant."

"I was wondering which place to take her. That's a great idea. Thanks."

"You bet. And you guys have fun."

"Thanks."

When Mason got home, he noticed there was a third car in the driveway. It was a 1960s model Ford Mustang. He and his dad had talked a lot about how they liked Mustangs. He guessed one of his dad's friends had one and was visiting. He was surprised when he walked inside and found just his mom and dad home.

"Hey, Son," his dad said.

Before Mason could respond, his mom said, "Mason, were you still expecting to borrow the car tomorrow for your date with Amy?"

"Yes, ma'am."

"I don't think that's going to be possible," Joy said.

"Oh," Mason said, obviously disappointed.

"And I'm afraid I'll have to have the truck for a big job tomorrow," Woody added.

"I guess we could just do things here at the beach tomorrow," Mason said.

"Why would want to do that when you could take YOUR car?" Joy said, smiling.

"Excuse me?"

"Surely, you saw the Mustang in the driveway," Woody said.

It took a moment for Mason to get through the set-up his parents had staged and put two-and-two together."

"You mean what I think you mean?"

"Yep," Woody said. "The Mustang is yours, but there is just one catch."

"I know, I'll have to pay you for it."

Woody laughed, "No, just for your own gas, but you will have to let me drive it every once in a while when I feel a middle age crisis coming on."

They all laughed. Woody tossed the keys to Mason and added, "Go take it for a spin."

"Thanks, I can't believe it. You guys are the best. I can't wait for Amy to see it."

"We figured you would want her to be your first passenger," Joy said.

Mason stepped outside and stood beside the Mustang, taking in the fact it was now his car. For almost five minutes he just looked at it before he finally got in the driver's seat and started it up. Woody and Joy were looking out of the sliding glass doors in the kitchen.

"Look at that," Woody said. "He's driving it like it's made out of glass. I remember me being like that with my first car."

"You always said you would never buy your son a car, that he would appreciate it more if he bought it. What changed your mind?" Joy asked.

"Amy. Well, the way he treated Amy the other night. That's one boy that really appreciates every good thing that comes his way."

"We are lucky," Joy said as she wrapped her arm around Woody's waist, watching their son drive off in his first car.

As Mason was pulling out of his driveway, Amy was sitting at her aunt's kitchen table in Sunset Beach. They had walked down to the Kindred Spirt Mailbox and spent almost two hours reading new notes and letters placed in the box.

"You're very quiet, Aunt Mary. Is something wrong?"

"No, not really. I was just thinking about that letter that man wrote to his wife. The one I showed you at the mailbox."

"You mean the one from the man who wrote it a few days after she died?"

"Yes, the very one. When all you see in the news these days about how marriages never last, it really stands out when you see some that not only last, but ones where they stay in love. If people weren't so darn selfish, more marriages would be like that. Why can't people learn that you only get when you're willing to give?"

"I think I learned that from listening to you all these years," Amy said.

"So, you really were listening, huh?"

"Yes, ma'am," Amy said.

"That's why I think you'll be like one of those people who stay in love when you find Mr. Right."

"I hope so."

"I shouldn't say this, especially at your age, but I'm kind of wondering if you haven't been lucky enough to find Mr. Right already?"

Amy looked at her aunt and blushed. "I sure hope so. He's the most unselfish person I've ever met."

"Normally, I'd discourage anybody your age from getting serious anytime soon," Mary said. "But, you and Mason are really different. You're both wise beyond your years."

Amy smiled. She loved the way her aunt always made her feel better.

"And speaking of Mason," Mary said. "Guess we better get to heading back to Carolina Beach so you'll have plenty of rest before the big date tomorrow. Besides, I need to get some donuts to go before they close."

Amy laughed and said, "I'll go get my things."

Chapter Fifty-Five

"Have you talked to Amy and told her what to expect when she gets back from your sister's?" Paul asked his wife.

"No, I haven't."

"Doesn't she have a date planned with Mason tomorrow? Maybe we should call and tell her they may want to change that date to tonight, since we have to leave early to get to that meeting with the CPA."

"You want to make their parting even worse by giving them another evening together?" Catherine asked. "She's young with a whole life ahead of her. If he's as serious as he says he is about her, then he'll be willing to wait until we can get back down for another visit, maybe over the holidays."

"I guess you're right, but she's going to be really upset. Maybe I should just delay my trip up just one day and let you have that meeting with the CPA first."

"Paul, I told you. This is more serious than you know. I need you at the meeting. If you want to come back down in a week or two with her to see that boy, that's fine, but this is an emergency for our company."

"Okay, but you'll have to be the one to tell her."

"And I plan on doing that tomorrow morning so she won't be up all night upset. We will be on the road before she can even think about it. I'll tell her you will bring her down for a visit one weekend as soon as things at the office calm down."

Paul said nothing. He picked up his coffee cup and walked out onto the back deck, watching the waves break. He was worried about his company and his daughter.

Amy needs Mason right now and here we are taking her away right after she was almost raped. Something doesn't seem right. And how in the world did the agency go from being the most economically sound ad agency in the Southeast to a company in a money crisis in a few weeks. That's something else that doesn't seem right.

It was a pleasant drive back to Carolina Beach. Amy was thankful for the visit with her aunt. She missed Mason, but knew he had to work. It was better to miss him while with her aunt, than sit in her room and relive what had happened to her there. The trip to Sunset Beach and the walk down to the Kindred Spirit Mailbox had been a good distraction from thinking about Drake's attack. Plus, looking forward to a long day with Mason would be an even better distraction. Amy began to think about the love letter she and her aunt had read at the mailbox, the one that revealed a man's lifelong love for his wife.

"Aunt Mary, I just made a decision."

"What's that, honey."

"When I get married, I want to have the ceremony at the Kindred Spirit Mailbox."

"I can't think of a better place to get married than a special mailbox by the sea."

"I like that, Aunt Mary. The mailbox by the sea."

Mason called Amy's house after he returned from a quick drive around the beach in the Mustang his parents had just given him. He was proud to have such classic car, but was mainly focused on how much he and Amy would enjoy going places together in it. Amy's mom, as usual, answered the phone.

"Hi, Mrs. Cole. Is Amy back from her aunt's yet."

"No, she isn't."

"Oh, okay, sorry to bother you. Please tell her I called and I'm looking forward to tomorrow."

Catherine said nothing and hung up the phone.

Amy said her mom was being nicer to her, Mason thought after she hung up on him. *I guess that doesn't mean being nicer to me. I'm not gonna let that bother me tonight because I get a whole day with Amy tomorrow.*

Chapter Fifty-Six

Amy woke up Friday morning in a very good mood despite the heavy atmosphere she sensed when she had returned home from her visit with Aunt Mary the evening before. She just assumed her parents had been involved in another disagreement. She even forgot about it when she spoke with Mason on the phone last night. As usual, her talks with him left her happy. It just made their plans to spend the day together all the more special.

The upbeat attitude began to take a drastic turn when Amy opened her closet door to decide what to wear for her all-day date with Mason. Almost all of her clothes were gone. She immediately headed downstairs and noticed suitcases piled by the door.

"Mom! What's going on?"

Catherine emerged from her office with a briefcase in her hand.

"There is an emergency back in Charlotte. We have to leave within the hour."

"What kind of emergency? Is the house on fire or something?"

"No, there is a problem at the ad agency. It is very serious."

Amy became more agitated.

"But, I have important plans with Mason today?"

"Important?" Catherine asked. Her old self was obviously back. "It certainly isn't as important as the business."

"Maybe not to you. But, my relationship with Mason is important to me. It's everything to me."

Amy went to the phone to call Mason and let him know what was going on. She picked up the receiver and there was no dial tone.

"I had the phones disconnected until we return here."

"Mom!"

Paul walked in the door and immediately heard the argument.

"What's going on?"

"Dad, I didn't know anything about us going back to Charlotte and I can't even call Mason and tell him our date is off. Mom had the phones cut off."

"Catherine, why did you do that?"

"With everything that's going on, it's the safe thing to do. Now, it's time to go. Amy, put on the clothes I left for you on your bed and get in the car," Catherine said.

Amy stormed up the steps. She stopped halfway up and asked, "Can we at least stop at Mason's long enough for me to tell him?"

"There isn't time," Catherine shot back.

While Amy was upstairs, Paul confronted Catherine. "What's wrong with you? Cutting the phones off, not even letting her do the courteous thing and tell Mason she can't make it. That's ridiculous."

"You won't think it's so ridiculous when you find out what is happening to the business. She can call from a pay phone if we stop to get gas, or she can call when we get to Charlotte and tell him what happened."

"Why can't she just use that expensive car phone you had put in?"

"Cause it needs to stay clear in case something gets worse in the business."

Paul cussed under his breath and stormed to the car. *Something bizarre is going on*, he thought.

Even though the Mustang was given to Mason in pristine condition and clean, Mason woke up early, washed his new car and waxed it. When he finished, he glanced at his watch and saw he was picking up Amy in an hour. He stepped inside to take a shower and get ready for the big day.

When he was dressed and ready, he went to the kitchen to tell his mom he was heading out. His dad had left for work just after Mason woke up.

"You look nice," Joy said. "You clean up really well."

Mason laughed and said, "See you sometime tonight."

"You two be careful and have fun. Love you."

"Thanks, Mom. Love you, too."

Mason had a bounce in his step as he approached and got in the Mustang. His mom watched him as he pulled out of the driveway. She thought, *Time sure does fly by.*

When Mason turned down the waterfront road to Amy's beach house, he noticed a car he had never seen in the driveway as he approached. A lady, nicely dressed, got out of her car as Mason pulled in the driveway. She reached in the trunk and pulled out a real estate for sale sign and put it in the front yard.

When Mason got out of the car, thinking the real estate lady must be making a mistake, he noticed there were no other cars in the driveway. He assumed one of them must have been placed in the one-car garage underneath the home on stilts. He started towards the steps.

"Can I help you with something?" the real estate lady said.

"No, ma'am, I'm just here to pick up Amy for a date."

"Amy Cole?"

"Yes, ma'am."

"I'm sorry, but she's not here. She and her parents left to go back to Charlotte about an hour ago. Her mom hired me to sell the house."

Mason was too shocked to say anything. He walked in a daze back to his car and drove away. About a block away, he thought the real estate lady had to be mistaken. He drove to Britt's Donuts, went inside and asked Bobby if he could use the phone."

"Sure, aren't you about to go on the big date with Amy?"

"I thought so," Mason said. There was a quiver in his voice and Bobby immediately knew something was wrong. Mason dialed the number to Amy's house. He got a recording.

"The number you have called is not in service at this time, please check the number and try again."

Mason tried again and got the same recording. He placed the phone back on the hook and walked out the back door of Britt's Donut Shop. Bobby went to the phone and called Mason's home.

Chapter Fifty-Seven

Woody James was on site with his crew remodeling a kitchen on Carolina Beach's northern extension when Joy came pulling quickly into that home's parking lot. She jumped out of the car and ran to her husband.

"Woody, something's wrong with Mason. Bobby called and said Mason came into the shop without Amy and left looking very upset. I've driven all over the place and can't find him. I went by Amy's house and there is nobody there, and there's a for sale sign in the yard."

Joy was talking so fast it took a moment for Woody to understand what she was saying. He had never seen her that upset.

"Did Bobby say if Mason said anything before he left?"

"Nope, he just tried to make two phone calls. Apparently, nobody answered and he just left. Bobby said Mason looked really upset."

"I'll go look for him. Maybe you ought to call Debbie at the police department. Maybe she could put the word out to look for him."

Woody told his crew he had to leave. He hopped into his truck and drove off. Amy decided to drive to the Carolina Beach Police Department.

As Mason's dad drove up and down roads on the beach, looking for the Mustang they had just given him, he kept thinking, w*here would he go*? Then, it hit him. He remembered Mason tell him about where he and Amy had gone on a recent date. Woody made a U-turn on the road and started heading south, to Fort Fisher.

Catherine insisted Amy ride with her. Since Paul seemed to be waffling on how important it was to get to Charlotte right now, she didn't want Amy talking him into making a stop at Mason's house or changing his mind and staying another day so Amy could go on that date.

Traveling westbound near Laurinburg on U.S. Highway 74, Catherine said she needed to get gas and took the next exit. When she pulled to the pumps at a convenience store, Amy jumped out of the car and ran to a pay phone beside the store. She knew Mason and his parents would let her call collect. She called Mason's home number three times, each time no answer. Joy had gone to the police department to talk to Sgt. Miller in person. Amy slowly walked back to the car, got into the back seat and started to cry.

Chapter Fifty-Eight

As soon as Woody passed the entrance to the port for the Southport-Fort Fisher Ferry, he saw Mason's Mustang ahead at the Rocks. He breathed a sigh of relief that he had found his son, but he was still concerned. Something bad had obviously happened.

Woody pulled beside the Mustang. He saw Mason sitting against the hood, looking out into the river. He looked distraught.

"Son, what's going on?"

Mason knew if he tried to speak at that very moment, he would fall apart. He stared out at the water, pulling himself together. Woody put his hand on his son's shoulder and waited. Finally, Mason said, "She's gone, Dad. Amy's gone."

Woody convinced Mason to let him drive them both home in the Mustang while he locked up his truck to leave in the parking lot at the Rocks. Mason told his dad all the details of what had happened that afternoon; no one being home when he went to pick Amy up, the real estate lady and the phone being disconnected when he tried to call Amy from the donut shop.

"That makes no sense at all," Woody said. "But, I can bet you Amy is not the type to not tell you she couldn't go on the date. Something must have come up fast."

"I thought the same thing, Dad, but how would you get a real estate agent signed up that fast?"

"That's a good point. I bet something was going on that Amy knew nothing about. I think it's best if we just go to the house and wait by the phone. I'm sure you will hear something before the day is over."

"Yes, sir," Mason said and hoped his dad was right.

In Charlotte, Paul was the first to arrive at the house. He noticed there seemed to be people around at the Crabtree's house next door. Since Catherine had told him they had taken Drake to their mountain home after they bonded him out of jail, Paul just assumed they were some people the Crabtrees had hired to do some work around their house.

Five minutes later, Catherine and Amy pulled into the driveway. Paul had come to get a few more things out of the truck of his car and noticed Amy had obviously been crying. He opened the passenger side door to let Amy out.

"Are you okay?"

"No, Dad, I'm not. I tried to call Mason when Mom stopped to get gas, but there was no answer. What if he's so mad at me that he isn't answering the phone?"

"I bet they're just not home. Why don't you come in and try again?"

Amy slowly made her way inside. She definitely wanted to talk to Mason, to tell him everything that had happened so fast that morning, but she was almost scared to try and call again. She was afraid there would still be no answer or that if he did talk to her, he would be so disappointed he would never feel the same about her again.

She went into her room and closed the door. She slowly picked up the phone and began to dial Mason's number back at Carolina Beach. On the third ring there was an answer. It was Mason's mom.

"Mrs. James, is Mason there?"

"Hi, Amy, I'm sorry he's not. I don't want to worry you or anything, but we are trying to find him. We haven't been able to locate him since he left to pick you up earlier. Are you okay?"

"No, ma'am, not really. Everything is awful right now. My mom made me leave for Charlotte this morning with her and I couldn't call Mason to tell him I wasn't coming because she had the phone disconnected."

"Is that where you are now? In Charlotte?"

"Yes, ma'am."

"I'm so sorry, Amy. I know how much you and Mason were looking forward to the day. I guess when he couldn't find you, he must have gone somewhere . . wait a minute, he's pulling into the driveway now. I'll get him to the phone."

Thank, God, Amy thought. *I hope he understands.*

Joy ran outside to find both Woody and Mason in the Mustang.

"Are you okay?" she asked her son.

"Kind of."

"Well, you better hurry inside. Amy is on the phone."

Chapter Fifty-Nine

Mason grabbed the phone on the kitchen table.

"Amy, are you okay? Where are you?

"I'm in Charlotte."

"Charlotte?"

"Please don't be mad at me, Mason. I woke up this morning and Mom made me get ready and get in the car. I didn't know anything about this."

"Are you not coming back at all? Why are you selling the house down here?"

"What? What are you talking about, selling the house?"

"When I went to pick you up, there was a real estate lady putting a for sale sign in the yard."

Amy was in shock.

"Mason, I don't know anything about that either. I have no idea what's going on. I just don't want you to be mad at me or give up on us because of this."

"I could never be mad at you. It just sounds like something weird is going on with your parents. I'm just glad to know you are okay."

"I'm not okay. I was looking forward to spending the day with you like I've never looked forward to anything in my life."

Mason could tell Amy was about to cry.

Through the tears, Amy said, "Mason, please do not let this come between us. Please. I love you and I will find a way to see you soon, even if I have to take a bus down there."

"I love you, too. More than anything. And you won't have to worry about finding a way down here. I can come see you there. That was another surprise I had for you today. Mom and Dad gave me a car."

"They gave you a car?"

"Yep, a Mustang."

The phone conversation was helping both of them calm down. Just knowing each other was all right, despite the crazy actions of Amy's mom, helped them relax. Within a few minutes, they had both settled into their usual telephone routine. They talked for a long time, focusing on what they would do when they saw each other again.

After they finally wrapped up their call, Amy ventured downstairs to find her mom, dad, and a man she had never seen before sitting in the living room. The man had a briefcase opened on the kitchen table and was handing some papers to her parents. Catherine looked up and saw Amy.

"This is our daughter, Amy. Amy, this is David Wallace, the new CPA for the agency."

"Mom, he isn't handing you papers about selling the house, is he?

"We're not selling this house, Amy. It's where you grew up. Why would you even think that?" her dad said.

"Not this house, the house at the beach," Amy said.

"We're not selling any house," Paul said.

"I just talked to Mason and he said he saw a lady putting a for sale sign in the yard when he came to pick me up. He said the lady was a real estate agent and she said Mom had signed a contract with her to sell the house."

Before Paul could respond, Catherine jumped in and said, "Amy, we have company right now, so it's not the right time to talk about our personal family business."

Paul looked agitated and looked at his wife.

"Catherine, did you sign a real estate contract on the beach house?"

"I said it's not the time to discuss it with company here."

"You're right. David, I'm going to have to ask you to leave. I will contact you tomorrow about whatever this is going on at the agency. I have to deal with some family matters right now."

"Paul, don't be silly," Catherine said. "We can discuss house matters anytime. David, you stay right there. He needs to hear what is going on with the business."

"David, like I said, I'm asking you to leave."

Catherine jumped up from the couch and stormed out of the room. David Wallace put the papers back into the brief case and left. Paul looked at Amy, still standing in the doorway with a look of shock on her face.

"What's going on, Dad?"

"I don't know, honey. But, I'm going to find out."

Paul found Catherine sitting in the library. She had a look of defiance on her face.

"What's this about selling the beach house without even talking to me about it? We just had it built."

"If you hadn't acted so immaturely and let David show you everything, then you would see we don't have any choice but to sell it. We will need that money to cover the cost of the embezzlement."

"What embezzlement?"

"The embezzlement going on at the agency. That accountant you thought so much of, and insisted we bring her on, has apparently been taking a lot of money."

"Gail? She's as honest as they come."

"You won't think so when you see what David has to show you."

"How come none of this ever surfaced until you went out and got another CPA on a whim?"

"There you go, questioning my business sense again," Catherine said. "I guess that CPA you had hired years ago was incompetent."

"If that's the case, explain to me why there has never been issues with accessing our funds, or having to sell a house, until just this month?"

"I'm through trying to talk to you when you're unwilling to listen. You'll just have to get David to explain it to you."

Catherine walked out of the room. Paul was angry and decided to go outside and cool off a little before he went to check on Amy. She had been through enough of her mother's impulsive actions for one day.

Walking onto the back patio, Paul heard a riding mower at work in the Crabtree yard next door. He glanced over to see who was mowing the grass while the Crabtree family was out of town. Driving the mower was Drake Crabtree.

Chapter Sixty

Paul Cole walked around to the front of the house and crossed the street. He rang the doorbell at the home of Doris and Jason Barkley, they were both attorneys in Charlotte. Jason answered the door.

"Hi, Paul. You guys back home from the beach already?"

"Yes, I guess so. I hate to bother you, but are you aware of what happened with my daughter involving Drake Crabtree?"

"I did hear about that, Paul. I heard another attorney talking with the Crabtrees' lawyer about it. I'm so sorry. I hope Amy is okay."

"She's had a rough time. Thanks for asking, but, I wanted to ask you something. Catherine said she had spoken with Doris and she said they had gone to their mountain place after bailing Drake out at the beach. But, I just saw Drake mowing their grass."

"Catherine must be mistaken about who she talked to, Paul. Doris has been up in Pennsylvania for almost two weeks helping her mom who had a mild stroke."

"I'm sorry to hear that. Again, sorry to bother you, I was just trying to make sense of why Drake is here when Catherine said he was in the mountains."

"I don't think they've been to the mountain place in a while. I've seen Drake outside every evening I get home from the office since he was bailed out."

It was all Paul could do to conceal his anger from his neighbor across the street. He thanked him and walked back home. Inside, he tracked down Catherine, who was now at the kitchen table, looking at some papers.

"I thought you said Drake Crabtree wouldn't be here. I just saw him mowing the grass!"

"Then, I guess they must have decided to come back," Catherine said.

"You said Doris Barkley said they had taken him to the mountains because they were trying to avoid embarrassment over his arrest."

"That's what she told me."

"And where was she when she told you that?"

"What's this third-degree for? She was at home. She told me she saw them leaving."

"What's going on with you, Catherine! You're lying! I just talked to Jason Barkley and his wife has been in Pennsylvania with her mother for two weeks because she had a stroke. What is going on? What else are you lying about?"

"If you are going to lower yourself to start calling me a liar, then this conversation is over."

"If it wasn't for Amy, this marriage would be over."

"Be careful, Paul Cole. I have to keep reminding you that you were nothing until I came along. I'm the reason the company became successful."

"Oh, really? So, none of my ad designs or campaigns meant anything? What would your precious sales team have to sell if we weren't producing advertising that worked and made the clients happy?"

"Obviously, it means little since your selection of an employee has almost thrown the company into bankruptcy."

"I don't believe that anymore than I believe the story you told about Drake being taken to the mountains. And, I want to know, again, where did you find this David Wallace guy?"

"He is the best CPA in the area. I had to give him 25 percent of the company to bring him on board."

"What?!?! You sell the beach house and give away a quarter of the company and never even ask me?"

"That's right, because you are incapable of thinking clearly. That's why you believed Amy's story over Drake's. The truth is somewhere in the middle. If you cared about your daughter, you would know Drake is capable of giving her a lifestyle she is accustomed to and that donut boy at the beach is not."

"Catherine, are you now telling me, after lying to Amy and me about apologizing, that this contract you signed at the beach is about getting Amy away from Mason so she'll get with a guy that almost raped her?"

"Selling that house is killing two birds with one stone. It will fix the money disaster at the agency and give Amy a chance to see what's really best for her."

Paul and Catherine heard a loud gasp from the doorway. They didn't know Amy had heard the commotion downstairs after talking with Mason on the phone and had been listening to most of their conversation.

"Mom, you knew Drake was here and you were lying when you said you were sorry about trying to keep Mason and me apart?"

"One of these days you'll learn I always look out for your best interests."

Amy, still a wreck of emotions, slid to the floor and began to cry so hard she could hardly breath.

"Look what you've done now, Catherine!"

Paul had raised his voice on rare occasions in the past, but no one had ever heard him with the anger and distraught sound coming from him now.

"What . . . what . . . what is wrong . . . with you . . ."

The words coming from Paul were becoming broken. His eyes seemed to glaze over and he fell silent, staring ahead. He grabbed his chest and had the look of enormous pain on his face. Then, he collapsed to the floor.

"Dad!" Amy cried out.

"I guess I better go call an ambulance," Catherine said, sounding more annoyed than concerned.

Chapter Sixty-One

For almost two hours Catherine and Amy sat in the waiting room for the ER at Carolinas Medical Center. Amy was nervous and worried, but she noticed her mom looked completely disengaged from what was happening. Finally, a doctor showed up to talk with them.

"Mrs. Cole?"

"Yes."

"I'm Doctor Bass. I'm a cardiologist here at the hospital. Is this your daughter?"

"Yes, her name is Amy."

"We have your husband stabilized. We completed an EKG and some other tests. There appears to be 80 percent blockage in an artery around his heart and I believe we need to perform a catherization right away."

"Is Dad going to be okay?"

"Fortunately, we believe we caught the blockage early, but it's a little early to tell what the long-term effects will be."

"What can they be?" Amy asked, her mom just standing there.

"In some cases, he may need additional surgery, but we won't know the extent of any actual damage until the catherization."

Amy began to cry. The doctor placed a hand on Amy's shoulder.

"I'm so sorry, but I can tell you we are going to do everything we can to give your dad the best care."

"When can I see Dad?"

"That will have to wait until after the catherization, as long as your mother gives us the go-ahead to proceed."

Catherine seemed to be paying no attention to what the doctor was saying, looking as if her mind was on anything other than what was happening to her husband.

"Mom, did you hear the doctor?" Amy asked.

"What did you say?" Catherine finally said to the doctor.

"We need your permission if we are going to proceed with the heart catherization."

"Go ahead."

"I'll get the nurse to bring you a release to sign. Do you have any other questions, Mrs. Cole?" the doctor added.

"No," Catherine said and returned to her seat. Amy sat beside her.

A few moments after the doctor left, Amy stood up.

"Where are you going?" Catherine asked.

"I'm going to find a phone and call Mason."

"You sit back down. He is not family."

"He is to me, Mom."

"You best listen to me and sit down. Besides, I called Dr. Crabtree when I went to the rest room a while ago and asked him to come assess your father's situation. He should be here any minute."

Amy's tears dried up instantly.

"What? You called the father of the guy who tried to rape me to look in on Dad?"

"Yes, I did. He is a respected doctor."

"Mom! He's an orthopedic surgeon. He's not a heart doctor!"

Amy stormed out of the room and down the hall. She was looking for a phone.

Joy knocked on Mason's bedroom door. She slowly opened it to find Mason reading in his bed.

"Honey, Amy's on the phone."

Mason jumped up and ran to the phone in the kitchen.

"Hello."

"I'm sorry to be calling so late."

"You know you can never call me too late, or too much. Is everything okay?"

"No," Amy said, trying to hold herself back from breaking down again. "Dad collapsed at the house. We're at the hospital."

"Oh, no. I'm so sorry. Is he going to be okay?"

"The doctor says it's too early to tell. They are going to do a heart catherization. He has an artery that is 80 percent blocked. I wish you were here."

"I do, too."

"There is something else I have to tell you. I heard Dad and Mom arguing about several things. There is something going on at their company and Dad found out Mom wasn't telling the truth about Drake being in the mountains. Dad saw him today mowing grass in his yard."

"Why would she lie about that?"

"Because she had one goal. To get us all back to Charlotte. Dad didn't even know she had placed the house down there on the market."

"That doesn't sound good."

"It's not. I think she got Dad so upset and that's why he collapsed."

"I'm sorry to hear that. I like your dad. He was always nice to me when I saw him."

"He likes you, too."

"Do you know how long he will be in the hospital?"

"I'm not sure, but I'm sure he won't get out really soon."

"Have you been able to talk to him?"

"Not yet. The doctor just left from talking to us a few minutes ago. I passed his nurse in the hall on the way to find the phones and she said someone will come get us when he is in recovery."

"I hope he's okay."

"There's one more thing."

"What's that?"

"Mom called Drake's dad, who is a doctor, to come evaluate Dad."

"What? That makes no sense. Why would she do that?"

"I don't know. It's like she's gone crazy. The guy's not even a heart doctor. He probably only agreed to come see Dad thinking it might help get his son off the hook."

"You don't think he'll bring Drake with him to the hospital, do you?" Mason was beginning to sound irritated over Amy's mom.

"If he does, I'm calling the police. Drake would be in violation of the no-contact order the judge issued against him. He is not supposed to be anywhere near me or even talk to me."

"Will you let me know if he does bother you?"

"Yes, I'll never be afraid to hold anything back from you again."

"I'm glad to hear that."

"I love you, Mason."

"I love you, too. Always."

"You made me feel better by talking to me. You always do. I guess I better get back to the waiting room."

"Okay. Please let me know how things go."

"I will. Love you. Bye."

"Love you, too, Amy."

Mason hung up and filled his parents in on what had happened with Amy's dad. He also told them about her mother's weird actions.

"I shouldn't say this, but that woman sounds like a piece of work. Something isn't right about all that," Woody said.

"Mom? Dad?"

"Yes," they both said, almost in unison.

"I want to drive the Mustang to Charlotte tomorrow."

Chapter Sixty-Two

At 4:30 in the morning, the doctor came into the cardiac care unit waiting room. Catherine had left an hour before and told Amy to call her if there was any news. Amy was very sleepy, but still awake.

"Hi, Amy, is your mother here?"

"No, sir. She went home and told me to call her if you had any news."

"Oh, okay. Well, your dad is in recovery. The catherization went well. We think we can treat the blockage, but we will need to keep him here for the treatment and for observation for about a week and then reassess the situation."

"I understand," Amy said, fighting back tears.

"He's still very groggy in recovery. If you would like to go home, I'd be glad to arrange someone to take you there and we will call you the moment he is able to see you."

"I'd rather wait here."

"I understand. I'll contact housekeeping and have them prepare a place for you to sleep here."

"Thank you," Amy said.

"Would you like me to call your mother and give her the details?"

"I'll call her, but thank you."

Amy ventured to the public phones in the hallway outside of the waiting room. She called home and the phone rang for over five minutes. Her mom never answered. Amy went back inside the waiting room and within minutes a hospital housekeeper walked in and took her to a private room so she could get some sleep.

About five hours after Amy had drifted off to sleep, she was awakened by her mother.

"They told me you were in here," Catherine said.

"How's Dad?"

"I don't know. I just got here."

Hearing her mother had waited hours to come check on her husband bothered Amy, but she was too tired and concerned about her father to even think about responding. She got up and ventured with her mother to her dad's hospital room.

Amy fought back tears when she entered the room and saw her dad hooked up to wires and tubes. He looked like a different man and he looked very weak. He was fighting to keep his eyes open. He looked around the room and saw Amy. He gave a little smile. She went to his bedside and took his hand.

"Need anything, Dad?"

He was barely able to say, "I'm not sure."

"Just rest, Dad. I'll be here if you need anything. I'll let Mom talk to you now."

Catherine just stood at the foot of the bed and didn't move.

"Mom? Aren't you going to talk to Dad?"

"He knows how I feel about all of this," Catherine said with coldness in her voice. "He never has eaten right or taken care of himself."

"Mom! This isn't the time to say anything like that."

Before Catherine could respond, they were interrupted by a knock at the door to the hospital room. They all looked to see who it was. It was Mason.

"Mason!" Amy said and ran to him, giving him a hug. "You didn't have to come all the way here."

"Yes, I did," Mason said, and then he whispered to Amy, "For both of us."

Amy hugged Mason even tighter. She stepped to Mason's side with her arm around him.

"Look, Dad, Mason came to see you."

Her dad, Paul, managed another smile and weakly said, "Thanks, Mason. That means a lot."

Catherine walked up to Mason.

"How did you get in here? Only family should be allowed."

"I'm sorry, ma'am. They didn't say anything at the desk about it being family only."

"Mom, he came all the way here because he cares about me and about Dad. He's like family to me."

"Oh, please," Catherine shot back. "Mason you need to leave now."

"Yes, ma'am. I didn't mean to cause any trouble."

"Well, you have," Catherine said. "Besides, I have Doctor Crabtree coming here any minute to check on my husband."

For the first time since he had met Amy's mother, Mason challenged her.

"Why would you ask Drake's dad to come here?"

"Because he is our neighbor and he's a well-respected physician."

Amy became visibly upset and was about to speak when they all jumped. A coffee cup hit a wall in the room and coffee splattered everywhere. They realized it had been thrown by Amy's dad.

Chapter Sixty-Three

Within seconds of Paul throwing the coffee cup, a nurse entered the room and saw the mess.

"Is everything okay?" the nurse asked.

Paul motioned for the nurse to come to his bed.

Struggling, he said, "I need a pen and something to write on."

"Yes, sir. I'll grab a pad for you," the nurse said as she handed him a pen from her pocket.

Mason, uncomfortable with being the one that seemed to cause the disturbance had turned to leave. Paul made a sound and pointed to Mason who was already leaving the room.

"Mason, Dad is wanting you," Amy said.

Mason sheepishly came back into the room and approached Paul.

"Don't go anywhere, son," Amy's dad said. "You are my guest."

It took a lot for Paul to get the words out. He was glad when the nurse came in with a legal pad. He leaned up and started writing.

"Catherine, I don't want Dr. Crabtree or anyone in his family in this room. I also don't want you being disrespectful to Mason. If you can't be nice, then go home."

He held the legal pad in the direction of Catherine. She took it, read Paul's words, cast the pad at the foot of the hospital bed, and she stormed out of the room.

Amy's dad motioned for her to hand the legal pad back to him. He wrote her a note.

"I'm feeling better. You and Mason go get something to eat. I'll be fine until you two get back. Where did they put my wallet?"

After reading the note, Amy looked around the room and found a small plastic bin that had her dad's name on it. She looked inside and saw it was filled with his personal belongings that were with him when he first arrived at the hospital. She took the bin to him. Paul fished out his wallet, opened it and handed Amy a hundred-dollar bill.

Mason saw it and said, "That's okay, sir. I have money to get us something to eat."

Paul took a breath and was able to say, weakly, "Please take it. It means a lot that you came to be with Amy today. If nothing else, use it for gas money for coming all the way to Charlotte."

Amy took the money and said, "I'll see to it he takes the money. Thanks, Dad."

"That's not fair," Mason said. "She has power over me."

For the first time since he arrived at the hospital, Paul laughed a little. Amy walked to her dad's bedside and squeezed his arm lightly.

"We'll be back in a little while," Amy said.

"Take your time and enjoy Mason's visit," Paul said, still weak in his voice. "I'll be fine. I feel like I could sleep a little more."

As soon as Mason and Amy left the room, Paul pushed the call button beside his bed. When a nurse arrived, he had already scribbled a note on the pad. It read, "If a Doctor Crabtree arrives to come see me, I don't want to see him. Don't let him in my room."

"I understand, Mr. Cole."

Paul nodded.

Chapter Sixty-Four

Amy and Mason walked to the hospital parking lot. Mason had taken Amy's hand on the elevator and had not let go. He could tell she was still worried about her dad. Plus, he was feeling very guilty about being the source of a confrontation in her dad's hospital room.

"I'm sorry about causing so much trouble. I shouldn't have come," Mason said.

Amy stopped walking and stepped in front of Mason, facing him.

"You have nothing to be sorry for. I'm the one who needs to apologize. My mom had no business acting like that."

"I wish I knew what I've done to make her so mad at me."

"You did nothing. When it comes to me, she thinks I need to be with somebody rich or some millionaire's son, whether I love them or not."

Mason didn't respond. They started walking through the parking lot again. In just a few more spaces they arrived at Mason's car.

"Here we are," Mason said, pointing to his car.

"Mason! That's your car? It's beautiful!"

"Thanks," Mason said as he opened the passenger side door for Amy.

After Mason sat down in the driver's seat and shut the door, Amy said, "I'm really serious about the car. I love classic Mustangs. Where'd you find it?"

"Dad found it and he and Mom gave it to me."

"What a great gift," Amy said.

"It really is, but, ah, I'm going to find some way to pay them back. My dad's business does pretty good, but he pays the guys who work for him more than any of the other contractors at the beach, so he isn't rich or anything. Oh, I don't know anything about Charlotte. Where would you like to eat?"

"There's a great pizza place a few blocks from here," Amy said. "You in the mood for pizza?"

Mason smiled and said, "It's hard to go wrong with pizza."

"I know, and they're not really expensive."

At the edge of the parking lot, Amy pointed in the direction Mason had to turn to head to the pizza restaurant she recommended. He was very quiet on the drive and said nothing after they parked. He jumped out of the car and opened the car door for Amy. A waitress welcomed them the moment they walked in the door and led them to a booth. She took their drink orders and walked towards the kitchen.

Amy and Mason sat down across from each other in the booth. Amy had barely sat down when she jumped up and moved to the same side of the booth where Mason was and sat right beside him, scooting up to be close. She took his hand.

"Mason, what's wrong?"

"Um, I'm still worried about the thing with your mom."

"Please don't worry about it. She will never change how I feel about you, ever. I love you."

"I love you, too," Mason said, still looking sad. "And, I guess I also . . . never mind."

"Mason, please tell me. I want you to be able to tell me anything."

After hesitating a moment, Mason said, "I just worry your mom is right. What if I can't give you the life you're used to and you deserve."

Amy held Mason's hand tighter.

"We talked about this on the beach, remember? The only thing that's changed since then is that I love you even more. Listen, when you told me you wanted to find a way to pay your dad back for the car, you have no idea how that made me feel. I don't just love you, I respect you. You would never hear that from any guys in my school or the people my mom wants me to hang around with. All they care about is what they are going to get next. They're spoiled brats. All of them."

Mason didn't say anything. He was hoping Amy completely believed what she was saying and always would. But, he still worried. He was glad when the waitress came to take their order.

Chapter Sixty-Five

As they ate their pizza, Amy asked about how things were at the beach and what Mason's plans were when school went back after the summer.

"I was able to get in this program that lets me get out of school at Noon and head to the *Star-News* for my intern work."

"That sounds perfect for you," Amy said and kissed him on the cheek.

"I hope I can live up to their standards."

"Mason, I love you, but you worry too much. I know you'll be great."

Mason loved the way Amy supported him. He wished she would go to school in Wilmington so she would be there to always encourage him.

After they ate, they ventured back to the hospital. Mason drove up to the front drop-off area of the hospital.

"What are you doing?" Amy asked.

"I thought I better let you out here in case your mom is still in the room."

"I looked in the parking lot as we pulled in. Her car is gone. Please come up with me."

Mason pulled into the parking lot and walked with Amy back to her dad's hospital room. When they entered, a nurse was taking her dad's blood pressure. He was sitting up a little more in the bed and looked like he had just a little more energy.

When he saw Amy and Mason walk in, he said, "Hey, guys, how was lunch?"

"It was good, Dad. We had pizza."

"Pizza sure sounds good," Paul said. He turned to the nurse. "How about ordering me some pepperoni pizza?"

"You've got to be kidding me, right?" the nurse said. "You're going to be on a special diet for a while."

"With these room rates, I should be able to order whatever I want," Paul said and smiled.

The nurse turned to Amy.

"Your dad is not being very cooperative. Maybe you can convince him to behave."

Paul had a mischievous grin on his face as the nurse left the room.

"Dad, you better do what they say. I don't want you back in here."

"Me, either," Paul said. "Speaking of doing what people say, come over here."

When Amy walked over to her dad's hospital bed, he handed her some keys.

"What's this, Dad?"

"They're my car keys. The doctor was in here while you were out and said they don't want me driving for a few months, just in case. They want to make sure I'm stable before I get behind the wheel, so you use my car until I get the all-clear. Then, we'll go pick you out a car."

"Thanks, Dad. I didn't expect all this."

"That's not all. I called the real estate agent at the beach and put an end to the sale of the beach house. There is still two weeks left before school starts, so I want you to go back there until it's closer to school time."

"But, Dad, I don't want to leave you here and go to the beach."

"Listen, I'll be fine. I think it would be best if you and Mason headed on down there. I have some things I need to do here to get your mom to calm down and find out what's going on at the agency."

"Dad, you sure that's a good idea until you're better?"

"I won't get better until I take care of all of this. It's the stress that put me in here in the first place. I don't want you thinking bad about your mom. She just needs to stop being so intense."

Amy and Mason stayed with her dad about an hour when he told them they should get on the road so they would not be getting to Carolina Beach too late.

"If you want to just ride with Mason and get the car when you get back, that's fine."

"Thanks, Dad."

"Now you guys get out of here so I won't worry about you driving after dark."

Mason and Amy went back to his car. After they were inside, Amy said, "I need to go by the house and get some clothes and things."

Going to Amy's house was something Mason wasn't looking forward to. The last thing he wanted was another encounter with her mother.

Chapter Sixty-Six

Amy and Mason both breathed a sigh of relief when they pulled into the driveway at Amy's house. The only car there was her dad's. Her mom was obviously out somewhere.

"I'll be right back," Amy said. "Hopefully, I can get everything together before Mom gets back."

"That would be great," Mason said and smiled.

Amy leaned over and gave Mason a quick kiss before she left the car. Before she could even take a few steps, someone appeared at the edge of her driveway. It was Drake Crabtree.

"How's your dad, Amy?"

Amy was shocked and didn't respond. Then she jumped when she heard a noise. It was Mason's car door slamming shut.

"Isn't there a court order for you to stay away from Amy?" Mason said. He sounded angry.

"This isn't any of your business and this isn't your neighborhood, so shut up, donut boy."

Mason started towards Drake with fire in his eyes. He was stopped by Amy.

"Mason, it's not worth it. Just come inside with me and we'll call the police.

Mason glared at Drake as they walked by him. Drake responded by giving him the finger. Mason didn't take the bait and followed Amy into the house.

After they had shut the front door, Amy asked, "Do you think we really ought to call the police?"

"Yes," Mason said. "He seems like the type who thinks rules don't apply to him."

"You're right."

Amy picked up a phone and called the police. While she was explaining the situation to the dispatcher, Mason stood in the hallway of the huge house. It was obvious there was nothing in there that wasn't the best money could buy. Amy finished the call and motioned for Mason to follow her. She led him into the library.

"Since you like writing, I thought you might want to wait in here while I pack a bag. As you can see, my dad really likes books and I think he has read them all."

"It's incredible," Mason said.

He heard Amy heading upstairs as he looked around. With the exception of cutouts for the door and windows, every bit of wall space was filled with mahogany bookcases. It was beautiful. There was also a row of waist high bookcases in the center of the room and two very-comfortable-looking chairs with reading lamps and small tables beside them both. Mason searched the book spines and noticed a wide range of genres. There was lots of well-known fiction and tons of non-fiction books dealing with everything from business to U.S. history.

It only seemed like a few minutes before Amy was back in the library with a backpack filled and ready to go.

As they made their way to the door, Mason stopped and asked, "What did the police say?"

"Oh, I'm sorry. I should have told you. I was just anxious to get my things so we could be on the road before Mom got here. Anyway, they said they're on their way to Drake's house to have a talk with him.

"That's good to hear."

Back in the driveway, Mason opened the trunk and placed Amy's backpack inside before he opened the passenger side door for her. In a minute, they were on their way to Carolina Beach.

Twenty minutes after Amy and Mason left, Catherine returned home. She had arranged a meeting with the CPA she had handpicked to carry out her schemes. About an hour later, the phone rang and Catherine answered it. On the other end of the line was her neighbor, Dr. Crabtree.

Chapter Sixty-Seven

Barely ten minutes out of Charlotte, Mason noticed Amy had fallen asleep. He turned the radio off. He was glad she was able to finally relax. He knew everything she had been through, involving her dad, Drake and her mom, had to be exhausting to deal with.

After passing through the series of towns just east of Charlotte along U.S. Highway 74, Mason finally reached the stretch of road where it was smooth sailing. While Amy slept, Mason's mind drifted back to everything that had happened while he was in Charlotte. He replayed the cold and angry reception he got from Amy's mom at the hospital and how much he wanted to punch Drake Crabtree in the face, not for his arrogance towards him, but for what he had done to Amy.

Eventually, Mason thought about Amy's house. It was a place you would see on the cover of a real estate magazine or on TV. To think Amy had grown up in all that luxury brought him back to worrying whether he could ever begin to keep her happy. He thought he could take on some freelance writing work after he was established at a newspaper, but when would he have time to spend with her? Maybe he should rethink his career plans. He began going through a list of jobs in his head where he could make more money than working for a newspaper somewhere. His pondering was interrupted when he felt Amy reach over and place her hand on his knee.

"I'm sorry," Amy said. "I guess I was more tired than I thought. I didn't mean to fall asleep on you."

"I'm glad you were able to relax some. I think you really needed it."

"I love you, Mason. You are the most unselfish person I've ever known."

"I love you, too, but I'm really too selfish when it comes to you. I want you all to myself."

"That's the kind of selfish I can live with," Amy said.

As usual, they settled into a long, comfortable conversation during the drive. They went through a McDonald's drive-thru in Lumberton and then continued east on Highway 74. Because they enjoyed each other's company so much, it seemed like no time before they were crossing the bridge over the Cape Fear River in Wilmington and making the turn down Highway 421 headed to the beach.

Back in Charlotte, Catherine had completed her talk on the phone with Dr. Crabtree quite a while ago. She was angry and staring at the clock waiting for the evening visitation hours to begin at the hospital. Five minutes before those hours began, she was in her car and headed to have a talk with her husband.

Catherine stormed into her husband's hospital room. She found him sitting up, looking a bit more energetic and watching television.

"Are you aware Amy is out with that Mason boy somewhere?"

"Yes, I am."

"Do you know where they are?"

"What time is it?"

"It's just after 7:00 in the evening. What does that have to do with anything?"

"That means they should be getting to Carolina Beach in about an hour."

"What?!?! You let her go with him to Carolina Beach? You mean you told her she could stay at his house tonight?"

"No," Paul said, still remaining calm. "I told her she could stay at our house at the beach until the day before school starts."

Catherine was still angry, but she hesitated a moment.

"Well, there is something you don't know. I had the power and phone cut off there to save money."

"And there's something you don't know, Catherine," Paul said as he turned off the TV with the remote and faced his wife. "You don't know that I know about your scheme to sell the house. I put a stop to that, and the phone and power are back on."

"You did what?"

"You heard me, Catherine. Now sit down."

She had never heard her husband use the tones he had used with her recently. She knew for all her plans to come to fruition she would have to carefully pick her battles for a while. So, she bit her tongue and sat down.

"I don't know what you think you're doing, Catherine, but it has to stop now. You are going to make Amy never want to come home again once she is out on her own. You are too controlling. You have been like that almost the entire time I've known you, but it's gotten worse. I'm tired of you running everybody's lives and I'm tired of you thinking you can run the company and even whether we sell a house or not without discussing it with me. That all ends today."

"Or, what?" Catherine asked, coldly.

"Or, I file for divorce and exercise my right as the president of the company to oust you. Plus, if that happens, where do you think Amy will want to live?"

Catherine jumped from her seat and headed towards the door of the hospital room. She stopped and turned around.

"You have no idea what I'm going through, Paul. I got a call from Dr. Crabtree today. Do you know Mason almost attacked Drake in our driveway this afternoon?"

"Almost attacked? He sure has more restraint than I would have if I had seen him in our driveway. That means Drake was in violation of the no contact order."

"You just don't get it. That boy Amy is with has ruined our relationship with our neighbors."

"No, you just don't get it, Catherine. That boy's name is Mason and it's that worthless boy next door that has ruined the relationship between our families. I still don't understand why you don't seem to care that he almost raped our daughter."

"That's one side of the story."

"And it's the side I believe because Amy has never given me a reason not to believe her anytime in her life."

"I don't like the tone you have with me. I'm going home."

Catherine took one step and heard Paul call her name firmly.

"Catherine. I meant everything I said."

Chapter Sixty-Eight

Amy and Mason were driving over the bridge at Snow's Cut into Carolina Beach.

"I guess I should stop off at the house and let them know I'm back," Mason said. "Is that okay with you?"

"Of course," Amy said. "I'd love to see your mom and dad."

Joy and Woody heard Mason's car pull into the driveway. They were at the door to welcome him home when he opened it. They were both surprised, but happy, to see Amy with him.

"Hi Amy!" Joy said, giving her and Mason a hug. "It's great to see you again. How is your dad?"

"He seemed better when we left the hospital. In fact, he was the one who insisted I come back to the beach with Mason."

"Well, we are certainly glad to have you. I can get the spare bedroom ready for you in no time."

"That's a very nice offer, but I'm actually staying at our beach house while I'm down. I'm going back the day before school starts."

"Oh, I thought the house had been sold," Woody said.

"It kinda was, but Dad put a stop to the sale. Mom had put it on the market without talking to him first."

Joy and Woody gave each other a look.

"Do you guys need some dinner?" Joy asked.

"Thanks, Mom, but we stopped and ate in Lumberton on the way here," Mason said. "Since Amy's had a few rough days, I thought I'd run by the donut shop on the way to her place and pick up a dozen and get her to her place so she can rest."

"Sounds like a plan to me," Joy said. "And Amy, please let us know if there is anything you need while you're here."

"Thanks, I really appreciate that. Having your son as my driver was more than enough."

Joy gave Amy a hug.

Woody and Joy stood on the front porch and waved as Mason and Amy were leaving.

"I sure do like her," Woody said.

"I do, too," Joy said. "I think they're perfect for each other. Reminds me of you and me when we first met. If only her mother would stop being so crazy."

"I was just thinking the same thing," Woody said.

Mason and Amy walked into Britt's Donuts and Bobby broke into a huge smile. He was standing at the counter talking with a few customers, but he walked around to greet them.

"You're back!" Bobby said. "And you brought this lovely lady with you."

Amy smiled and Mason said, "Yes, sir. We just got back a little while ago. I wanted to drop by and let you know I can work again, plus, we wanted to pick up a dozen to take with us."

"I'm glad," Bobby said. "It's not the same around here without you. I don't know how I'll manage when you become a famous newspaper reporter and end up at the *New York Times* or some other place far away."

"You don't have to ever worry about me ending up in a place like New York," Mason said. "I don't think I could handle living in a big city."

The minute Mason said that, he cringed. He remembered Amy was going to go to Juilliard and that would put her in New York City. He looked at Amy, but she had not changed her expression. She was still smiling.

"I bet you guys are tired from all that driving," Bobby said. "Let me get you those donuts."

When he returned, he had two bags filled with two dozen donuts.

"Oh, I just needed a dozen," Mason said.

"The other bag is not for you, it's for your folks. You don't think they'd turn them down do you?"

Mason and Amy laughed. Mason reached in his pocket for money to pay for the donuts.

Bobby held up his hand and said, "Nope, your money is no good here."

"I can't keep taking free donuts from you," Mason said.

"They're not free. They're a bribe to try and convince you to come into work tomorrow at noon. I know you just got back in town, but I could sure use you."

"You don't have to bribe me for that. I'll be here. But, thanks a lot for the donuts."

"Yes, thanks for the donuts," Amy added.

"It's the least I could do for one of my favorite couples."

Being referred to as a couple wasn't lost on Amy or Mason. They both liked the sound of that.

Chapter Sixty-Nine

When Amy and Mason walked into her beach house, the phone was ringing. Amy had no doubt who was calling. Her mother.

"I'll call her back later," Amy said. "I can't deal with that right now."

Mason put his arm around her. He wished there was something he could do to end all the stress Amy was under.

"I've got an idea," Mason said, smiling.

"Yeah? What's that?"

"Let's eat some donuts."

Amy laughed out loud. "I'm all for that. They can heal anything. But, there's just one problem."

"What's that?" Mason asked.

"Why are you filling me up on all these donuts? Are you trying to fatten me up so nobody else will want me?"

"I haven't thought about that, but it's not a bad idea."

Amy laughed again and playfully punched Mason.

Mason sat down beside Amy at the table in the breakfast nook.

"I need to tell you something serious," he said.

"Is everything okay?"

"Yes, but I think I need to tell you I shouldn't have said what I did about New York to Bobby. I know you're going to Julliard and I'll come see you there whenever I can."

"It's funny you bring that up. I've been thinking about that a lot lately. I don't think I want to go to Julliard. I don't want to be that far away from you."

"Now, you're really making me feel guilty. I don't want to keep you from your dream. I could look into some journalism schools up there."

Amy scooted her chair right beside Mason.

"I'll let you in on something I haven't told you. Julliard is not my dream. It's my mother's dream. I'd be happy playing music anywhere. I've even thought about being a music teacher."

Mason took her hand. "You are so talented. People should hear you play all over the world. I don't want to keep you from that."

"Mason, please listen to me. I know almost everybody thinks we're too young to be serious. Too late. I am serious. What is being some famous musician if I'm not happy? I have never been as happy in my life as I am with you. That's more important to me than anything."

"I love you more than anything. I don't want to be the reason you don't go through with going to Julliard. What if you didn't go and you ended up with regret?"

"The only regret I'd have is losing you," Amy said. "Just the thought of that tears my heart out."

"Not being with you would tear me apart, too. But, we have all senior year to make those decisions. Plus, we're both tired from all you've been going through. Not a good time to be making big decisions. In fact, I should go and let you get some rest."

"You mean you got me all sugared up on donuts and now you're going to leave me here all by myself? No way, let's watch a movie."

Mason was glad for the suggestion. He wasn't really ready to leave her anyway.

Amy picked a DVD to watch from a few she brought with her in her bag. They only watched about ten minutes and turned it off. They spent the next two hours kissing and talking. As always, it all came naturally.

Chapter Seventy

The sound of the phone ringing woke Amy up from the first peaceful sleep she had been able to have in almost two weeks. She glanced at the clock. It was 7:30 in the morning. She hoped it might be Mason calling as he was getting ready for work. No such luck.

"Where have you been?" her mom belted out before she could even get out a "hello."

"I was sleeping, Mom. I've been here."

"Is that boy there?"

"You mean, Mason? No, he brought me home last night, we watched some of a movie and then he went home."

"You should not have boys in that house."

"You mean like you had Drake Crabtree in here?"

"Don't get smart with me. I'll be leaving here in an hour to come get you."

"Dad said I could stay until it's time for school to start."

"You heard me. I'll be on my way."

Catherine hung up. Amy found herself getting upset again. She had been though enough of that feeling recently and the thought of being taken away from time with Mason again, not to mention the thought of being subjected to the long drive back to Charlotte with her mother, was almost more than she could bear. She needed to find a way to keep that from happening. She had an idea. She called Aunt Mary.

"That woman could make the Pope cuss," Mary said after Amy filled her in on everything that had transpired the past few days. "I tell you what. Just sit tight. I'm coming to get you. It's hard to pick you up if you're not home."

"She'll go ballistic," Amy said.

"I'll deal with that. I'll call her before she leaves and tell her what I'm going to do."

"She'll just come to Sunset Beach and get me."

"Not if we are down at the Kindred Spirit Mailbox. You know she won't walk a mile on the beach."

"I just hate to be away from Mason. He brought me back and I want to spend as much time with him as possible before school starts."

"You guys are really in love, aren't you?"

"Yes, ma'am, we are."

"Well, I can't think of anybody else as good as Mason is for you. We'll work out a way for you to see him and avoid being drug back to Charlotte, too. But, I better get off of here so I can get ready and head your way."

"Thanks, Aunt Mary. You're the best."

"It's the least I can do for my favorite niece."

"I'm your only niece."

"What does that have to do with anything?"

Amy laughed and said, "Love you."

"Love you, too."

Catherine was aggravated hearing the phone ring while she was trying to get a few things done before she left to go get Amy. She answered it anyway.

"What do you do, get up every morning and ask yourself what you can do to make somebody's day a living Hell?" It was Mary.

"I don't have time to talk to you right now or listen to your silliness. I am getting ready to leave."

"I know why you're getting ready to leave," Mary said. "That's why I'm calling. Don't you come down here because Amy won't be home, she'll be with me."

"My daughter is none of your business. If you don't stop interfering, I'll put a stop to you ever seeing her."

"Go ahead and try. You know I don't give a damn about that business you want to control, but I did invest a lot to help you and Paul when you were growing it. If you try and keep me from seeing my niece, I'll just get with Paul and we'll vote you out."

There was silence on the other end. Mary never talked much about the agency because she was never motivated by money. But, she did have a lot of power because of her investment when they were expanding the company.

"If anything happens to her, I'm holding you personally responsible," Catherine said, changing her tune a bit.

"What's going to happen to her, other than having a little peace away from you?"

Catherine slammed down the phone and Mary went to get Amy.

Chapter Seventy-One

Mary picked Amy up and they both went to the donut shop so Amy could see Mason and fill him in on what was going on.

"It sure is nice for you to help Amy so much," Mason said to Mary.

"She's very important to me and I want both of you to be happy. I'm going to take her with me today just in case her mom is crazy enough to come down here, but I'm going to bring her back tomorrow so you guys can spend some time together. It's too close to school starting back up for you guys not to spend as much time as you can together."

"I can't tell you how much I appreciate that," Mason said.

"Aunt Mary's the best," Amy said.

"You two stop before you make me do something I haven't done in 40 years, blush."

They all laughed.

"Are you going back to the mailbox?" Mason asked.

"Of course. I'll let you know what we find when I call tonight. Are you still getting off at 8:00?"

"Yes."

Amy kissed Mason and told him she couldn't wait to talk to him tonight.

"You two are so sweet, we better get out of here before a swarm of bees fly in here," Mary said, before she waved goodbye to Bobby who was at the cooker preparing another batch of donuts. He came running out and handed Mary a bag of a dozen donuts.

"Bobby, you're the reason I'm not a size five anymore, but I love ya anyhow."

Amy and Mary said their goodbyes to Mason and Bobby and left.

Bobby turned to Mason and said, "You're a lucky guy, you know that? Amy and her aunt are really good people."

"They sure are," Mason said, while on the inside he still wondered if he was good enough for Amy.

After work, Mason went home and hopped into the shower. He had not been out long when his mom said Amy was on the phone. He ran to the kitchen to take the call.

"I'm glad you called. I've been missing you all day."

"I've been missing you more," Amy said, playfully.

"That's not possible. Did you and your aunt go to the mailbox?"

"We sure did. There was a huge stack of new letters in it. A bunch of them were love letters and they made me think about you. When I took a break from reading them, I started daydreaming about you and me getting married there. That doesn't scare you, me talking about getting married, does it?"

"Not at all. It makes me feel great."

"Good, cause the thought makes me feel great, too. I really do love you, Mason."

"I love you more," Mason said.

"Now, that's not possible," Amy said.

As usual, they settled into an easy conversation for the next two hours. Neither of them wanted to be the first to hang up.

Chapter Seventy-Two

The days before school was scheduled to resume had passed by too quickly. Mary had brought Amy back to Carolina Beach so she could stay at the beach house and spend as much time with Mason as possible. Luckily, Amy's mom never showed up. She called everyday to check on Amy, but never even mentioned Mason.

The day before Amy had to leave to return to Charlotte, she was dreading her mom coming to get her. Mary came to the rescue for that, too. She told Catherine she was going to take Amy home so she could visit with Paul to see how he was recuperating.

The next afternoon, Mason had taken off work to see Amy off. It was hard on both of them to say goodbye. Finally, Amy got into Mary's car and he watched them drive off. He felt a tear streaming down his cheek.

In Charlotte, Amy's dad was doing well and was about to be released from the hospital. He called Amy from his hospital room just as she was about to leave the beach house with Aunt Mary and head to Mason's house to say bye. Amy was glad to hear her dad's voice on the other end of the phone.

"Hi Dad!"

"Hello back at you. I think they're sick of me at this hospital, so they're sending me home."

"That's great news," Amy said, and Paul heard Amy tell Mary about his release to go home.

"You're coming home today, right?"

"Yes, Aunt Mary is here and we are just about to leave."

"Okay, I won't keep you from getting on the road, so I'll let you go. You and Mary be careful on the drive back."

"We will. Ah, Dad?"

"I bet you're about to ask about your mom."

"Yes, sir. Is she still really mad at me?"

"She's at the office right now, but I had a long talk with her earlier. She seems to be backing down. I think I got through to her this time."

"Thanks, Dad. I was just worried about what to expect when I get home."

"I'll tell you what you can expect. You can expect to be driving around in your car. I decided to keep my car and just told James at the office to go pick up your new car."

"Wow, Dad! I didn't expect that!"

"Well, you deserve it. And besides, if Mason gets a car, you should get one, too. That way you have a way to get to see each other when you get breaks from school."

"Dad, I don't know what to say, except thank you and I love you."

"I love you, too. Now you and Mary get on the road. I don't want you guys driving much after dark."

"We're leaving in just a minute."

Amy filled her aunt in on the conversation with her dad as they walked to the car.

"I'm glad to hear your mother is calming down. Maybe your dad and I finally got through to her."

"I sure hope so," Amy said.

Chapter Seventy-Three

Catherine was at the ad agency and sitting across from her was David Wallace, her hand-picked CPA. She had summoned him into her office and shut the door.

"We've had this conversation before, but it's imperative I know where your loyalties are." Catherine said.

"You know my loyalty is to you. It has to be. I'm in this as much as you are," David said.

"That's exactly right. Did you file the new incorporation papers?"

"First thing this morning."

"I need to see a copy."

"I knew you would want to see them, so here they are," David said as he handed her a file folder.

Immediately, Catherine turned to the last page. That's where the signatures were, along with witnesses. She was impressed. Paul's signature was beyond passable. It looked exactly like his signature. She had never heard of the notary that signed the paper.

"Good job. Did you do these yourself?"

"No, I know a guy who is really good at it."

"You mean you have involved somebody else? I made it clear this has to be off the radar."

"He only saw a copy of the signature. Trust me. I handled a big mess he was in with the IRS over his taxes for six years. He owes me. He would never talk."

"I'll take your word for it. What about the notary that witnessed the signature?"

"She lives in Monroe. The guy who did the signature also did a great job of pretending to be Paul."

"Didn't she have to see an I.D.?"

"Yes, I had that covered."

"How did you pull that off?"

"Let's just say there are some things it's best you not actually know for your own protection."

Catherine sighed. She felt comfortable that David Wallace was on her side. After all, he stood to gain a lot financially with the plan. David stood to leave, thinking she was through with the inquiry.

"Wait a minute," Catherine said. "Sit down. I need to talk to you about something else."

David sat down.

"I have a problem with my daughter. She has become smitten with a boy who is no good for her. I've tried several things to break them up, but she's being stubborn, just like her father. I need a way to break them up for good."

"I'll get right on it, but I need his name."

"Just come up with an idea and run it by me, but don't do anything yet. The boy lives in Carolina Beach and she's on her way back home today. I'm hoping being back in school will bring all that to an end, but I want something in place if that doesn't happen. She'll be turning 18 next year and I want to stop that relationship before I lose any control over her. I have already enrolled her in the Julliard School of Music and I don't want anything to threaten that."

"I'll work on it."

It was a very calculated move for Catherine to involve David Wallace in her plan to break Amy and Mason up. She had just witnessed her sister, her husband and Amy challenging her. She was not stupid. She knew she had to back off, but that didn't mean she couldn't get someone else to do her dirty work. That way, she could look like a "changed woman" to her family, while still getting what she wanted done. She knew Wallace was just the guy to pull it off without her appearing to be involved.

Chapter Seventy-Four

Amy was very relieved to get the news from her dad that her mom had appeared to calm down. However, that didn't keep her from still being happy to find her mom's car was not in the driveway when she and Mary arrived at her house.

When they walked in the door, they heard her dad shout from the library.

"Amy? Is that you?"

"It's me," Amy said when she walked into the room. She was a little taken aback to see her dad was in a wheelchair. "I thought they said you were okay?"

"Oh, this thing? My doctor must want some more money from the insurance company because he wants me to take it easy for a week."

"That makes sense," Amy said. "I don't want you to push your recovery too fast."

Mary walked into the library. She was moving a little slower than Amy.

"Hi Mary!" Paul said. "I sure do appreciate you bringing Amy home."

"I don't mind at all. You know I love every minute I get to spend with my niece. But, I also wanted to check on you. Is there anything I can do?"

"Not at all, but thanks. You've done plenty making that long drive. You're not planning on heading back tonight are you?"

"I'm getting too old to drive that much. I'll wait until tomorrow if you don't mind me taking over the guest room for tonight."

"Not at all. You know you're welcome to stay as long as you'd like."

They both heard the front door open and the alarm system beep as it did anytime a door was opened when the system was not engaged. In less that a minute, Catherine walked into the library. Mary and Paul both saw Amy tense up.

"What's going on in here?" Catherine said, shocking everybody with her tone. It almost sounded playful.

"Amy and Mary just got here. Mary's going to stay tonight before heading back," Paul said.

"That's good. I'm glad you made it back safely."

Mary and Amy glanced at each other and raised their eyebrows.

Aunt Mary's right. They must have gotten Mom to change her mind about Mason, Amy thought.

"I'm going to go call Mason," Amy said. "I told him I'd call him when I got home."

"I'm sure he'll be glad to hear you made it home," Catherine said.

This time, it was Paul and Mary who looked at each other with raised eyebrows.

"Hello."

"You answered on the first ring," Amy said. "You must be sitting by the phone."

"I am," Mason said. "I've been waiting for you to call. You back home?"

"Yep. We just made it back a few minutes ago."

"How's your dad?"

"He looks a lot better, but I was shocked when I walked in because he's in a wheelchair. He says it's just doctor's orders for him to take it easy this week."

"Sounds like good advice."

"I know," Amy said. "What have you been up to?"

"I've been sitting by this phone waiting for you to call. I've had my meals brought to me and I've restrained all body functions."

Amy laughed. "Wow, you missed your calling. I see a stand-up comedy career in your future."

"Like that's going to happen," Mason said.

"I already miss you," Amy said.

"I missed you the minute you got into your aunt's car."

"I love it when you say things like that. It just makes me love you even more. Oh, I've got some news."

"What's that."

"Actually, two things. First, Mom has been really nice since I've been back. Mary thinks she and dad finally got through to her. She even sounded nice when I told her I was going to call you."

"Wow, I hope she stays like that."

"Me, too, but that's not all. Dad says he's buying me a car so you and I can get to see each other during breaks."

"That's great to hear. I can't wait for us to be together again."

"Me either," Amy said. "I was thinking I'd come back down on Thanksgiving."

"I was thinking Labor Day weekend."

Amy laughed. Labor Day was the weekend right after school let back in.

"That would be nice, but I do need to study some. Plus, don't you start your internship at the *Star-News* tomorrow."

"Yeah, but it doesn't hurt to dream does it?"

"Not at all. I'll be there in spirit every day."

Amy then filled Mason in on the conversation she and Mary had on the way home. Before they knew it, they had been through another two-hour conversation. When they hung up, Amy went into the kitchen for something to drink. Her mom and aunt were sitting at the table talking.

"How's Mason?" Catherine asked, shocking Amy and Mary again with her sudden interest in Mason.

"He's great," Amy said.

"You have something on the counter there," Catherine said.

Amy walked to the kitchen counter and found a large envelope. It was from the Julliard School in New York. She opened it.

> We are proud to be able to advise you
> of your acceptance into the
> Julliard School music orchestra
> string program. Your first-year tuition
> has been paid and we look forward to
> welcoming you next year.

Her mom had been acting too nice to get into a conversation about her change of interest in attending Juilliard. She didn't want to throw a wrench in the evening's atmosphere.

"Thanks, Mom," she said. "I'm going to grab some tea and get ready for bed."

Chapter Seventy-Five

After school resumed, Mason and Amy fell into the routine of high school for their senior year. Mason would head to the newspaper office every afternoon after school and would work there until about 8:30 in the evening.

Since it was a morning paper, the deadline for the portions he worked on came early in the evening. The last pages prepared for the press were the front page and the front page of the local news section. That's so they could put any last-minute breaking news in with the most up-to-date information.

Every night around 9:00, he and Amy spoke on the phone. It was a time when cell phones were becoming more and more popular and their cost had come down. Their parents had bought them both one, but since the unlimited plans had not yet become routine, they both tried to keep their minutes down by talking on their home phones as much as they could.

Two months into the school year, during their nightly call, Amy didn't seem herself.

"Is everything okay?" Mason asked.

"I hope it will be."

"What's wrong?"

"I guess I should look at the good news part, but it has some bad news with it."

"Oh, no, what's the bad news?"

"Dad wants me to go with the family to see his brother in Tennessee for Thanksgiving. He says since it's my senior year, he wants this to be a special family Thanksgiving. If I go, that would mean I couldn't come down for Thanksgiving weekend like we talked about."

"I guess I see what he's saying. He will miss you when you head off to college, so he wants to spend as much time with his daughter as he can before that happens. It is probably on his mind even more after being in the hospital."

"There you go again, putting everything into perspective and making sense. That's one of the many reasons I love you."

"I love you, too, Amy. But, I sure was looking forward to seeing you on Thanksgiving. I could use the good news now."

"I talked about it with Dad and we made a deal. If I go with him on the Thanksgiving trip, he says I can come down there for the whole Christmas break."

"The whole break? Two weeks?"

"Yep."

"That makes losing you for Thanksgiving a lot more bearable."

"I thought so, too," Amy said.

They were quiet for a moment, both daydreaming about what a great Christmas they could have spending two weeks together. Mason broke the silence.

"I got my first official story assignment at the paper today."

"That's great. What's it about?"

"The editor wanted to give me a long time to work on this one. Speaking of Christmas, it's a story about the World's Largest Living Christmas Tree."

"Where is that?"

"It used to be in Wilmington and everybody around here loved it. During Christmas season, they'd have programs at the tree with school groups singing and appearances by Santa."

"How come I never heard of it."

"Sadly, the tree they used, which was actually an old southern live oak tree, began to die and became a fire hazard. So, they couldn't take the risk of the lights on the tree anymore. They never found another tree around town to replace it."

"That is sad," Amy said. "I'm sure people who used to see it will have a lot of memories come back when they read your story."

"That's the goal. I have several other more current features to do, mainly about some local people, but that is supposed to be the big one that will have a color photo of the tree taken the last year the tree was used."

"I can't wait to see that story."

"I can't wait for you to see it because that will mean you'll be here."

"I love you, Mason."

"I love you, too."

Chapter Seventy-Six

When Amy's best friend Hope dropped her off at home after school the next afternoon there was a car she did not recognize in the driveway. At first, she thought it may the car her dad had talked about getting her. On second glance, she knew her dad would not buy her a car that looked like some kind of unmarked cop car.

As soon as Amy walked into the front door, her dad called her to come back into the library. When she walked into the room, Paul introduced her to the two men wearing suits. They were a detective from the New Hanover County Sheriff's Department, Henry Eakins, and an investigator from the district attorney's office in Wilmington. His name was Bob Cooper. They were there to ask questions about Drake Crabtree and his actions on the night he tried to rape Amy.

"I have to ask you some questions and they may be uncomfortable to hear," Investigator Cooper said. Paul and Amy were not impressed with his demeanor.

"Okay," Amy said as she sat down in a chair beside her dad.

"I need you to go through all the details of exactly what happened the night you claim Mr. Crabtree attempted to rape you." He seemed to emphasize the words "claim" and "attempted."

"Wait a minute," Paul said. "She isn't claiming anything. What she said is not a claim, it's a fact."

"I need you to not interfere with the questioning," the man curtly said.

"And I need you to treat my daughter with respect, or I'll end this interview now and we can wait for my attorney to get here."

"It's okay, Dad," Amy said. "I have nothing to hide. I'll just tell him the truth."

"Okay," Paul said, looking back at the investigator. "But keep the tone up with my daughter and this is over. Remember, she's the victim here."

The D.A. investigator seemed unmoved by either Amy's willingness to continue the interview or her dad's warning. He turned to Paul.

"Actually, we are investigating the possibility Mr. Crabtree was the victim of an assault by you."

"You've got to be kidding me!" Amy shouted. "My dad kept him from raping me!"

Paul stood up and walked towards the two men.

"If you have no compassion for the victim of an attempted rape, then it's time for you to leave. I'll contact my attorney. If you have no intention of prosecuting the criminal in this case, then leave. We'll pursue this case in civil court."

The detective from the New Hanover County Sheriff's Department had not uttered a word during the interchange. He waited until he and the D.A. investigator were in the driveway getting ready to leave.

"What the hell are you doing?" Detective Henry Eakins said.

"What are you talking about?" Cooper said, being just as arrogant with Eakins as he was with Amy and Paul.

"Your attitude with a young girl who appears to have almost been raped is not acceptable," Eakins said. "Most sex assault victims are scared to come forward because of people like you."

"I'm doing my job."

"Your job is to prosecute criminals."

"Her father may be guilty of a crime. You read the report. The suspect had injuries obviously done by her father."

"Oh, for God's sake. It's a miracle they didn't have to take him out on a stretcher. Can you imagine walking into a girl's room and finding a punk trying to rape your daughter? Do you think he hit the punk for no reason?"

"I need to talk with the suspect. That's his house next door, right?"

"Yes, that's his house. But, I'm doing the talking this time. If you interfere, I'm going to file a grievance against you when we get back. I've been with the department for 22 years. You've been at the D.A.'s office for what, eight months? Who are they going to listen to? Get off that law school arrogance they drill into you and let me do some real police work."

Cooper looked angry, but he didn't respond. He knew a grievance from a long-time detective could affect his career. He let Eakins do the questioning of Drake Crabtree. However, they had to wait a while since Drake's father insisted they wait for his attorney to arrive.

Chapter Seventy-Seven

With the attorney for the Crabtrees sitting next to Drake at the kitchen table, Detective Eakins began asking Drake questions. His attorney interrupted almost every other question, telling Drake he didn't have to answer it. When Drake did respond, he was cocky and arrogant.

"I didn't rape anybody," Drake said at one point. "The little bitch wanted me. What are you going to do about her stupid ass dad trying to beat me up?"

Eakins could tell the Crabtrees' attorney was trying to kick Drake under the table.

"Let's watch your language here," Eakins said.

"My client has good reason to be angry," the attorney said. "He was assaulted by a crazy man."

"Since this isn't getting anywhere because your client is not cooperating, we will just head over to the school," Eakins said.

"What's the purpose of going to his school?" the attorney said.

"There is a no contact order against your client to maintain distance from the victim," Eakins said, emphasizing "victim."

"I strongly object to that," the attorney shot back.

"You know as well as I do it's our job to make sure no contact orders are enforced. So, object all you want. We're going to the school."

Eakins and Cooper stood up and left the house. Drake acted as if he didn't care what they did. The next morning, his attitude changed when he arrived at school. A school resource officer met him at the door and escorted him to the office. Inside the office was the principal and his tennis coach.

"What's all this about?" Drake said.

"A no contact order was brought to the school yesterday afternoon. You are required to stay at least 50 feet away from Amy Cole," the principal said.

"Yeah, so?" Drake said.

The school resource officer jumped in. "How are you going to do that when you are in a few of her classes and have to share the same halls?"

"The whole thing is bullshit," Drake said.

"An order from the court isn't bull and you need to watch your language," the principal said.

"You have any idea how much money my father gives to this stupid school!"

"That doesn't affect this court order."

"Stick that order up your ass," Drake said.

The principal calmly turned to the officer.

"Escort Mr. Crabtree off this campus, please. I will call Dr. Crabtree and advise him his son is being suspended for disrespect of school personnel and for violating our profanity rules."

The school resource officer stood, grabbed Drake by the arm and started pulling him out of the office. Drake let out a string of profanity until the officer lead him outside the front door of the school and then locked the door.

Drake stormed to the parking lot where he angrily paced back and forth around his car. He looked like a caged animal. He was not accustomed to not getting his way. Finally, he stopped. He looked towards the school and saw the school resource officer standing in the door watching him. Drake gave him the finger and got into his car.

"This is all that stupid ass donut boy's fault," Drake said to himself. He started his car and pulled out of the school parking lot. Instead of turning right to head to his house, he turned left in the direction of Highway 74. He was going to Carolina Beach.

Chapter Seventy-Eight

"You've got to kidding me. Are they all idiots?" Mason was angry when Amy told him on the phone what had happened with the investigators.

"Dad said they hope they're just playing a detective game with me to make sure I'm just not some girl making up a story to get back at some guy."

"It's not like this is some he-said, she-said thing," Mason said. "Your dad witnessed what was happening."

"That's the other thing. The detective was telling dad he should be charged with assaulting Drake."

"What? A dad can't intervene when his own daughter is getting attacked?"

"That's exactly what we were all saying."

It was quiet for a moment before Mason had another question.

"Did your mom agree with you and your dad this time?"

"I have no idea," Amy said, sounding sad this time. "She's nowhere around."

Catherine wasn't around because she was still at the ad agency in another meeting with her hand-picked CPA, David Wallace.

"Have you found a psychiatrist willing to say Paul is not of sound mind to handle the affairs of the company?"

"Yes, but I'm afraid it will cost us dearly."

"Give me the bottom line. How much?"

"About half a mil."

Catherine didn't even flinch. "Considering the payoff for both of us, that's fine with me. But, let's not jump on this until after we deal with the situation with Amy."

"You're the boss," Wallace said before he got up and left the office.

Back in Catherine's neighborhood, Dr. Crabtree was on the phone with the principal who was advising him of Drake's suspension and his dismissal. He was livid at first, but then realized his own reputation was just as much at stake as his son's.

"Thank you for letting me know. I'll deal with it. Maybe we can meet soon to discuss Drake's future there."

"That will be fine, Dr. Crabtree," the principal said, hiding the fact she hoped Drake would be a former student from now on.

Realizing Drake was dismissed at least an hour before and was not yet home, his dad called his cell phone. He was surprised Drake answered when he saw who was calling.

"Where are you, Son?"

"I'm on my way to Carolina Beach, Dad. That stupid donut boy got me suspended from school."

"No, he didn't. You got yourself suspended. You're not helping your case."

"I don't give a shit about my case, I'm gonna kick his ass."

"Drake, I've always been on your side, but this has crossed the line. Turn around right now and come back home. That's not a request."

"I'll come home tonight after I take care of this."

"No, you'll come home now. You have to get gas and something to eat eventually, so as soon as I hang up, I'm calling the bank to put a hold on your credit and debit cards."

"Damn, Dad! Whose side are you on?"

"I know you don't realize this right now, but I'm actually on your side. Now, do what I told you."

As soon as he hung up with Drake, Dr. Crabtree made a phone call, but it wasn't to the bank, yet. Instead, he called his secretary.

"Beth?"

"Yes, Doctor."

"I need you to research some private boarding schools for Drake to attend."

"Yes, sir."

"And Beth, look for one out of state, maybe on the west coast."

After calling the bank to put a hold on Drake's cards, he knew his son was stubborn enough to ignore his order to come home. He wasn't sure how much cash Drake had on him which would make the credit and debit card holds a moot point. He knew Drake was now in violation of the court order that not only prohibited him from being in contact or close to Amy or Mason, but also prohibited him from being anywhere except home, school or any work. He called his attorney to tell him what was going on and ask for advice. Within minutes after the call, the Crabtree family attorney made a call to Carolina Beach.

"Is this Mrs. James?"

"Yes, it is. Who is calling?"

"Mrs. James, this is David Dobson in Charlotte. I represent the Crabtree family in Charlotte and I'm calling to . . ."

Joy interrupted, "I don't think you should be calling here, especially since my husband is not home right now and since this case is in the hands of the D.A.'s office."

"I normally would agree, Mrs. James, but I'm calling to let you know we believe Drake is on his way to Carolina Beach. His father thinks he may be wanting to take out the fact he was suspended from school today on your son."

"What? Have you called the police?"

"We want to do that as a last resort. His father has placed a hold on his bank cards, so we don't think he could make it all the way there without getting gas. But, I do have an obligation to let you know what is going on."

"Well, thank you for that," Joy said. "But, since you won't call the police, I will."

Joy hung up and called Sgt. Debbie Miller at the Carolina Beach Police Department, the one who originally had Drake arrested.

Chapter Seventy-Nine

Sgt. Debbie Miller called the New Hanover County Sheriff's Department to advise them of the call she received from Joy about Drake. They all agreed they would have a better case against Drake violating his court order if they let him cross the bridge into the Carolina Beach town limits.

Sgt. Miller was in an unmarked car on the beach side of the bridge when she got the call a sheriff's deputy, also in an unmarked car, had spotted Drake's car near Monkey Junction, just south of the Wilmington city limits. He was covertly following Drake now.

The moment Drake crossed the bridge at Snow's Cut, his car was surrounded by four law enforcement vehicles. Sgt. Miller was the one to approach his car.

"Let me see your license and registration please," she said to Drake, trying her best to remain calm.

"I want to talk to my lawyer," Drake said with arrogance in his voice.

"You haven't been charged with anything, yet," Sgt. Miller said.

"I refuse to show you anything."

"Okay, now you are being charged. Get out of the car and keep you hands where I can see them."

Drake seethed with anger, but he got out of the car. He said, "This is illegal. I know my rights."

"I know your rights, too, and we know who you are. In addition to other charges that are coming, you are being arrested for being in violation of a court order. Turn around and put your hands behind your back."

Drake started to turn around, but quickly took a swing at Sgt. Miller. Before his fist could make contact with her face, he felt a baton slam him in his side, bringing him to his knees. Then, he was tased. The deputy standing behind Drake was ready.

"Thanks," Sgt. Miller said to the deputy. "I was ready, too." She showed him she had her taser by her side.

Drake was taken to the New Hanover County Courthouse and placed in jail. A magistrate had placed his bond at $45,000 because of all the charges, including assault on an officer, in addition to the court order violation. Drake was allowed to call his father.

"Dad, come get me. These bastards locked me up."

"Not this time, Son. You've crossed the line and it's my fault. I gave you too much, including too much freedom, before you could handle it. You have done this not only to yourself, but you've put your whole family's reputation at risk. You'll just have to stay there at least a few days and we'll see if your attitude changes."

Drake slammed the phone on the floor. The deputy working in jail took him to a cell.

The next morning, Drake Crabtree's latest arrest had made the local news in Charlotte, both in the paper and on WBTV News. His father and mother saw the story. They both determined their son had ruined their reputation in Charlotte.

That afternoon, Dr. Crabtree called a hospital administrator in San Diego, California.

"Hi, Bill. Is the offer you made to me last year still in effect? My wife and I have decided we need a change of scenery."

Within three weeks, Dr. Crabtree had bailed Drake out with a promise he would be back for the trial. The next thing neighbors, including Amy's family, saw was a moving truck and a for sale sign in front of the Crabtree house.

That night, during their regular phone call, Amy told Mason the news.

"Finally, that jerk is out of our hair," Mason said.

"I know," Amy said. "Now Mom can't push me getting involved with him anymore. That means you and I don't have to worry about her being like that anymore. We'll have a great life now."

"Sounds perfect," Mason said. "I love you."

"I love you more," Amy said.

"I already told you. Not possible."

They both laughed. They didn't know Catherine's scheming was not over by a long shot. She was just waiting for the right situation and the right time. They both would come soon after Christmas.

Chapter Eighty

Any more problems coming from Drake Crabtree had gone to nonexistent. He and his family had moved quickly to San Diego in hopes of escaping the bad publicity his actions had created. That meant Mason and Amy could relax into the routines of school, Mason's internship at the *Star-News*, Amy's music practice and their favorite, the nightly phone calls. They were both busy enough for time to pass quickly. They were counting down the days until Christmas break when they could be together again.

As Thanksgiving vacation approached, Catherine announced at the last minute that she was not going on the trip to visit with Paul's brother. Amy and her dad made the trip alone. Neither of them voiced it, but they both had in the back of their minds this would likely be the last dad/daughter time they would spend together before she would venture out into the world on her own.

They had been listening to the radio until Paul cut it off while they were driving through the Blue Ridge Mountains, almost at the Tennessee border.

"How's that fella of yours?"

"He's doing great, Dad. The newspaper keeps giving him bigger assignments and he loves it."

"That's good to hear. It really makes a difference when somebody enjoys their work."

"Do you enjoy your work, Dad?"

Paul was quiet for a moment, hesitant to be brutally honest with his daughter.

"I used to," he finally said. "I miss the days I was just involved in the creative side of the business. It was fun to make up campaigns for businesses, especially when the ads were funny. Some business people don't understand the power of humor. It gives a business a great image."

"Don't you still do that?" Amy asked, upset with herself she never really knew much about her father's work.

"These days I mostly just supervise the creative staff. It's all administrative stuff. I'm tempted sometimes to add an idea or two, but I don't want the young creative ones on the staff to think I'm micromanaging them. Don't get me wrong, I'm very appreciative of the success of the agency, but it isn't the same."

Paul glanced over and noticed Amy looked sad.

"I'm sorry. I shouldn't have gotten so serious with you. This is supposed to be a fun trip," Paul said.

"Don't be sorry. I like it that you feel comfortable talking to me about things."

"It's hard for me to believe you'll be 18 next month," Paul said, changing the subject.

"Yeah, me, too."

"I just realized I have no idea when Mason's birthday is."

"It's January the 20th."

"Will he be 18 then?"

"Yes. sir."

"You mean Mason's dating an older woman?"

"Yep. I'm a real cradle robber."

They both laughed. Deep down inside, they both knew the trip would not have had the same atmosphere if Catherine had been along.

The visit with Paul's brother went very well. Amy enjoyed hearing her dad and uncle try to top each other with crazy stories of their boyhood. She shared all of them with Mason during their nightly calls.

Chapter Eighty-One

Amy was excitedly packing. It was the morning she was leaving to spend Christmas break with Mason's family. Plus, Joy had invited Aunt Mary to spend Christmas Eve and Christmas Day with them. That made her love Mason's family even more.

After putting her bags in her car, she came back in to tell her mom and dad goodbye. Her mom was waiting just inside the door.

"I think I should go with you."

"Why, Mom?"

"For your safety."

Before Amy could respond, she heard her dad's voice coming down the hall.

"Catherine, Amy is 18 now, so we have to stop treating her like she's 12. She'll be striking out on her own in June."

"I know how old she is, but she will still be dependent on us financially when she goes to college and that means we have some say so. But, go ahead."

"Thanks, Mom. Love you. Love you, too, Dad. I'll call you when I get down there."

With that, Amy left, headed for Carolina Beach and Mason. She was so excited she could hardly stand it.

At Mason's house, his dad looked at his mom and smiled before he spoke.

"Son, you okay? I don't think I've ever seen you like this. I'm afraid you're going to wear a trench in the hardwood floor walking back and forth like that."

"Sorry, Dad, I just hope Amy makes it okay. I've really missed her."

"We know you have," Joy said. "It will be good to have her."

Just before 3:30 in the afternoon, Amy pulled into the driveway at Mason's. He ran outside to greet her. Amy jumped out of the car and they both grabbed each other. They hugged and kissed as Joy and Woody watched through the sliding glass door in their dining room.

"They've got it bad," Woody said.

"Yes, they do," Joy agreed. "They remind me of a couple I know the year they met."

"Really?" Woody asked as he pulled Joy close. "They remind me of a couple I know now."

Amy walked in. Joy and Woody both gave her a hug, making her feel as welcome as she had ever felt anywhere. It was the beginning of a Christmas they would all never forget, for more reasons they ever realized at that moment.

Chapter Eighty-Two

"Here, talk some sense into her," Amy said, handing the phone to Mason. Amy's aunt Mary was on the phone.

"Hi, Mrs. Carter."

"Oh, you call me Mary. You're like family, Mason."

"Amy says you are thinking about not coming tonight for Christmas Eve."

"I just don't want to be a party pooper, crashing your family's Christmas time. I've never wanted to be the third wheel."

"Mrs. Carter, I mean, Mary, didn't you just say we were all like family?"

Mary laughed, "Oh, you're good. Even using my own words against me. No wonder Amy says you're so smart."

"I don't know about that, but I do know we will all be very disappointed if you don't come celebrate Christmas with us, especially Amy and me."

"That's right, Aunt Mary!" Amy shouted from the background.

"Well, I guess since all of you teamed up on me like that, I better come."

"That's right," Mason said. "Please come."

"You and your family are such good people, Mason. And I'm so glad you and Amy met."

"I am, too. I really love her a lot."

"I happen to know first-hand she feels the same way about you. Guess I better get off this thing if I'm going to make it there on time. Tell Amy I'll see her in a little while."

"I certainly will. Drive carefully."

Mary arrived right on time. She had really dressed up for the evening and had a small bag with her so she could spend the night. Joy had turned their in-home office into a bedroom for Mason for the night so that Amy could sleep in his room and Mary could have the guest bedroom.

On Christmas Eve, they all exchanged gifts and called out for three large pizzas to be delivered. Everyone had a great time.

The next morning, Amy, Mason, Mary and Woody woke up to the smell of bacon cooking. It had become an annual tradition to have pancakes and bacon for Christmas morning. After breakfast, they all gathered around the TV for another family tradition, watching "It's a Wonderful Life."

"That movie gets me every time," Mary said, wiping a few tears out of her eyes.

"Me, too," Joy and Woody said, almost in unison.

"Wow, that's an incredible movie," Amy said.

"Is that the first time you've seen it?" Mason asked.

"Yeah. My mom never wanted to watch it. She said she'd seen it before and it was a bunch of, what did she call it? Oh, yeah, sentimental hogwash. I didn't know cause I hadn't seen it, but it's great."

"It puts life in perspective to me," Woody said. "It's not all about the money."

That was something Amy had never heard her mom say.

At dinner, Joy had prepared a traditional feast of turkey, ham, gravy, rice, salad and a huge, three-layer chocolate cake.

"Thanks, Honey, for contributing to my sin of gluttony," Woody said after dinner.

They all laughed.

"It's not gluttony if you don't eat for two days after this," Mary said. "I don't think I can eat for a week. Joy, you sure are a great cook."

"Thanks, Mary. We are so glad you could be with us."

"I don't want to wear out my welcome, so I guess I better head back to Sunset Beach."

"But, Aunt Mary, it's after dark. Why don't you and I just stay at the beach house?"

"I guess I can do that," Mary said. "I just don't want to burden these folks anymore."

"You're always welcome here, anytime," Woody said.

"You folks are so nice. I feel like I have a second, very special family here."

"You do," Mason said.

Mason drove Amy and Mary to the beach house. Mary excused herself to get ready for bed while Mason and Amy sat in the library and talked.

Eventually, Mason got up to go home. He gave Amy and long goodnight kiss and told her he would see her tomorrow morning.

"I wish you didn't have to go," Amy said in Mason's ear as she hugged him tight.

"Me, too," Mason said. "One day, I hope I never have to leave you."

The next morning, Mary headed back home. Not long after, Mason came to get Amy and they went out to eat breakfast together.

Chapter Eighty-Three

The week went by too fast in Mason's and Amy's minds. They wanted this Christmas break to last a long time before they had to head back to the routine of school and other obligations, like music practice and writing stories for the paper.

On New Year's Eve, Amy and Mason decided they would bring in the new year at Amy's family beach house and watch the broadcast from Times Square on TV.

After the ball dropped, Mason and Amy welcomed a new year with a long kiss. Several more followed. At almost 1:30 in the morning, Mason said, "I guess I better go."

"Please don't. Not yet," Amy said. She pulled Mason back into her arms.

After more time kissing and hugging on a couch in the library, Amy stood up and held out her hand to Mason. He took it and stood up. She led him into her bedroom and shut the door.

Mason and Amy made love that night. They knew they were in love. It felt as natural as anything to them both. They wished they never had to part again.

"I guess I have to be the bad guy again and head home," Mason said at about 4:00 in the morning.

"I'm glad you have the strength to go. If it was up to me, I couldn't do it," Amy said, in a very peaceful voice. She was basking in pure contentment over the night.

"I love you," Mason said.

"I love you more," Amy said.

"I keep telling you that's not possible."

They both wanted to feel this way for the rest of their lives. Mason drove home knowing one day they would never have to be apart. He had just experienced the best night of his life with the only girl he would ever love.

Chapter Eighty-Four

The day after New Year's Day meant it was time for Amy to head back home for the remainder of her senior year. Mason was at her family's beach house to help her pack and to see her off for the drive back to Charlotte.

It was very difficult for both of them to say goodbye. It had been a perfect visit for both of them and they did not want it to end.

"I guess we're just going to have to focus on this coming summer," Mason said after another long kiss.

"You're right," Amy said. "It's only five months, right?"

"Yes. It will give us time to plan our future."

"Our future. I like the sound of that."

"Me, too," Mason said, pulling Amy closer.

Since Mason did not want Amy driving at night, he encouraged her to begin her trip.

"Please call me the minute you get home."

"I will," Amy said, her voice starting to break. "Just remember one thing, Mason James. I will always love you."

"You have no idea how happy it makes me for you to say that because I will always love you, too. Always."

With that, Mason watched Amy get into her car and drive away. Instead of getting into his car and heading home, he walked in the direction of the beach. It was cold and windy, but he needed some time alone.

Once again, Amy and Mason fell back into a routine of school, work, music practice and their nightly phone calls, which always lasted at least two hours. Knowing the call was coming got them both through each day.

A week after Amy had returned to Charlotte, Mason ran an idea by Amy.

"Valentine's Day will be here in just about a month. How do you feel about me coming up that weekend for a visit? I know I can't stay at your house, but I have enough put away for a hotel room. The paper raised the amount they're paying me for my internship."

"That sounds great on all the above," Amy said. "I was hoping we could find a way to see each other before school's out. I miss you something awful."

"Me, too. Then it's a date."

"It's a date!" Amy said.

Their spirits went through the roof knowing it would be just a matter of weeks, instead of months, when they would see each other again.

That night, they both hung up focused on the newly scheduled visit. Mason was also focused on another plan associated with that visit. The next afternoon, after he finished his work at the *Star-News*, he was going to a jewelry store owned by his aunt in Wilmington. He decided that no matter how young everybody else thought he and Amy were, he knew their feelings were real and he was more than ready to prove how he felt to Amy.

With the help of his aunt, Mason bought the best ring he could afford. His aunt insisted on selling it to him at a big discount over Mason's objections.

"You're my nephew and no nephew of mine is going to get engaged without the best ring he could give his girl. And based on what your mom tells me about Amy, she's worth it."

"Yes, ma'am, she really is."

Mason walked out of the jewelry store with a ring he never thought he would be able to afford. He couldn't wait for Amy to see it and he couldn't wait to put it on her finger.

That night, during their usual call, Amy sensed something in Mason's tone.

"What are you up to?" Amy asked him.

"What are you talking about?"

"You can't hide from me. I can tell in your voice you're up to something."

"Well, I am. I'm planning my trip up for Valentine's Day and I'm just excited about that."

"Oh, okay, but, I still think there's something else going on."

"You'll just have to wait and see."

"Now, that's cruel," Amy said.

"No, I'm just trying to be a mysterious guy. Isn't that what girls want? A mysterious guy?"

"I tell you what I want. I want you, Mason."

"And I want you, too."

Chapter Eighty-Five

On the last day of January, Amy was eating lunch with her best friend, Hope, in the school cafeteria. They had been friends since elementary school and they both now played in the high school orchestra. Hope played the flute. Amy was filling Hope in on the latest with Mason.

"I wish you'd tell me more details," Hope said. "I'm having to live my whole love life vicariously through you."

They both laughed. Then, Amy began to feel lightheaded. Hope could see it in her friend's face.

"Are you okay?"

"Yeah, I think so," Amy said. "I just feel kind of sick to my stomach all the sudden."

Amy got up quickly from the table and made a beeline for the rest room. Once inside, the feeling began to ease up. She thought she had been too excited talking about Mason's upcoming visit. Before she could return to the cafeteria, Hope walked in.

"I came to check on you. Are you sure you're okay?"

"I am now," Amy said. "I feel better."

Hope looked around to make sure there was no one else in the rest room before she said, "Amy, what if you're pregnant?"

The color went out of Amy's face.

After school, Hope drove Amy to a drug store. Hope went in to buy a pregnancy test knowing that Amy's mom would go ballistic if she happened to see Amy buying the test. When Amy got home, she was glad her mother was not home. She used the test kit.

That night, it was Amy's turn to call Mason. Before she made the call, she called Hope.

"I'm pregnant," Amy said. "How can I tell Mason? What if it ruins everything?"

"Based on what you've told me about the guy, nothing could ruin how he feels about you."

"I like to think that, but this is serious, it's life changing."

"You could just have an abortion and he would never know."

"I can't do that. I would always know I had kept a secret from him. He has a right to know."

"Amy Cole, you are the last of the honest people on Earth. I believe Mason will stand by you no matter what."

"I hope so. I've got to go. It's time for me to call him."

"You're not going to tell him on the phone, are you? It's just a few weeks till he comes up, I'd wait till you can talk face-to-face."

"That's sounds like a good idea," Amy said. "But, I think I should tell him now. He has a right to know."

"I hope everything goes okay, Amy."

"Thanks. I'll let you know what happens tomorrow at school."

Amy hung up the phone. At the same time, her mother hung up the downstairs phone. She had heard the entire conversation.

Catherine jumped up from her desk to go confront Amy right now. When her hand grabbed her home office door she stopped. She remembered what Paul had told her about Amy now being 18. She had to navigate these waters carefully. She sat back down at her desk with her mind flying through a collection of ideas.

Knowing Amy was on the house phone by now, talking to Mason, which made her even more angry, Catherine reached into her purse and pulled out her cell phone. She hit the send button underneath David Wallace's number. He answered on the second ring.

"It's kind of late, Catherine, is everything okay?" David said.

"No, it's not. You and I have to talk first thing in the morning. So, be at the office by 7:00."

"Okay, I'll be there."

"One more thing," Catherine said with a more serious tone than he had ever heard from her. "Is the man who did the signatures for you good with copying anybody's handwriting? If he is, bring him with you."

Chapter Eighty-Six

After Amy left for school the next morning, Catherine entered her room. She looked through Amy's desk and found her diary and a large stack of papers that was schoolwork where Amy had written a lot. She took them to her office in the house and made copies of all of them.

Less than an hour later, Catherine was in her office. David Wallace and a man she had never seen before were waiting for her. She shut the door.

"What's your name?" Catherine asked the stranger.

David Wallace intervened. "He doesn't want you to know that. It's safer for both of you if you don't know."

"Okay," Catherine said. "Since that's the case, though, if something goes wrong or gets out, I'm holding you responsible, David."

"That's fine, but I can assure you neither one of us wants to be involved in a legal nightmare if this gets out. I assume this is about your daughter."

"Yes," she said as she pulled a large folder out of her briefcase. She handed it to the stranger.

"Do you think you can write a letter that looks like it was written by my daughter?"

The man looked over the papers Catherine handed him for well over a minute. He seemed very studious about what he was doing and that made Catherine more comfortable he could pull off what she wanted.

"Yes, I can." A man of few words, but that also made David and Catherine comfortable.

Catherine reached back into her briefcase and pulled out two pieces of notebook paper with her own handwriting on them. She handed them to the stranger.

"Write this on this paper in my daughter's handwriting," she said, handing the man several pieces of stationary Amy used to write friends.

"When do you need this?" the man asked.

"Now," she said and pointed to a small conference table in her office. "There is $1,000 in it, if I think it's passable, and another $1,000 for another letter I need you to write."

The stranger said nothing. He took the papers and went to the conference table. He pulled a magnifying glass out of his tattered briefcase and went to work. Catherine and David lifted their eyebrows to each other. A strange man, they both were thinking, but he was doing a strange job.

David and Catherine left the room and went down the hall to David's office where they had a private conversation about the new incorporation papers she demanded for the ad agency. They returned to her office 20 minutes later where they found the stranger sitting stoically in the chair in front of her desk where he sat when he first arrived. When they walked in, he placed papers on her desk. She read the letter he had written in an amazingly exact copy of her daughter's handwriting.

Dear Mason,

I now realize I am a weak person because I do not have the nerve to tell you this in person.

This situation I'm in now makes me realize how immature I am. I love you, but the thought of having a baby has changed everything. I know I'm not ready for any commitments. I know you are and I can't do this to you. I don't want to put you through waiting and wondering if I will ever be ready.

I've decided to end the pregnancy and focus on school and music until I get my head together. Please don't try and reach me until I am ready. It will just make this harder. I'll let you know when I'm ready to talk.

Love, Amy

"Well done," Catherine said to the stranger. "Here's the other one. The only handwriting I have for that one is a Christmas card sent to my daughter. But, I know they use a typewriter in their house and just sign letters. So, you only need to copy her signature. I've already typed the letter."

The man studied the card. It was a card sent from Mason's parents and signed by his mother with a message about how much they have loved getting to know her. The stranger nodded, took the letter Catherine gave him and returned to the conference table. It only took him a few minutes to make a passable signature.

Amy,

My family is in shock over the news. Mason told us you were the one who led him into the situation where you now find yourself. He is heartbroken. We all believe you might have done this deliberately, but why? You knew Mason loves you. You didn't need to set a trap for him.

Mason knows I am writing this letter. He needs and wants time to think about this and what it means for his future. He will call you when he's ready to talk.

-Joy James

After reading and checking the letters, Catherine handed the man two envelopes to address in the handwriting of Amy and Joy. He did them quickly. Catherine reached into her purse and paid the stranger $2,000 in cash. He nodded. Catherine turned to David.

"Take this letter, the one to Mason, to the post office and send it overnight. I've got to run to Wilmington."

By 4:00 that afternoon, Catherine was in a post office branch in Wilmington not far from the *Star-News* office. She sent the letter with overnight postage to Amy and drove right back to Charlotte.

Chapter Eighty-Seven

The evening before, Amy had told Mason the truth. Mason could tell there was something bothering Amy by the sound of her voice. He was hoping it was not another issue involving her mother or he hoped her dad had not taken a turn for the worse.

"I can tell something is wrong," Mason said. "What is it?"

Amy started crying.

"Amy? What is it? Is it your dad? Is he okay?"

"No, he's fine," Amy said between the sobs. "It's me."

"Oh, God, are you sick?" Mason said with obvious fear in his voice.

"I was going to wait until you came here for Valentine's Day, but you have a right to know now. Oh, God, I'm so scared to tell you."

"Please, Amy, tell me."

"I'm, uh, I'm pregnant."

For a moment, Mason was quiet.

"Amy, I'm so sorry. I didn't mean for that happen. I mean, not yet, until we were married."

"I'm the one that's sorry, Mason. I'm the one who made you go with me to my room."

"You didn't make me do anything I didn't want to do."

"Oh, God, what am I going to do?"

Mason, in his typically quiet demeanor, focused on Amy. He was scared, too, but he always put her above his fears.

"Amy, please don't be upset. We'll figure this out together. I know it's not easy to do, but please try and relax. I'll be up in less than two weeks and we'll talk about it and decide what's best to do. I promise, we're going through this together."

As always, Mason made Amy feel better. She knew he would focus on what was best for her. Mason felt better, too, hearing Amy's desperation begin to ease as they talked. They both knew everything would somehow be okay because they loved each other.

Amy and Mason had no idea their lives would be forever changed when letters arrived at their homes the next afternoon.

Chapter Eighty-Eight

Knowing Amy was in the habit of checking the family mailbox every afternoon after she arrived home from school, Catherine deliberately did not get the mail when she went home for lunch.

Amy grabbed the mail and went into her house. Scanning through the letters, most were for her parents. She then saw the letter from Mason's mother and was shocked to see it had been sent by overnight mail. Her heart began to beat harder as she opened the envelope. She read the letter and collapsed into a chair at the kitchen table and began to cry.

Oh, God, what have I done? They hate me.

Mason did not read the letter he received until after he arrived home from his internship work at the newspaper. On the drive home, he was thinking about being able to talk to Amy during their nightly call. He was determined to make sure she knew he stood beside her, no matter what. He wanted her to know they were going through this as a couple.

He had been open and honest with his parents and told them about Amy's call not long after they hung up.

"I know you are disappointed in me," Mason had told Joy and Woody.

"Why would we be disappointed?" Woody asked. "You have told a girl you love you will stand by her and deal with this as a couple."

"That's right," Joy said. "And please remember this, Son. People are quick to judge a pregnancy, but anybody worth a darn will ever judge the child."

Walking into the house, Joy told Mason he had a letter on the kitchen table. He went to read it. Mason walked back into the living room. He looked deeply disturbed.

"What's wrong, Son?" Woody said, who was sitting on the couch reading the paper.

Mason couldn't speak. He handed the letter to his dad and walked out on the porch.

"What is it?" Joy asked.

Woody handed her the letter.

Joy read it and said, "Oh, no."

They both walked onto the front porch and Joy put her arm around her son.

"I'm so sorry. I'm sure she'll call you soon. She's just upset right now and probably very confused."

Mason told his parents he was going for a walk on the beach. Despite the cold wind, he walked for almost an hour. He kept hearing his mother's voice saying, "I'm sure she'll call you soon." That kept him sane. He kept telling himself not to go crazy, just to be patient.

Sadly, the call from Amy never came.

Both of them did not want to violate the trust or request that they be given time to make a decision. They both assumed the decision of the other was to bring their relationship to an end.

Over the next several years, Amy and Mason had thought several times of trying to contact the other. Each time, the words in the letters they had received, that they would make contact when they were ready to talk, haunted them. They never wanted to be someone who harassed somebody who didn't want to talk to them.

A year after the letters had arrived, Mary told Amy she wanted to contact Mason's parents to see if Mason was okay.

"Please don't, Aunt Mary," Amy said as tears filled her eyes.

Mary never brought Mason up to her again for a long, long time.

Chapter Eighty-Nine

17 Years Later

After graduating high school, Mason accepted a full-time staff writer position at the *Star-News*. Amy stood by her decision to not attend the Juilliard School. Instead, she attended the University of North Carolina in Asheville to receive a degree in music education. She had become a middle school music teacher.

Rarely a day went by that Mason did not think about Amy. Even after all the years that had passed, he wondered why she never called.

Mason's friends frequently tried to talk to him about his single-minded focus on work. Even the editor of the paper, his friend Don Langley, who he had worked with ever since they were involved with the high school newspaper, tried to have a heart-to-heart talk with him.

One afternoon, Don called Mason into his office.

"I'm worried about you," Don said. "You used to laugh all the time. I haven't heard you laugh since you were hired here after the internship and that was a long, long time ago."

"I'm okay," was all Mason said. He had the same response when he would go back home to eat Sunday dinner with his parents. They were heartbroken knowing their son had never recovered from Amy.

Mason had moved to a small apartment in Wilmington after he graduated and only went back to Carolina Beach to visit his parents on Sunday. Bobby, at Britt's Donuts, asked about Mason frequently. Joy told him about the broken heart of her son.

"I sure wish that would have worked out," Bobby said. "They just looked perfect together."

Mason never ventured anywhere near the beach house Amy's parents had built, even though his father had told him the house had been placed back on the market and sold the month after he received the letter. Mason assumed her mother and father had both agreed to sell the house that time to keep Amy from having to be around him.

Mason was the first person in the newsroom in the morning and the last one to leave. He went to the same restaurant for dinner every night where he sat and read a book while he ate. Then, he would go to his apartment and let television bore him to sleep.

When spring started bringing some warmer weather to southeastern North Carolina, Don called Mason into his office.

"I've got a feature I'd really like you to do. Your writing style would be perfect for it."

"Sure," Mason said.

"There's this mailbox down at Sunset Beach this couple put up, right at the ocean, years ago and people go there and put messages into the mailbox. Have you ever heard of it?"

"Yes. It's called Kindred Spirit."

"Oh, great, you have heard of it. Why don't you head down there and spend a couple of days, try to catch some people leaving messages and maybe find the couple that put it up."

"Can I please ask you to give this one to someone else?" Mason said.

"Um, yes, is something wrong?"

"I'm okay," Mason said. He got up and left the editor's office. Don was in shock. Mason had never turned down a story assignment before.

Mason stepped outside and sat on a bench near the entrance to the newspaper office. Hearing about the Kindred Spirit Mailbox brought back memories of Amy that seemed like he had just spoken with her yesterday. Before the letter came, he had promised they would make the trip to see the mailbox together right after they graduated. He knew how much she loved going to read the messages in the mailbox when she went to visit her Aunt Mary.

For the first time anyone at the newspaper could remember, Mason was the first one to leave the newsroom and head home for the day.

On the drive home to his apartment, the memories brought on by the mention of Kindred Spirit Mailbox left Mason wondering how Mary was. He had always liked her and hoped she was doing well after all the years that had passed. He even wondered if she was still living. Little did he know, he would have an answer to his questions about Mary, and Amy, before the next Christmas came around.

Chapter Ninety

On August 11th, a little over four months after Mason had turned down the assignment to write a feature story on the Kindred Spirit Mailbox, Amy got a call from her mother.

"I just wanted to let you know Mary had a stroke."

"Where is she? Is she okay?" Amy asked.

"She is at the hospital near here. She was visiting when she had the stroke."

Amy knew when her mother referred to the "hospital near here," she was talking about the same hospital her dad had been in when he had the heart procedure 18 years ago.

"Are you there? Can I talk to her?"

"She was resting, so I came on home. But even if I was still there, she couldn't talk to you. The doctor said this was one of those strokes that has seriously affected her ability to speak. He doesn't think she'll ever be able to speak normally again."

Amy felt tears falling down her cheeks. She loved Mary and had spent many vacations with her after she graduated from high school. They talked on the phone almost every other night and Mary was the most encouraging person she had ever known. The thought of not hearing her aunt's voice again and her feisty retorts was heartbreaking.

"Are you still there?" Catherine asked.

"Yes, Mom, I'll be down by Friday evening."

When Amy arrived in Charlotte at the hospital, she was happy to see Mary awake and alert. She had a huge smile when Amy walked into the hospital room and hugged her tightly. When Mary pulled back, she started motioning in the air like she had a pen in her hand. Amy knew she wanted something to write with and some paper.

Amy went to the nurse's station and asked for some paper. She already had a pen in her purse. She handed the paper and pen to Mary.

"Your dad called last night and the nurse had to tell him everything cause I can't talk," Mary wrote. "Please tell him how much I appreciate him calling."

"I will," Amy said. "I'll probably take 74 back to Asheville so I can stop to see him on the way back home."

Fifteen years ago, Amy's mother and father had divorced when he found out about the attempt to have him declared incompetent so her mom and David Wallace could take over his part of the ad agency. Paul agreed not to press charges and even gave them his share of the company in exchange for her buying half the house from him. Catherine considered it a bargain to gain control and he considered it the wisest move towards peace he'd ever made.

Paul bought a small home on Lake Lure, in the mountains, and started a freelance business doing illustrations for magazines, websites, books and advertising. He set up a studio on the second floor of the house with a picture window looking out over the lake and the mountains. He loved it.

Mary was released from the hospital in a week. Since she was still unsteady when she walked, she agreed to stay at Catherine's home for a few weeks.

When Thanksgiving came around, Mary was still recovering and still couldn't speak. Amy had bought her a stack of legal pads and pens that became her voice.

Amy decided to spend Thanksgiving Day visiting her mother and Mary and then leave the next afternoon to spend the weekend with her father.

The morning after Thanksgiving, Catherine asked Amy to come with her for a little Black Friday shopping before she left. Mary wrote on the back of a napkin at breakfast that she was too tired to go and asked them to please pick her up some more legal pads.

About an hour after Amy and Catherine left, Mary began to think of several things she wanted to share with Amy before she left, including hoping she would think about spending as much of Christmas vacation with her as she could. She wanted Amy to know she was ready to go back home to Sunset Beach.

Out of paper, Mary started searching around the house. She went into Catherine's home office and opened several drawers hoping to find some kind of writing paper. The only blank paper she found was business stationary for the ad agency and it looked too expensive to write on, so she kept looking. When she opened up the bottom left drawer, several handwritten papers came moving to the front of the drawer. The handwriting looked like Amy's. She pulled the papers out and read them.

While Mary was reading what she had found, Amy and Catherine were inside of a Macy's store in a Charlotte mall. Catherine was holding up an expensive dress when she heard the rack beside her fall over. She looked to find Amy had collapsed on the floor.

Chapter Ninety-One

A week after Thanksgiving, Mason was sitting at his desk working on a story about a local World War II vet. The newsroom clerk dropped some mail on his desk. As he scanned through the letters, one stood out. Instead of the usual pre-labeled envelopes with press releases, this one was handwritten and was addressed to him personally. In big block letters on the bottom left of the envelope were the words, "Personal and Important." Then, he looked at the return address. It was from Mary at Sunset Beach. Mason's heart began beating harder as he opened the letter.

My Dear Mason,

I sure hope you remember this old lady after all these years. This is Amy's aunt, Mary. I would have called you, but I had a stroke in August and it left me unable to talk. I bet some people are glad about that.

On a serious note, I have something
very important to ask you to do.
PLEASE come down to Sunset Beach
on December 10th. Please be at that
mailbox Amy and I talked about at
1:00 that afternoon. There is
something you need to know and
have a right to know.

I wish I could tell you everything now,
but I can't. Just please be there. You
will understand why when you arrive.

I hope I haven't interrupted your life
with this letter, but I couldn't live with
myself if I didn't write it.

Please be there, Mason. Dec. 10th at
1:00.
                    Thank you,
                    Mary

Thoughts began to fly through Mason's
mind. Has Amy died? If this is about her, why
didn't Amy write? What in heaven is it that I
need to know and have a right to know?

Mason was unusually anxious. The thought
of having to wait over ten days to find out what
this letter is all about was almost unbearable.

But, from everything he remembered about Amy's aunt, she was a wonderful lady. He knew she had to have a reason to set a date and time like that. He had no choice but to wait. Since he had never been to the Kindred Spirit Mailbox, he needed to find out how to get there. He went online to search for directions. He found a story about the mailbox and directions in an online story on the *USA Today* website.

Later that night, Mason called his parents to tell them about the letter. Knowing how the break-up from Amy had affected Mason's entire life since then, Joy and Woody were skeptical of the letter. They hoped it wasn't a set up for another heartbreak.

"Are you sure you should go?" Joy asked.

"Your mom's right, Son. We just hate to see any old wounds come back. You've been through enough. You're not a boy anymore, but we still love you."

"Thanks," Mason said. "I know how much you care, but I have to go."

Mason also shared the letter with his boss and friend Don Langley at the newspaper. His concern sounded very much like his parents.

"This explains why you didn't want to do the story on the mailbox," Don said. "There is a connection with Amy, huh?"

"Yes," Mason said.

"As your friend, I hope you're doing the right thing. It's been a long time. How many years has it been since you've even seen Amy?"

"Seventeen," Mason said. "But I still have to go."

Mason began counting down the days to Dec. 10th. He had to know what the secret behind the letter was all about.

Chapter Ninety-Two

When Dec. 10th arrived, Mason was discouraged by the weather reports. A nor'easter was forming off the coast and the winds along the beaches in southeastern North Carolina were picking up, along with the possibility of rain. He hoped it would not affect whatever was waiting for him at the Kindred Spirit Mailbox. For all he knew, there could just be another letter waiting for him.

With the directions printed off beside him, he left the *Star-News* office headed south. Within a little over an hour, he was crossing a bridge onto Sunset Beach. He located the road where there was parking and the beach access mentioned in the article.

Worried that a letter would be all that was waiting for him, Mason had purchased a notebook at a dollar store the evening he received the letter from Mary. Every night, he wrote something in the notebook about Amy. How much he missed her. How much he still loved her. How often he was tempted to call her despite her request not to and how hard it was to live up to that request. By the time the 10th arrived, the wire bound notebook was filled with stories, memories and his feelings about the only girl he had ever loved.

Worried the approaching weather would damage the notebook, he had put it in a large plastic bag with a pull lock on it. In the event there was only a letter to him in the mailbox, he wanted to leave something in its place in case someone came to see if he had actually come.

Fighting the wind and the sea spray whipped up by the nor'easter, Mason kept walking until he, despite being almost blinded by the wind, spotted an American flag on a pole a mile-and-a-half from where he started walking south on the beach. By the article he read, that was where the mailbox was.

Mason finally saw the mailbox and started walking faster. Focused on the mailbox itself, his knee slammed into one of two benches placed around the mailbox where people could sit and read the messages and letters left in the mailbox.

I should have remembered the benches! I know Amy talked about sitting on them to read.

The wind eased up enough for Mason to get a good look. There it was. On the side of the mailbox planted in the middle of nowhere on a place called Bird Island were the letters, Kindred Spirit.

Mason looked around and didn't see anyone. He guessed his assumption was right. There must be a letter inside for him. He opened the mailbox and began reading all the messages inside. There was a notebook and pencils inside for people to write a message if they had not brought something with them. He looked through the notebook, too. There was nothing he could see that had anything to do with him, Amy or Mary.

Disappointed, Mason assumed the weather may have prevented Mary or someone from getting to the mailbox to leave him a message. Considering Mary said she had a stroke, that made the most sense. So, he carefully placed the notebook he had filled with stories inside the Kindred Spirit Mailbox. He left it inside the plastic bag hoping it would preserve his memories of Amy for whoever found it.

Still fighting to see in the increasing winds, Mason pulled up the sleeve to his coat to look at his watch. It was now 20 minutes after 1:00. That's 20 minutes after the time Mary said he should be here. Despite the weather, he felt compelled to wait a little longer at the mailbox that had captivated Amy so many years ago. He pulled out all the notes and letters and read them one more time just in case he had missed something. Nothing referred to him or Amy. He decided he should just return to Wilmington and hope another letter with an explanation would come from Mary.

Taking one last glance around, Mason began the slow walk back to his car. He had only walked about 20 feet when he heard something. It sounded like a voice, but in the wind he wasn't sure. Then, he heard it again.

"Excuse me!" the voice said.

Mason turned around to find a girl standing at the mailbox. Despite wearing a hooded jacket, she looked soaked and scared. From where he stood, she looked like a teenager to him and he wondered why she was out alone in all this weather.

He took a step in her direction and gave a wave, hoping to not make her anymore afraid than she already appeared. "Are you okay?"

"Can I ask you a question?" the girl said.

"Of course," Mason said. "Do you need help?"

The girl took a step closer to Mason, looking intensely into his face.

"Are you . . ., uh, is your name . . . Are you my father?"

Chapter Ninety-Three

Mason approached the girl who just asked him the most shocking question he had ever heard in his life. He studied her face, first looking into her eyes. He noticed her eyebrows, her mouth and her nose. His eyes slowly moved back to hers before he spoke. Somehow, he knew the answer to her question.

"Yes, I am."

Mason did not know what to do. A big part of him wanted to take her in his arms, but he didn't want to scare her. He wanted to know everything about her. As his mind raced with questions, she came to him and hugged him. They both cried. Through the tears, Mason spoke softly.

"I'm so sorry. I didn't know you, uh . . . I didn't know you existed."

"I know," the girl said. "Aunt Mary found out the truth about everything."

Mason wanted to know the truth, but he was focused on this beautiful girl in front of him that looked so much like her mother.

"I wish I was there for you. I missed everything," Mason said, still choking back tears.

"It's not your fault, Dad."

Not only did this young girl sound so confident, just like her mother, Mason loved to hear her call him "Dad." Then, he sadly realized he didn't even know the name of his own daughter. It was as if she had just read his mind. She pulled back from their hug, still holding his arms in her hands.

"I'm Kristie," she said and smiled. "Kristie Marie."

Mason smiled before a chill went down his spine.

Why is she here alone? Where is Amy?

"Is your mom married?" Mason asked.

"No, she never got married."

The way the response was given in a past tense scared Mason. He was almost afraid to ask.

"Your Mom, is, ah, is she okay?"

"Please come with me to Aunt Mary's house," Kristie said. She took her dad by the hand.

It was a long, quiet walk back. Mason was afraid of what he may hear when he got to Mary's home. Kristie said nothing during the walk, but kept holding his hand. When they entered Mary's house, Mason's heart sank. Sitting in the living room in a recliner was Amy. She looked as beautiful as ever, but very weak. Mary was sitting in a chair and holding Amy's hand. Amy looked up, saw Mason and tears began to stream down her face.

"Thank God, you came," Amy said.

Mason walked to Amy and got down on his knees. The look on his face told Amy that Kristie had not told him any of the details.

"I'm sorry I can't get up. I just had the last of my chemo treatments this morning and I'm still pretty weak. But, the doctor says I am doing really good and he thinks I'm headed to a full remission. Kristie and I have been here with Aunt Mary ever since she discovered what Mom had done to us both."

"What did she do?"

Amy told Mason everything Mary had discovered. The made-up letters. The lies. Mary had confronted Catherine after Amy had been released from the hospital after her collapse in the mall. Catherine had no choice but to confess.

"I just wish I knew. I could have been here for everything. For you and for Kristie."

"None of us knew," Amy said.

Mason hesitated. It was obvious he wanted to say something, but he wasn't sure he should.

"What is it? I can tell something is wrong?" Amy said.

"No, nothing's wrong. It's just I need to know something."

"What's that?"

"I never stopped loving you. You were the only girl I ever loved and still do. I guess I'm wanting to know . . ."

"Yes," Amy interrupted. "I never stopped loving you, too."

Mason and Amy kissed. Their kiss was interrupted by Mary shaking a piece of paper at them. Mason took the paper and held it where he and Amy could read what Mary had wrote.

"You guys just gave me the best Christmas present I ever had."

Kristie leaned over and the read the note from her great aunt.

"Me, too, Aunt Mary. The best ever."

Chapter Ninety-Four

It was a beautiful early spring day on Bird Island at Sunset Beach. A small crowd of friends and family gathered near the Kindred Spirit Mailbox. Mason's parents were there, as well as his friend and boss, Don Langley and his wife. He also saw Bobby, his old boss from Britt's Donuts. And of course, Mary was there, beaming.

An archway of flowers had been erected behind the mailbox. The flap to a privacy tent opened and Amy walked out in a simple, but beautiful dress. Mason watched as she walked up to the flowered arch with Kristie and Paul on each side.

Mason's father stood beside him, serving as his best man, as the minister began the ceremony. After a welcome to everyone there and a brief inspirational statement about the importance of the day, he turned towards Amy.

"Who gives this woman to be married to this man?" he asked.

"We do," Kristie and Amy's father said in unison.

After the ceremony, everyone was invited to Mary's house for a reception. As they all began the walk along the beach, Mason noticed someone standing in the distance on top of a dune. Amy noticed, too. It was Catherine. When she noticed they had seen her and when Mason and Amy waved to her, she walked away.

The small reception was enjoyed by everyone. It was a happy day. There were some gifts on a table in the dining room and Amy opened them all. She thanked everyone for being so kind and for being at the wedding. Paul, Joy and Woody all talked a long time and took their turns congratulating the new bride and groom.

After most people had spoken to the newlyweds, Mary approached them. She handed them a gift box. Amy opened it. Inside, there was just two keys.

"Aunt Mary, what's this?"

Still struggling with speech after her stroke, she was now able to talk for brief periods of time.

"A new family needs a place to live. I'm moving to that assisted living center just down the street. I have a lot of friends there."

"Mary! We can't take your house," Mason said.

"To heck you can't," Mary said as best she could. "Besides, it's a selfish gift for me. Now I have people to take me down to the Kindred Spirit Mailbox whenever I want to go."

Kristie walked up and was listening in on the conversation.

"Mom? Dad? Did I just hear what I think I heard? Did Aunt Mary just give us her house?"

"No," Mary said before Amy or Mason could respond. "I just gave my favorite people in the world THEIR house."

Acknowledgements

My childhood was split between two places, Carolina Beach and Wilmington in North Carolina. From birth until Christmas break of the fourth grade, my family lived at Carolina Beach.

I have very fond memories of being a beach kid, with one exception of almost drowning. That was a scary experience and it occasionally haunts me to this day. My early school days were at Carolina Beach School where I saw all my year-round beach friends, including Donald Langley, Rodney Klutz, Susan Gee, Gail Evans and a slew of others I remember very well. I also remember my great teachers there, Mrs. Lambeth, Mrs. Eakins, Mrs. Neilson and Ms. Brothers.

My early summers were spent staying at my grandmother's small hotel across the street from the ocean while my parents worked. I would venture down to the boardwalk and always enjoyed a stop to have one of the best donuts on the planet, at Britt's Donuts. Well, more like three of those donuts.

When I decided to base this book at both Carolina Beach and Sunset Beach, I wanted people who knew the area to relate, so several events in the book happen at Britt's Donuts. I called Bobby Nivens, the owner, to ask if he would mind me not only using his famous donut shop in a work of fiction, but to actually write him into a few fictious scenes. He graciously agreed. Thanks, Bobby, for the permission, for the years of being a friend and for spending your summers churning out those famous donuts.

I sincerely thank everyone who made my Carolina Beach childhood one filled with great memories. My parents, my brothers, my grandparents, my cousins; including Joy Lee, her parents Grover and Blanch, and another cousin, Penny; as well as a slew of beach kid friends who made them happy days.

A huge thank you goes out to friends and family, as well as my agent, who encouraged this book project.

To my longtime friend, T.C. Freeman, thanks for letting me borrow you and your drone-flying skills to make the trek on a hot day to the Kindred Spirit Mailbox on Bird Island for a photo and video session there.

My daughter, Kayla, became my first reader and offered very valuable insight and ideas. I love you, daughter of mine.

I thank my brother Gary who is always providing me with good ideas and important aspects on the business side of being a writer. He acted as a valuable editor on the book.

Thanks, too, to Steve Frigiola for adding his services as a line editor.

To the list of family, I add my son, Michael, his wife, Megan, and my little two-year-old granddaughter, Miina. All of you are the reasons I want to keep on trucking and keep on writing.

Just before this book went to press, I got some great news. There is another grandchild on the way. I guess I better get to work writing more books so I can afford the Christmases coming my way.

Books by Mark Grady

Blaire's Bridge

Yes, Sir! Mr. President (co-author)

Coming Soon

Searching for Walden
The true story of one man's search for
meaningful success

Missing in Mississippi
A Romantic Comedy Novel

The Front Porch of Cracker Barrel
A young non-verbal autistic boy discovers his
gift of storytelling and hides a love story he is
writing for a girl he secretly loves.

Dog Daze
The Duplin Animal Clinic Series- Book One
A beloved veterinarian finds himself drawn
into a battle to stop a dog-fighting ring while
he also deals with a family tragedy.

Get the latest news on new books,
exclusive discounts and a free book by
subscribing to Mark's newsletter.

www.MarkGrady.com

Printed in the USA
CPSIA information can be obtained
at www.ICGtesting.com
LVHW041359130823
755092LV00001B/114